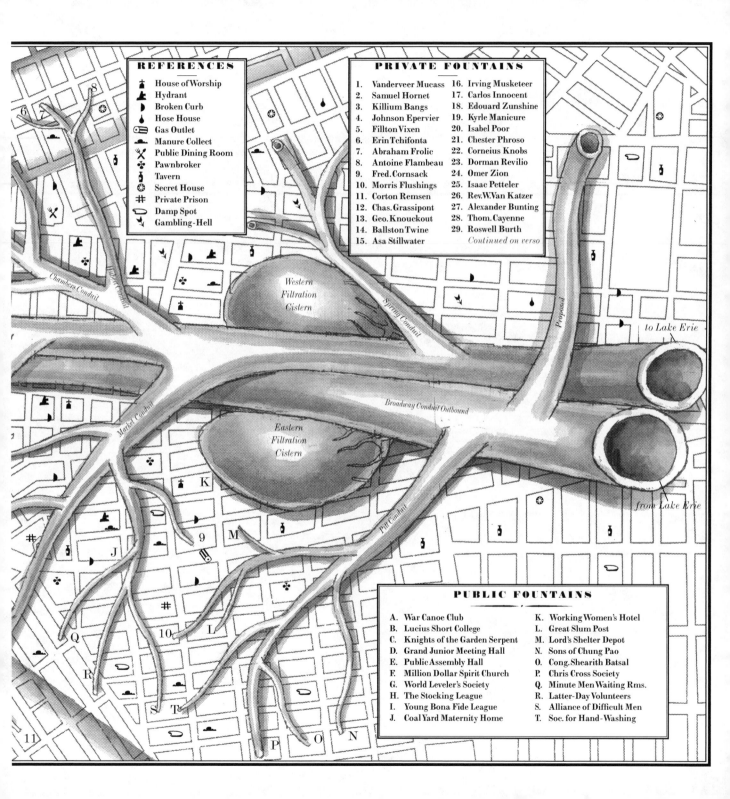

REFERENCES

- House of Worship
- Hydrant
- Broken Curb
- Hose House
- Gas Outlet
- Manure Collect
- Public Dining Room
- Pawnbroker
- Tavern
- Secret House
- Private Prison
- Damp Spot
- Gambling-Hell

PRIVATE FOUNTAINS

1. Vanderveer Mucass
2. Samuel Hornet
3. Killium Bangs
4. Johnson Epervier
5. Fillton Vixen
6. Erin Tchifonta
7. Abraham Frolic
8. Antoine Flambeau
9. Fred. Cornsack
10. Morris Flushings
11. Corton Remsen
12. Chas. Grassipont
13. Geo. Knouckout
14. Ballston Twine
15. Asa Stillwater
16. Irving Musketeer
17. Carlos Innocent
18. Edouard Zunshine
19. Kyrle Manicure
20. Isabel Poor
21. Chester Phroso
22. Corneius Knobs
23. Dorman Revilio
24. Omer Zion
25. Isaac Petteler
26. Rev. W. Van Katzer
27. Alexander Bunting
28. Thom. Cayenne
29. Roswell Burth

Continued on verso

Western Filtration Cistern

Eastern Filtration Cistern

Chambers Conduit

Talbert Conduit

Market Conduit

Spring Conduit

Broadway Conduit Outbound

Pitt Conduit

Proposed

to Lake Erie

from Lake Erie

PUBLIC FOUNTAINS

A. War Canoe Club
B. Lucius Short College
C. Knights of the Garden Serpent
D. Grand Junior Meeting Hall
E. Public Assembly Hall
F. Million Dollar Spirit Church
G. World Leveler's Society
H. The Stocking League
I. Young Bona Fide League
J. Coal Yard Maternity Home
K. Working Women's Hotel
L. Great Slum Post
M. Lord's Shelter Depot
N. Sons of Chung Pao
O. Cong. Shearith Batsal
P. Chris Cross Society
Q. Minute Men Waiting Rms.
R. Latter-Day Volunteers
S. Alliance of Difficult Men
T. Soc. for Hand-Washing

THE
JEW
OF
NEW YORK

——

Albany Direct

CANAL BOAT.

Nathan Kishon

Until SEPTEMBER 1st, 1832.

$ Twenty

This ticket shall be destroyed upon arrival in Albany.

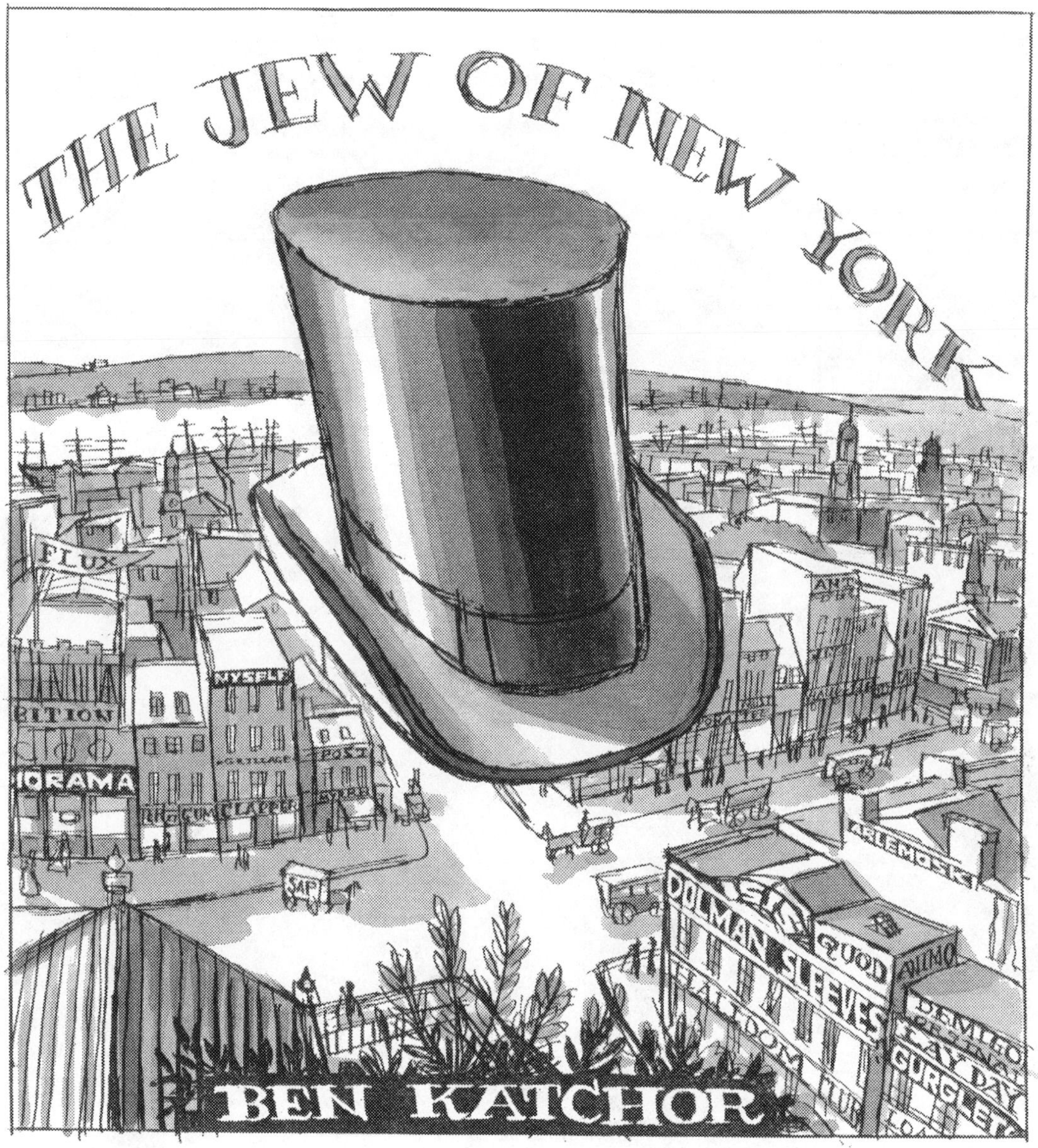
THE JEW OF NEW YORK
FLUX
MYSELF
SAP
ISIS
DOLMAN SLEEVES
QUOD
GURGLET
BEN KATCHOR

PANTHEON BOOKS
New York

Some material in this book was originally published in the *Forward*.

PUBLIC CITATIONS

Page 3. panel 5: Francisco Lopez de Gómara's *Historia de las Indias*. 1553.
Page 6. panel 8: M. M. Noah. *The National Advocate*. 1821.
Page 7: *The Ten Tribes of Israel Historically Identified with the Aborigines of the Western Hemisphere*. by Mrs. Simon. 1836.
Page 8: Ibid.
Page 11. panel 6: M.M. Noah. "Proclamation to the Jews." Sept. 15. 1825.
Page 19. panel 6: Berakhot. 9:1.
Page 23. panel 8: M. Valtinau. *Jerusalem in the New World*. 1828.
Page 24. panel 6: Dr. C. Leannox. *Communing with the Brutes*. 1829.
Page 27. panel 5: Joseph Priestly. *Experiments and Observations on Different Kinds of Air*. 1790.
Page 28. panel 3: Ibid.
Page 32: Abraham Abulafia. *The Book of Eternal Life*. 1280.
Page 36. panel 4: Rabbi J. Ollveys. "On Public Nakedness." 1927.
Page 36. panel 6: Anonymous. Unpublished Sermon. 1830.
Page 43. panel 9: *Niles' Register*. Nov. 28. 1829.
Page 47: Châteaubriand. *L'Intinéraire de Paris à Jérusalem et de Jérusalem à Paris*. 1811.
Page 72. panel 4: Deuteronomy. 4:25.
Page 89. panel 8: Christopher Marlowe. Machiavel from *The Jew of Malta*. 1633.
Page 92. panel 8: *The Evening Star*. Oct. 5. 1833.

LIBRARY OF CONGRESS
CATALOGING-IN-PUBLICATION DATA

Katchor, Ben.
The Jew of New York : a historical romance / Ben Katchor.
p. cm. ISBN 0-375-70097-8 I. Title. PN6727.K28J48 1999
741.5'973—dc21 98-23996 CIP

www.pantheonbooks.com

Designed by Ben Katchor and Misha Beletsky

First Paperback Edition

146122990

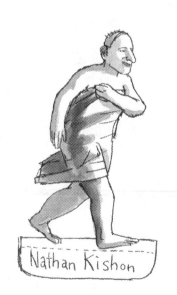

Nathan Kishon
Mr. Marah
Prof. Solidus
Isaac Azarael with stick

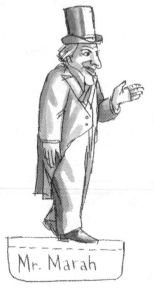

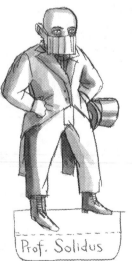

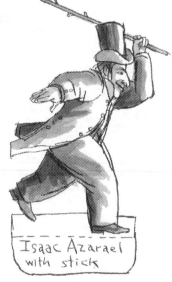

דהי
The

דזשו

Jew

אוו
of

ניו יארק

York   New

Yosl Feinbroyt   Francis Oriole   Enoch Letushim   Man in an India Rubber Suit

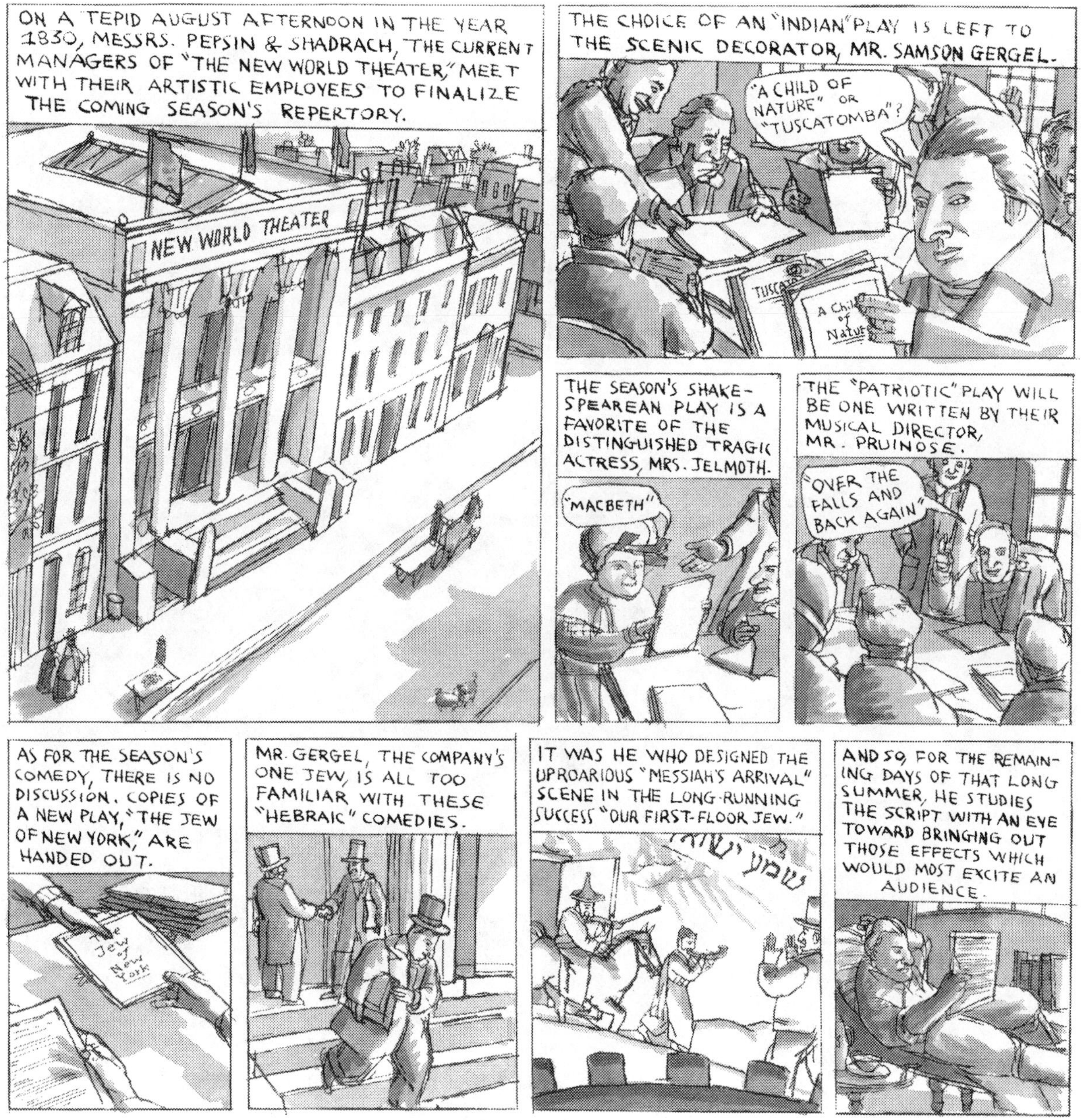

ON A TEPID AUGUST AFTERNOON IN THE YEAR 1830, MESSRS. PEPSIN & SHADRACH, THE CURRENT MANAGERS OF "THE NEW WORLD THEATER," MEET WITH THEIR ARTISTIC EMPLOYEES TO FINALIZE THE COMING SEASON'S REPERTORY.
NEW WORLD THEATER
THE CHOICE OF AN "INDIAN" PLAY IS LEFT TO THE SCENIC DECORATOR, MR. SAMSON GERGEL.
"A CHILD OF NATURE" OR "TUSCATOMBA"?
A Child of Nature
THE SEASON'S SHAKESPEAREAN PLAY IS A FAVORITE OF THE DISTINGUISHED TRAGIC ACTRESS, MRS. JELMOTH.
"MACBETH"
THE "PATRIOTIC" PLAY WILL BE ONE WRITTEN BY THEIR MUSICAL DIRECTOR, MR. PRUINOSE.
"OVER THE FALLS AND BACK AGAIN"
AS FOR THE SEASON'S COMEDY, THERE IS NO DISCUSSION. COPIES OF A NEW PLAY, "THE JEW OF NEW YORK," ARE HANDED OUT.
The Jew of New York
MR. GERGEL, THE COMPANY'S ONE JEW, IS ALL TOO FAMILIAR WITH THESE "HEBRAIC" COMEDIES.
IT WAS HE WHO DESIGNED THE UPROARIOUS "MESSIAH'S ARRIVAL" SCENE IN THE LONG-RUNNING SUCCESS "OUR FIRST-FLOOR JEW."
שמע
AND SO, FOR THE REMAINING DAYS OF THAT LONG SUMMER, HE STUDIES THE SCRIPT WITH AN EYE TOWARD BRINGING OUT THOSE EFFECTS WHICH WOULD MOST EXCITE AN AUDIENCE.

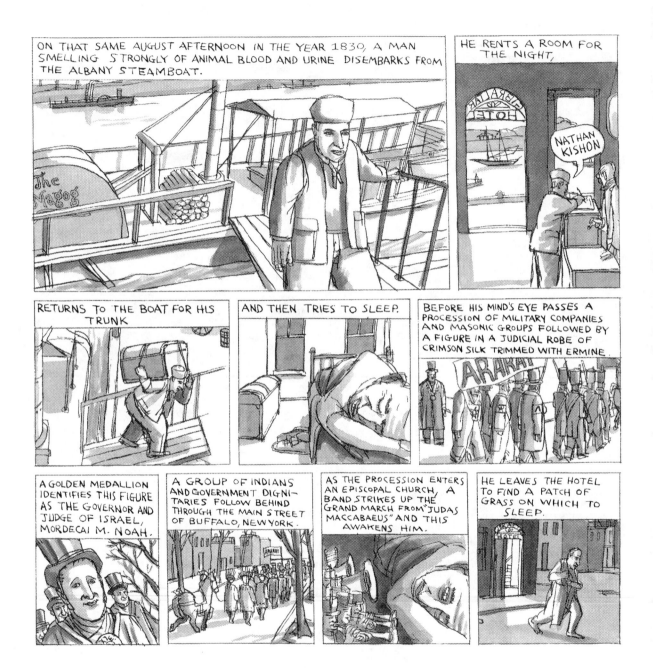

ON THAT SAME AUGUST AFTERNOON IN THE YEAR 1830, A MAN SMELLING STRONGLY OF ANIMAL BLOOD AND URINE DISEMBARKS FROM THE ALBANY STEAMBOAT.

HE RENTS A ROOM FOR THE NIGHT,

NATHAN KISHON

RETURNS TO THE BOAT FOR HIS TRUNK

AND THEN TRIES TO SLEEP.

BEFORE HIS MIND'S EYE PASSES A PROCESSION OF MILITARY COMPANIES AND MASONIC GROUPS FOLLOWED BY A FIGURE IN A JUDICIAL ROBE OF CRIMSON SILK TRIMMED WITH ERMINE.

A GOLDEN MEDALLION IDENTIFIES THIS FIGURE AS THE GOVERNOR AND JUDGE OF ISRAEL, MORDECAI M. NOAH.

A GROUP OF INDIANS AND GOVERNMENT DIGNITARIES FOLLOW BEHIND THROUGH THE MAIN STREET OF BUFFALO, NEW YORK.

AS THE PROCESSION ENTERS AN EPISCOPAL CHURCH, A BAND STRIKES UP THE GRAND MARCH FROM "JUDAS MACCABAEUS" AND THIS AWAKENS HIM.

HE LEAVES THE HOTEL TO FIND A PATCH OF GRASS ON WHICH TO SLEEP.

[2]

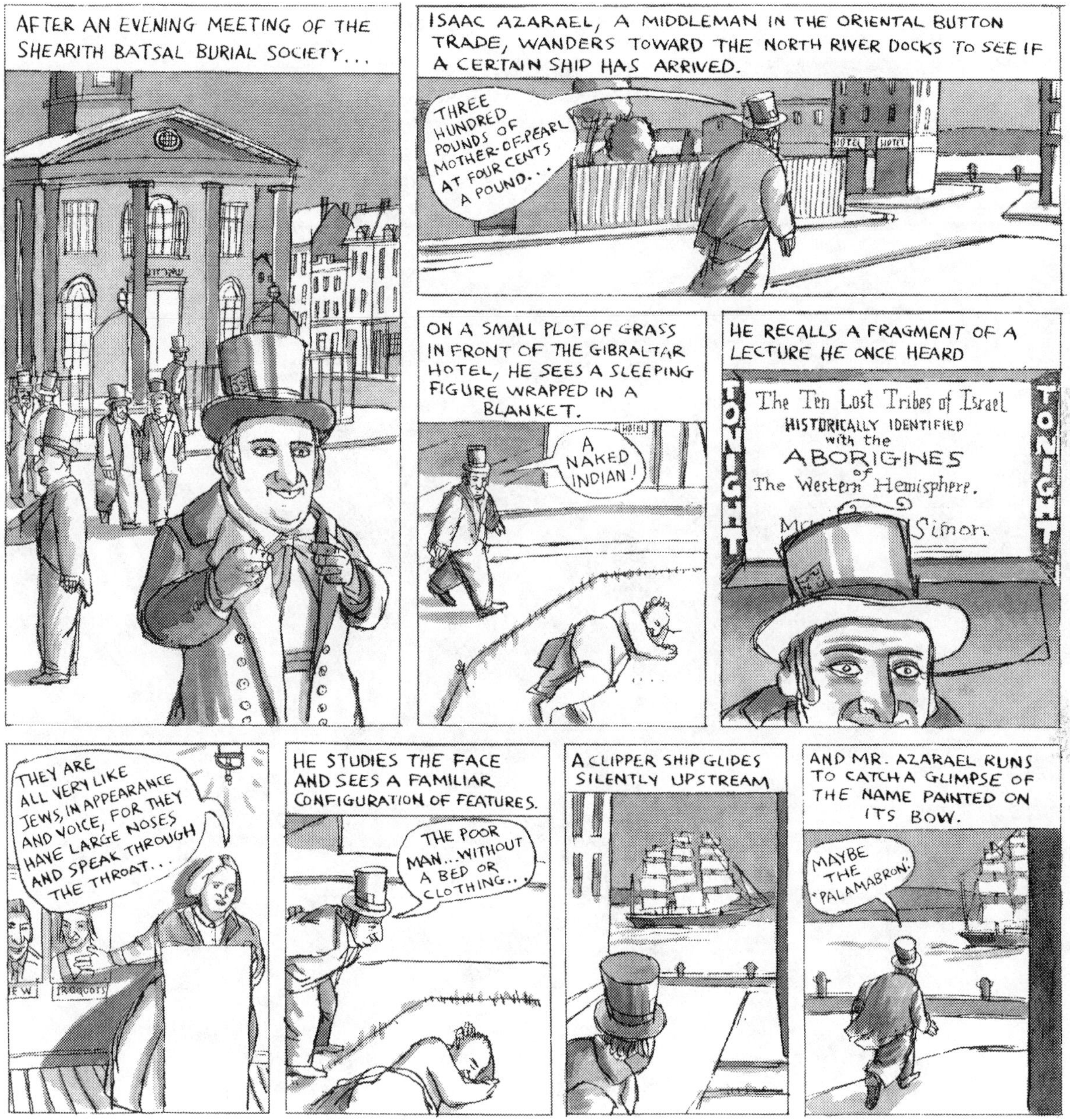
AFTER AN EVENING MEETING OF THE SHEARITH BATSAL BURIAL SOCIETY...
ISAAC AZARAEL, A MIDDLEMAN IN THE ORIENTAL BUTTON TRADE, WANDERS TOWARD THE NORTH RIVER DOCKS TO SEE IF A CERTAIN SHIP HAS ARRIVED.
THREE HUNDRED POUNDS OF MOTHER-OF-PEARL AT FOUR CENTS A POUND...
HOTEL
HOTEL
ON A SMALL PLOT OF GRASS IN FRONT OF THE GIBRALTAR HOTEL, HE SEES A SLEEPING FIGURE WRAPPED IN A BLANKET.
HOTEL
A NAKED INDIAN!
HE RECALLS A FRAGMENT OF A LECTURE HE ONCE HEARD
TONIGHT
The Ten Lost Tribes of Israel
HISTORICALLY IDENTIFIED with the
ABORIGINES
of
The Western Hemisphere.
Simon
TONIGHT
THEY ARE ALL VERY LIKE JEWS, IN APPEARANCE AND VOICE, FOR THEY HAVE LARGE NOSES AND SPEAK THROUGH THE THROAT...
JEW
IROQUOIS
HE STUDIES THE FACE AND SEES A FAMILIAR CONFIGURATION OF FEATURES.
THE POOR MAN...WITHOUT A BED OR CLOTHING...
A CLIPPER SHIP GLIDES SILENTLY UPSTREAM
AND MR. AZARAEL RUNS TO CATCH A GLIMPSE OF THE NAME PAINTED ON ITS BOW.
MAYBE THE "PALAMABRON."

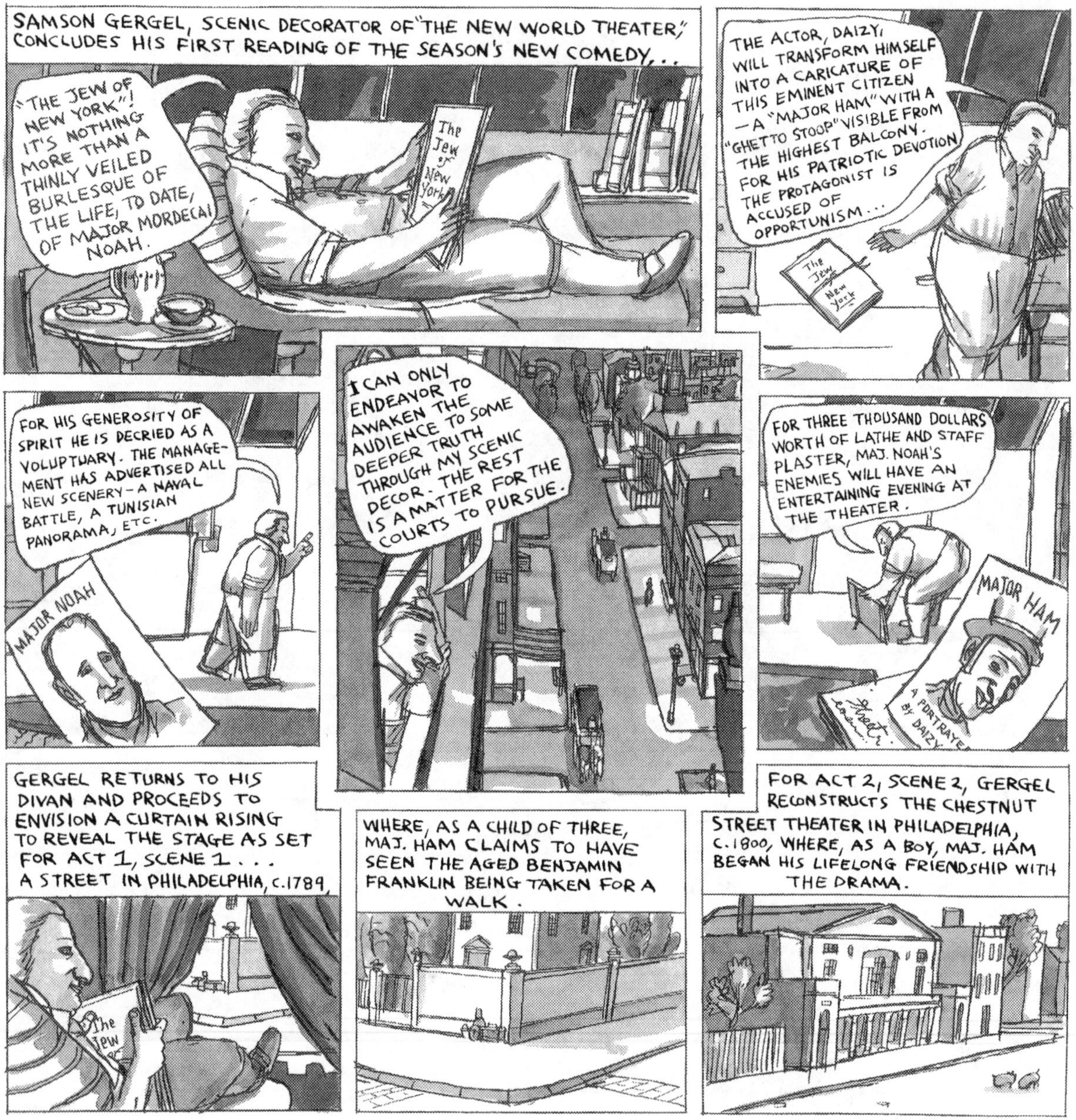
SAMSON GERGEL, SCENIC DECORATOR OF "THE NEW WORLD THEATER," CONCLUDES HIS FIRST READING OF THE SEASON'S NEW COMEDY, . . .
"THE JEW OF NEW YORK"! IT'S NOTHING MORE THAN A THINLY VEILED BURLESQUE OF THE LIFE, TO DATE, OF MAJOR MORDECAI NOAH.
The Jew of New York
THE ACTOR, DAIZY, WILL TRANSFORM HIMSELF INTO A CARICATURE OF THIS EMINENT CITIZEN —A "MAJOR HAM" WITH A "GHETTO STOOP" VISIBLE FROM THE HIGHEST BALCONY. FOR HIS PATRIOTIC DEVOTION THE PROTAGONIST IS ACCUSED OF OPPORTUNISM . . .
The Jew of New York
FOR HIS GENEROSITY OF SPIRIT HE IS DECRIED AS A VOLUPTUARY. THE MANAGEMENT HAS ADVERTISED ALL NEW SCENERY—A NAVAL BATTLE, A TUNISIAN PANORAMA, ETC.
MAJOR NOAH
I CAN ONLY ENDEAVOR TO AWAKEN THE AUDIENCE TO SOME DEEPER TRUTH THROUGH MY SCENIC DECOR. THE REST IS A MATTER FOR THE COURTS TO PURSUE.
FOR THREE THOUSAND DOLLARS WORTH OF LATHE AND STAFF PLASTER, MAJ. NOAH'S ENEMIES WILL HAVE AN ENTERTAINING EVENING AT THE THEATER.
MAJOR HAM
BY DAIZY
GERGEL RETURNS TO HIS DIVAN AND PROCEEDS TO ENVISION A CURTAIN RISING TO REVEAL THE STAGE AS SET FOR ACT 1, SCENE 1 . . . A STREET IN PHILADELPHIA, C.1789,
WHERE, AS A CHILD OF THREE, MAJ. HAM CLAIMS TO HAVE SEEN THE AGED BENJAMIN FRANKLIN BEING TAKEN FOR A WALK.
FOR ACT 2, SCENE 2, GERGEL RECONSTRUCTS THE CHESTNUT STREET THEATER IN PHILADELPHIA, C.1800, WHERE, AS A BOY, MAJ. HAM BEGAN HIS LIFELONG FRIENDSHIP WITH THE DRAMA.

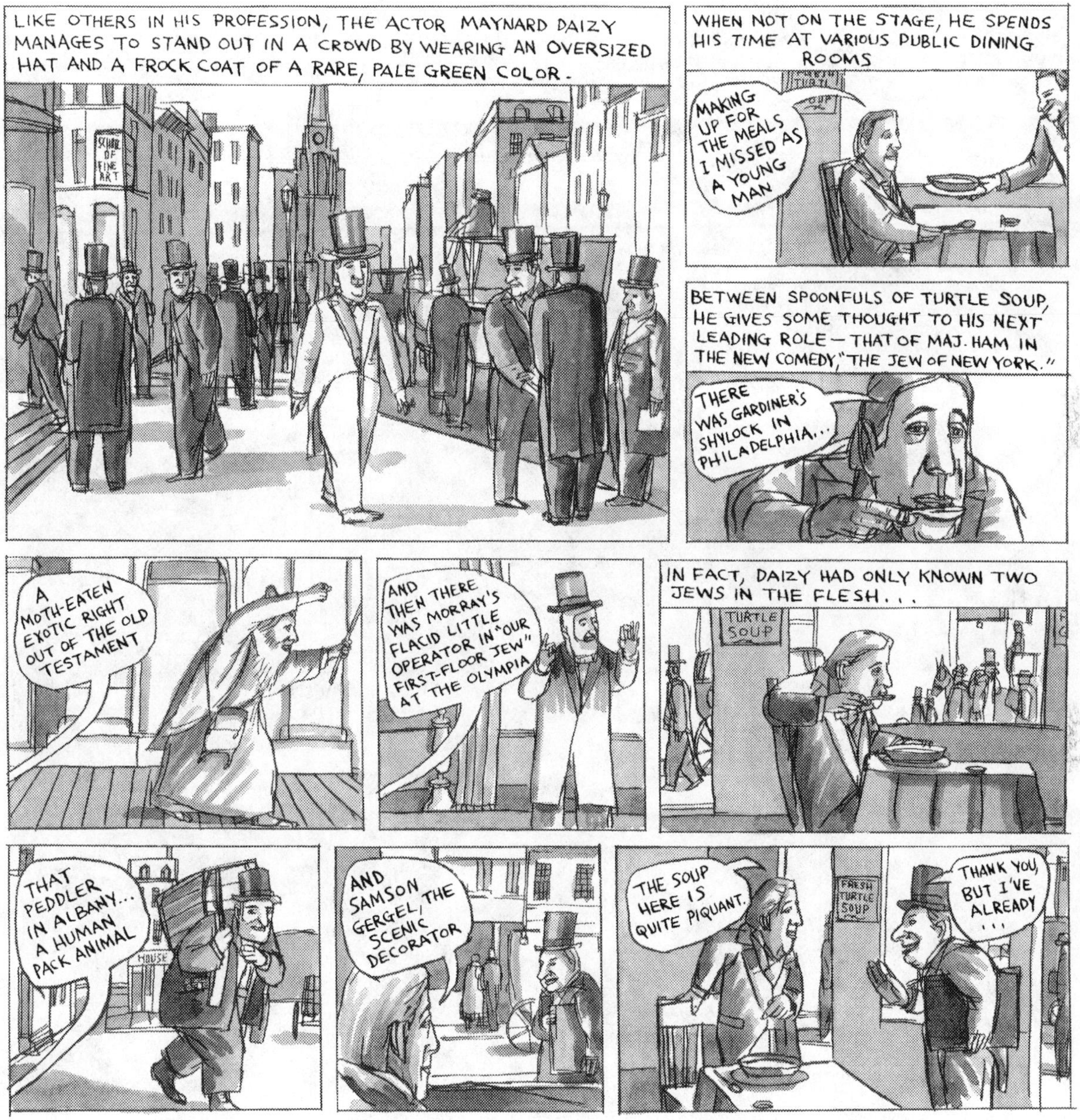
LIKE OTHERS IN HIS PROFESSION, THE ACTOR MAYNARD DAIZY MANAGES TO STAND OUT IN A CROWD BY WEARING AN OVERSIZED HAT AND A FROCK COAT OF A RARE, PALE GREEN COLOR.
SCHOOL OF FINE ART
WHEN NOT ON THE STAGE, HE SPENDS HIS TIME AT VARIOUS PUBLIC DINING ROOMS
MAKING UP FOR THE MEALS I MISSED AS A YOUNG MAN
BETWEEN SPOONFULS OF TURTLE SOUP, HE GIVES SOME THOUGHT TO HIS NEXT LEADING ROLE — THAT OF MAJ. HAM IN THE NEW COMEDY, "THE JEW OF NEW YORK."
THERE WAS GARDINER'S SHYLOCK IN PHILADELPHIA...
A MOTH-EATEN EXOTIC RIGHT OUT OF THE OLD TESTAMENT
AND THEN THERE WAS MORRAY'S FLACID LITTLE OPERATOR IN "OUR FIRST-FLOOR JEW" AT THE OLYMPIA
IN FACT, DAIZY HAD ONLY KNOWN TWO JEWS IN THE FLESH...
TURTLE SOUP
THAT PEDDLER IN ALBANY... A HUMAN PACK ANIMAL
HOUSE
AND SAMSON GERGEL, THE SCENIC DECORATOR
THE SOUP HERE IS QUITE PIQUANT.
FRESH TURTLE SOUP
THANK YOU, BUT I'VE ALREADY...

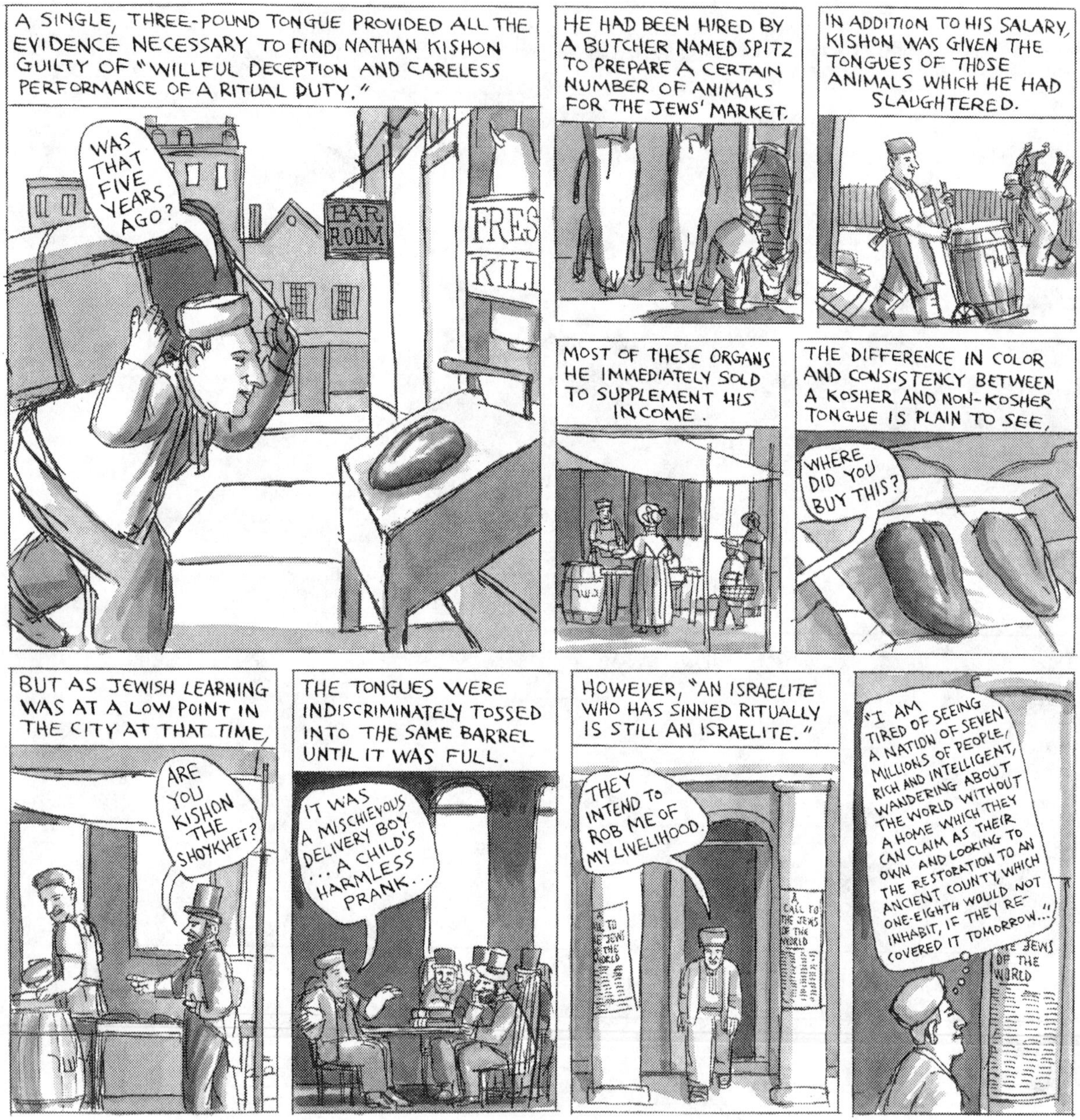
A SINGLE, THREE-POUND TONGUE PROVIDED ALL THE EVIDENCE NECESSARY TO FIND NATHAN KISHON GUILTY OF "WILLFUL DECEPTION AND CARELESS PERFORMANCE OF A RITUAL DUTY."
WAS THAT FIVE YEARS AGO?
BAR ROOM
HE HAD BEEN HIRED BY A BUTCHER NAMED SPITZ TO PREPARE A CERTAIN NUMBER OF ANIMALS FOR THE JEWS' MARKET.
IN ADDITION TO HIS SALARY, KISHON WAS GIVEN THE TONGUES OF THOSE ANIMALS WHICH HE HAD SLAUGHTERED.
MOST OF THESE ORGANS HE IMMEDIATELY SOLD TO SUPPLEMENT HIS INCOME.
THE DIFFERENCE IN COLOR AND CONSISTENCY BETWEEN A KOSHER AND NON-KOSHER TONGUE IS PLAIN TO SEE,
WHERE DID YOU BUY THIS?
BUT AS JEWISH LEARNING WAS AT A LOW POINT IN THE CITY AT THAT TIME,
ARE YOU KISHON THE SHOYKHET?
THE TONGUES WERE INDISCRIMINATELY TOSSED INTO THE SAME BARREL UNTIL IT WAS FULL.
IT WAS A MISCHIEVOUS DELIVERY BOY ... A CHILD'S HARMLESS PRANK...
HOWEVER, "AN ISRAELITE WHO HAS SINNED RITUALLY IS STILL AN ISRAELITE."
THEY INTEND TO ROB ME OF MY LIVELIHOOD.
A CALL TO THE JEWS OF THE WORLD
"I AM TIRED OF SEEING A NATION OF SEVEN MILLIONS OF PEOPLE, RICH AND INTELLIGENT, WANDERING ABOUT THE WORLD WITHOUT A HOME WHICH THEY CAN CLAIM AS THEIR OWN AND LOOKING TO THE RESTORATION TO AN ANCIENT COUNTY, WHICH NOT ONE-EIGHTH WOULD INHABIT, IF THEY RE-COVERED IT TOMORROW..."

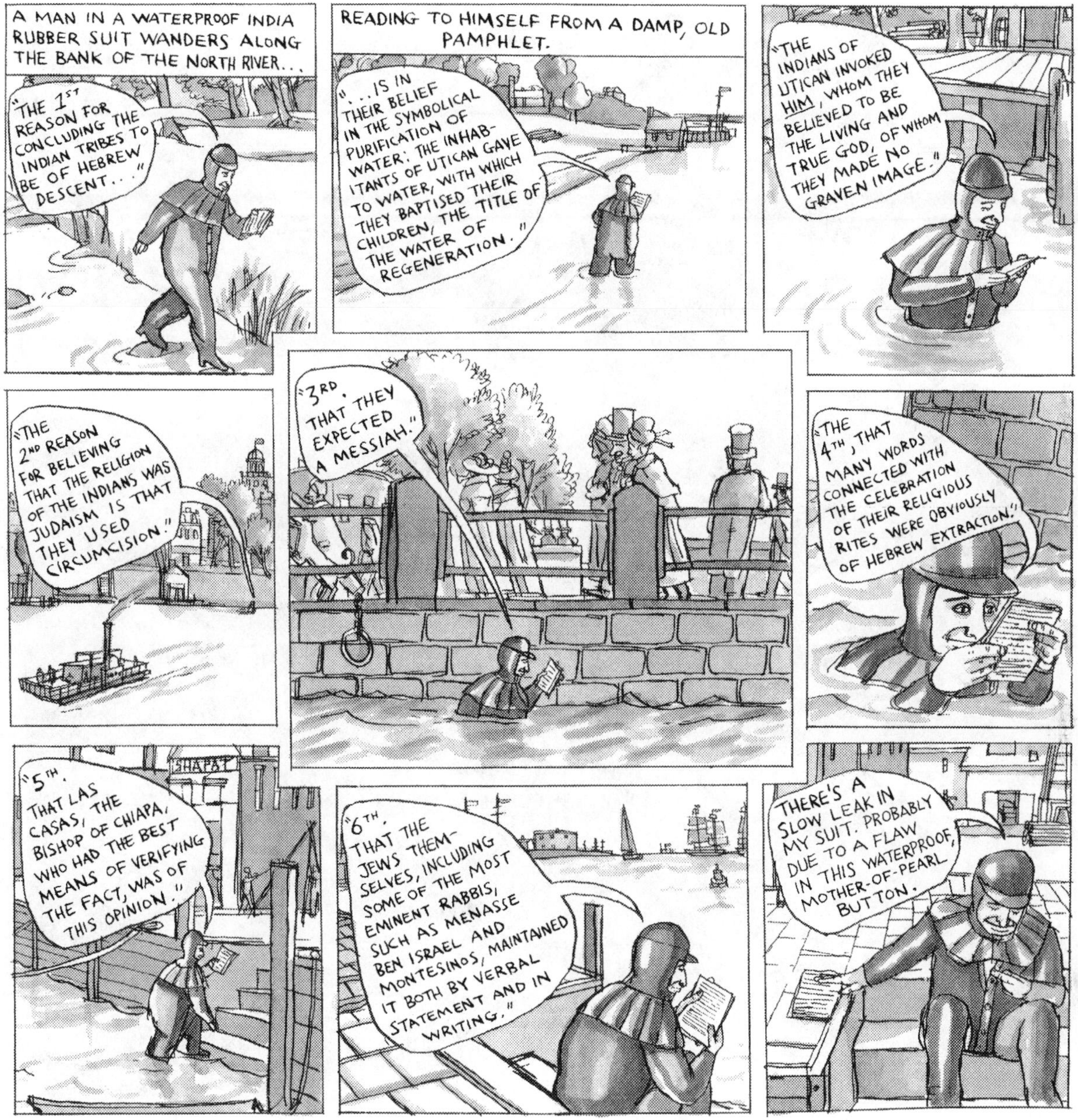
A MAN IN A WATERPROOF INDIA RUBBER SUIT WANDERS ALONG THE BANK OF THE NORTH RIVER...
"THE 1ST REASON FOR CONCLUDING THE INDIAN TRIBES TO BE OF HEBREW DESCENT..."
READING TO HIMSELF FROM A DAMP, OLD PAMPHLET.
"...IS IN THEIR BELIEF IN THE SYMBOLICAL PURIFICATION OF WATER; THE INHABITANTS OF UTICAN GAVE TO WATER, WITH WHICH THEY BAPTISED THEIR CHILDREN, THE TITLE OF THE WATER OF REGENERATION."
"THE INDIANS OF UTICAN INVOKED HIM, WHOM THEY BELIEVED TO BE THE LIVING AND TRUE GOD, OF WHOM THEY MADE NO GRAVEN IMAGE."
"THE 2ND REASON FOR BELIEVING THAT THE RELIGION OF THE INDIANS WAS JUDAISM IS THAT THEY USED CIRCUMCISION."
"3RD. THAT THEY EXPECTED A MESSIAH."
"THE 4TH, THAT MANY WORDS CONNECTED WITH THE CELEBRATION OF THEIR RELIGIOUS RITES WERE OBVIOUSLY OF HEBREW EXTRACTION."
SHAPAT
"5TH. THAT LAS CASAS, THE BISHOP OF CHIAPA, WHO HAD THE BEST MEANS OF VERIFYING THE FACT, WAS OF THIS OPINION."
"6TH. THAT THE JEWS THEMSELVES, INCLUDING SOME OF THE MOST EMINENT RABBIS, SUCH AS MENASSE BEN ISRAEL AND MONTESINOS, MAINTAINED IT BOTH BY VERBAL STATEMENT AND IN WRITING."
THERE'S A SLOW LEAK IN MY SUIT. PROBABLY DUE TO A FLAW IN THIS WATERPROOF, MOTHER-OF-PEARL, BUTTON.

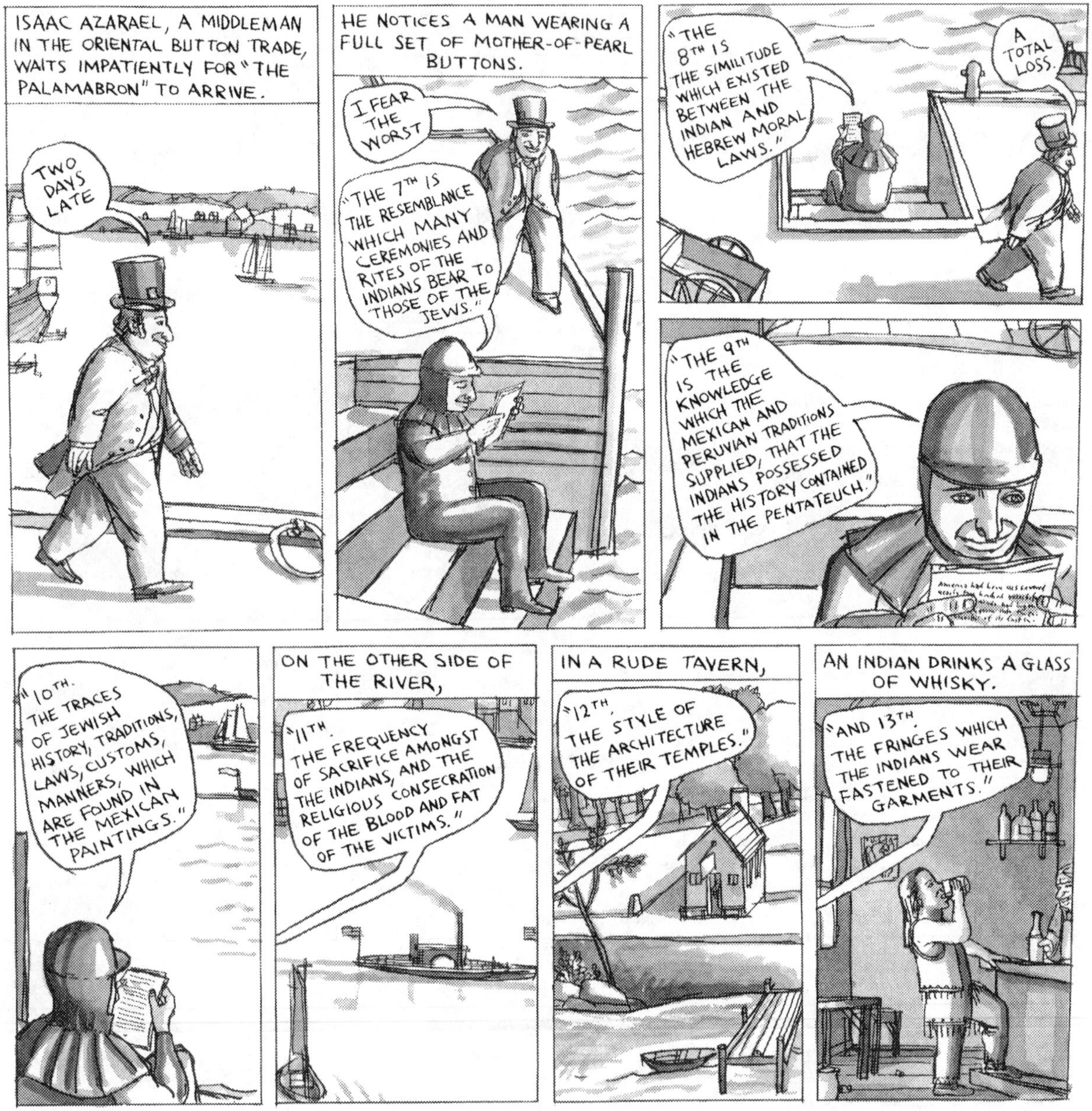
ISAAC AZARAEL, A MIDDLEMAN IN THE ORIENTAL BUTTON TRADE, WAITS IMPATIENTLY FOR "THE PALAMABRON" TO ARRIVE.
TWO DAYS LATE
HE NOTICES A MAN WEARING A FULL SET OF MOTHER-OF-PEARL BUTTONS.
I FEAR THE WORST
"THE 7TH IS THE RESEMBLANCE WHICH MANY CEREMONIES AND RITES OF THE INDIANS BEAR TO THOSE OF THE JEWS."
"THE 8TH IS THE SIMILITUDE WHICH EXISTED BETWEEN THE INDIAN AND HEBREW MORAL LAWS."
A TOTAL LOSS.
"THE 9TH IS THE KNOWLEDGE WHICH THE MEXICAN AND PERUVIAN TRADITIONS SUPPLIED, THAT THE INDIANS POSSESSED THE HISTORY CONTAINED IN THE PENTATEUCH."
"10TH. THE TRACES OF JEWISH HISTORY, TRADITIONS, LAWS, CUSTOMS, MANNERS, WHICH ARE FOUND IN THE MEXICAN PAINTINGS."
ON THE OTHER SIDE OF THE RIVER,
"11TH. THE FREQUENCY OF SACRIFICE AMONGST THE INDIANS, AND THE RELIGIOUS CONSECRATION OF THE BLOOD AND FAT OF THE VICTIMS."
IN A RUDE TAVERN,
"12TH. THE STYLE OF THE ARCHITECTURE OF THEIR TEMPLES."
AN INDIAN DRINKS A GLASS OF WHISKY.
"AND 13TH. THE FRINGES WHICH THE INDIANS WEAR FASTENED TO THEIR GARMENTS."

Misterall's
Characters & Scenes
IN THE
JEW OF NEW YORK
TAKEN FROM
THE
COMEDY BY

Professor V. Solidus
With a Book written expressly for the above.

4 Plates of Characters, 96 Scenes and Set Pieces
4 Part Wings

THE TEN TRIBES OF ISRAEL

HISTORICALLY IDENTIFIED

WITH THE

ABORIGINES

OF THE

WESTERN HEMISPHERE

By Mrs. Simon

. . . .

"Behold! I was left alone: — these, where had they been?—"
Isaiah XLIX. 21.

. . . .

PUBLISHED BY
THE SOCIETY FOR THE REDEMPTION
OF ISRAELITIC PEOPLES
CORNER STREET, LONDON
1830

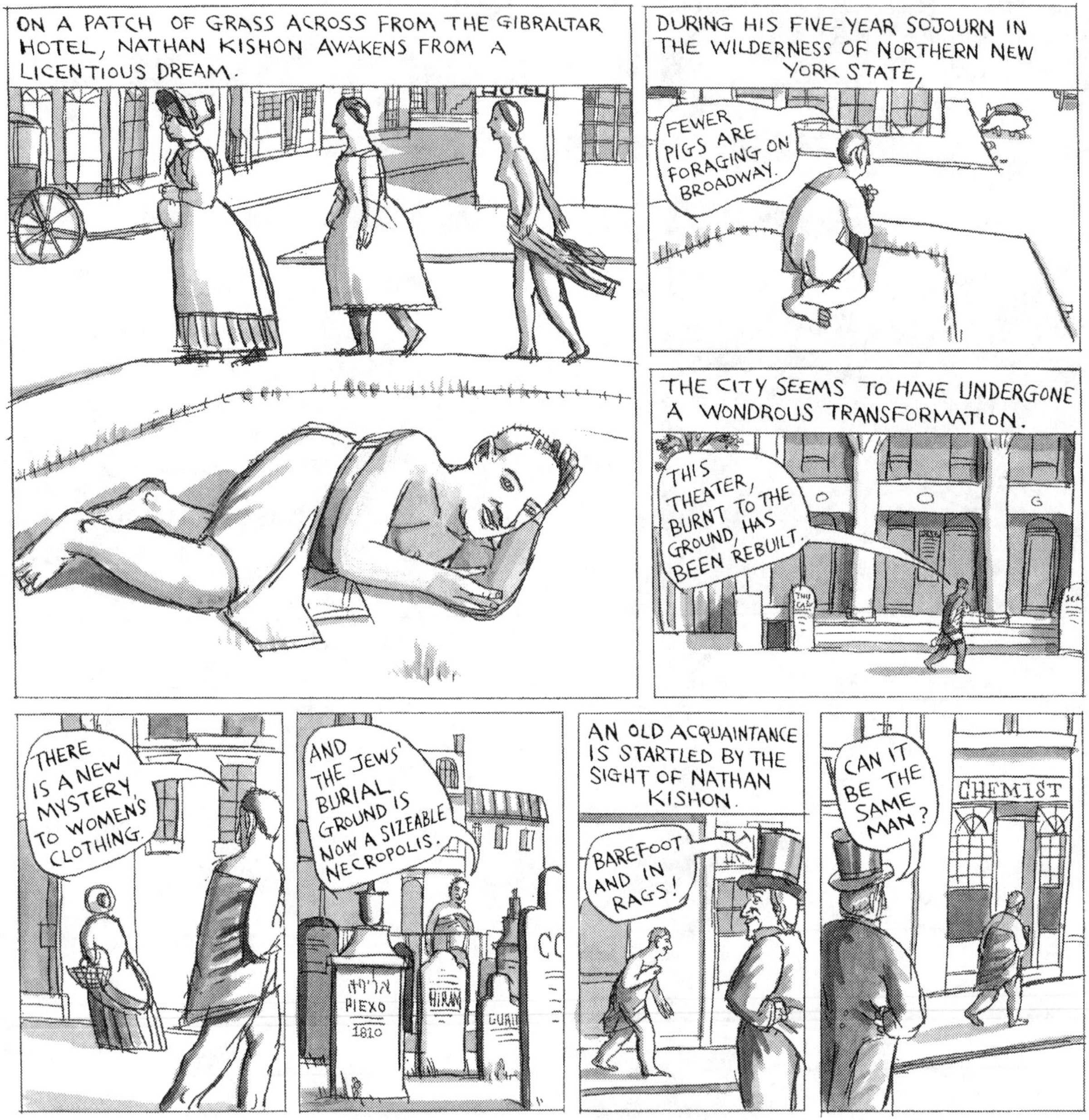
ON A PATCH OF GRASS ACROSS FROM THE GIBRALTAR HOTEL, NATHAN KISHON AWAKENS FROM A LICENTIOUS DREAM.
HOTEL
DURING HIS FIVE-YEAR SOJOURN IN THE WILDERNESS OF NORTHERN NEW YORK STATE,
FEWER PIGS ARE FORAGING ON BROADWAY.
THE CITY SEEMS TO HAVE UNDERGONE A WONDROUS TRANSFORMATION.
THIS THEATER, BURNT TO THE GROUND, HAS BEEN REBUILT.
THERE IS A NEW MYSTERY TO WOMEN'S CLOTHING.
AND THE JEWS' BURIAL GROUND IS NOW A SIZEABLE NECROPOLIS.
PIEXO
1810
HIRAM
AN OLD ACQUAINTANCE IS STARTLED BY THE SIGHT OF NATHAN KISHON.
BAREFOOT AND IN RAGS!
CAN IT BE THE SAME MAN?
CHEMIST

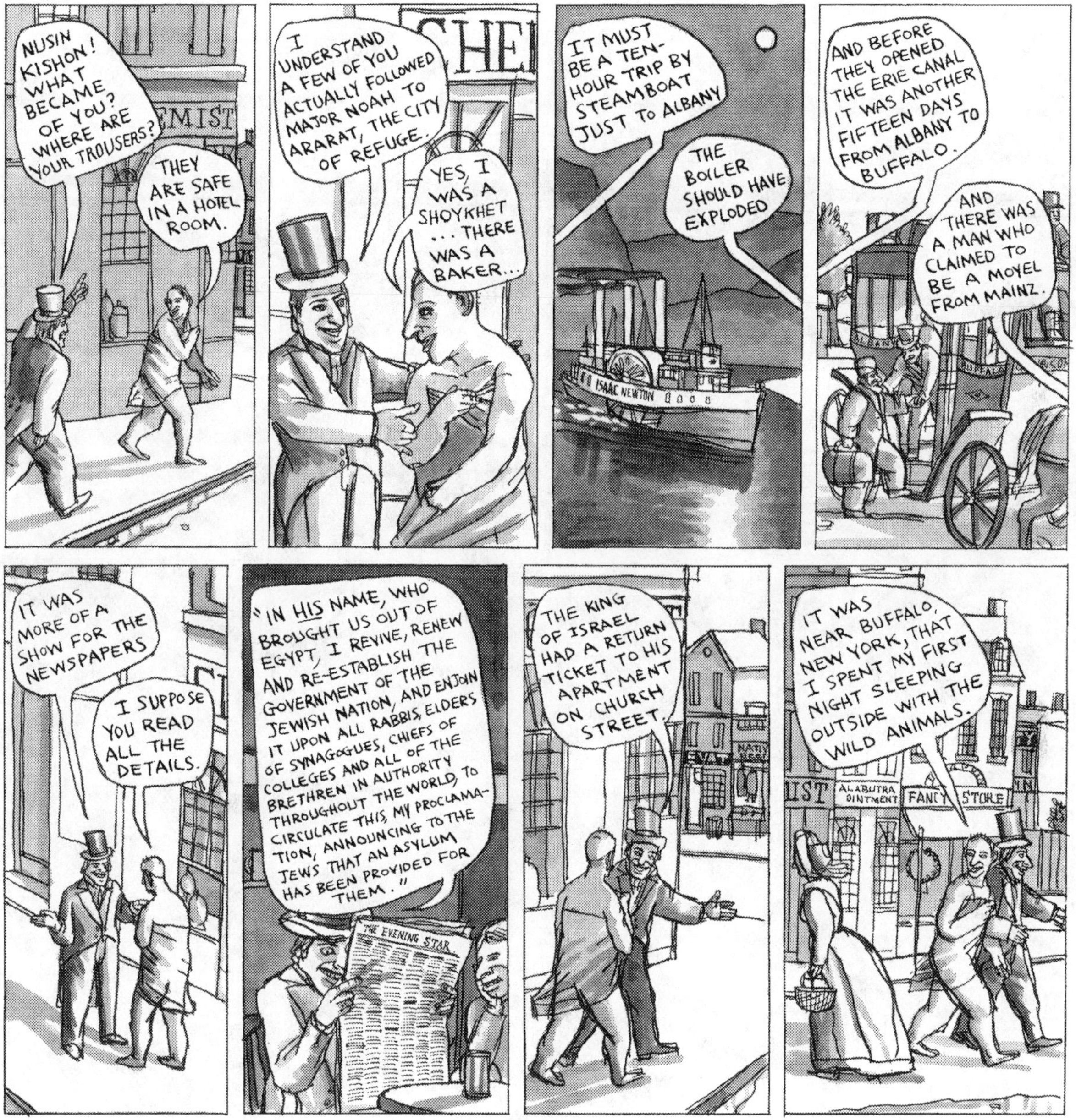
NUSIN KISHON! WHAT BECAME OF YOU? WHERE ARE YOUR TROUSERS?
THEY ARE SAFE IN A HOTEL ROOM.
EMIST
I UNDERSTAND A FEW OF YOU ACTUALLY FOLLOWED MAJOR NOAH TO ARARAT, THE CITY OF REFUGE.
YES, I WAS A SHOYKHET ... THERE WAS A BAKER...
SHE
IT MUST BE A TEN-HOUR TRIP BY STEAMBOAT JUST TO ALBANY
THE BOILER SHOULD HAVE EXPLODED
ISAAC NEWTON
AND BEFORE THEY OPENED THE ERIE CANAL IT WAS ANOTHER FIFTEEN DAYS FROM ALBANY TO BUFFALO.
AND THERE WAS A MAN WHO CLAIMED TO BE A MOYEL FROM MAINZ.
IT WAS MORE OF A SHOW FOR THE NEWSPAPERS
I SUPPOSE YOU READ ALL THE DETAILS.
"IN HIS NAME, WHO BROUGHT US OUT OF EGYPT, I REVIVE, RENEW AND RE-ESTABLISH THE GOVERNMENT OF THE JEWISH NATION, AND ENJOIN IT UPON ALL RABBIS, ELDERS OF SYNAGOGUES, CHIEFS OF COLLEGES AND ALL OF THE BRETHREN IN AUTHORITY THROUGHOUT THE WORLD, TO CIRCULATE THIS, MY PROCLAMATION, ANNOUNCING TO THE JEWS THAT AN ASYLUM HAS BEEN PROVIDED FOR THEM."
THE EVENING STAR
THE KING OF ISRAEL HAD A RETURN TICKET TO HIS APARTMENT ON CHURCH STREET.
IT WAS NEAR BUFFALO, NEW YORK, THAT I SPENT MY FIRST NIGHT SLEEPING OUTSIDE WITH THE WILD ANIMALS.
IST
ALABUTRA OINTMENT
FANCY STORE

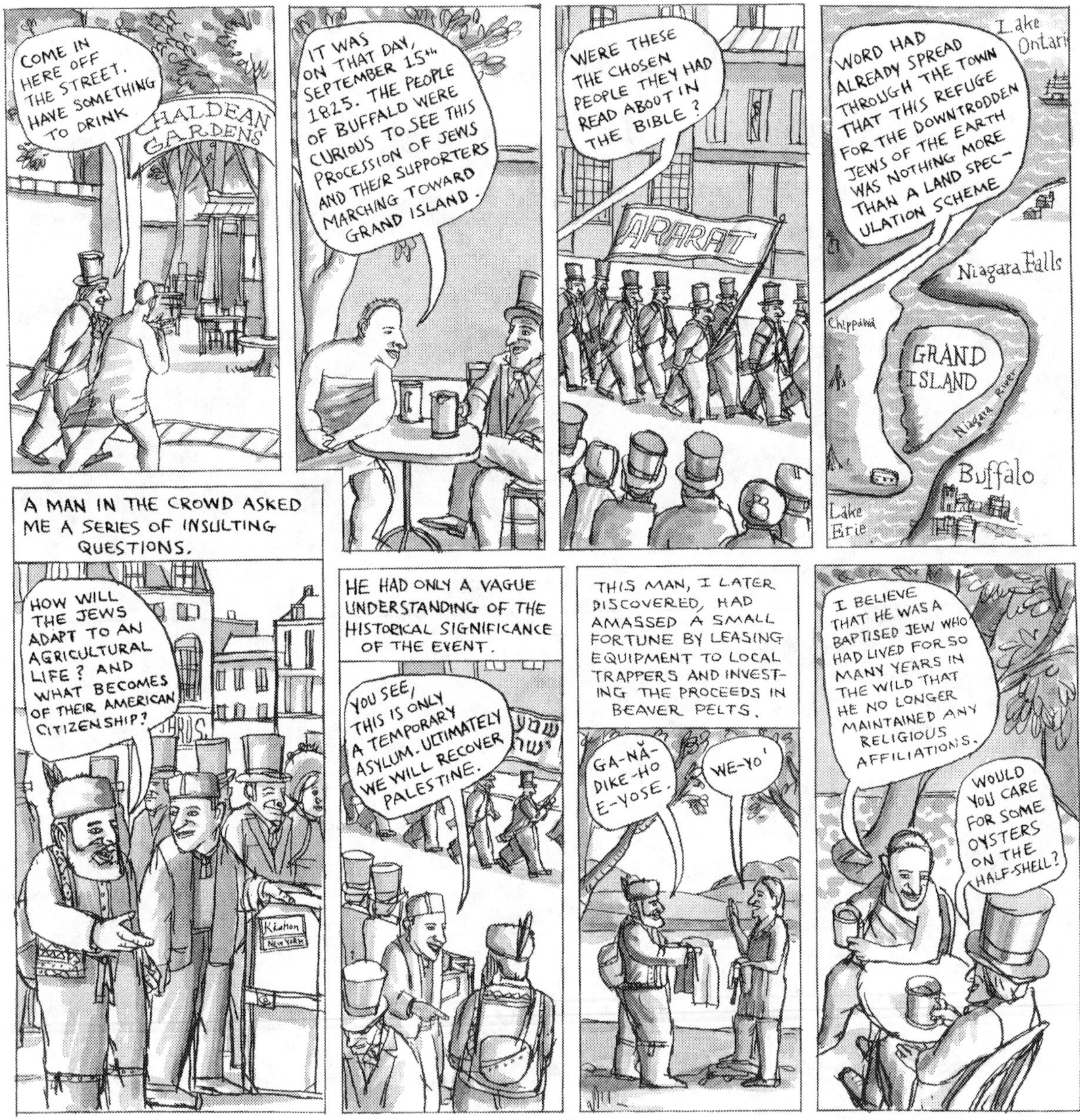
COME IN HERE OFF THE STREET. HAVE SOMETHING TO DRINK
CHALDEAN GARDENS
IT WAS ON THAT DAY, SEPTEMBER 15th 1825. THE PEOPLE OF BUFFALO WERE CURIOUS TO SEE THIS PROCESSION OF JEWS AND THEIR SUPPORTERS MARCHING TOWARD GRAND ISLAND.
WERE THESE THE CHOSEN PEOPLE THEY HAD READ ABOUT IN THE BIBLE?
ARARAT
WORD HAD ALREADY SPREAD THROUGH THE TOWN THAT THIS REFUGE FOR THE DOWNTRODDEN JEWS OF THE EARTH WAS NOTHING MORE THAN A LAND SPECULATION SCHEME
Lake Ontario
Niagara Falls
Chippawa
GRAND ISLAND
Niagara River
Buffalo
Lake Erie
A MAN IN THE CROWD ASKED ME A SERIES OF INSULTING QUESTIONS.
HOW WILL THE JEWS ADAPT TO AN AGRICULTURAL LIFE? AND WHAT BECOMES OF THEIR AMERICAN CITIZENSHIP?
HE HAD ONLY A VAGUE UNDERSTANDING OF THE HISTORICAL SIGNIFICANCE OF THE EVENT.
YOU SEE, THIS IS ONLY A TEMPORARY ASYLUM. ULTIMATELY WE WILL RECOVER PALESTINE.
THIS MAN, I LATER DISCOVERED, HAD AMASSED A SMALL FORTUNE BY LEASING EQUIPMENT TO LOCAL TRAPPERS AND INVESTING THE PROCEEDS IN BEAVER PELTS.
GA-NĂ-DIKE-HO E-YOSE.
WE-YO'
I BELIEVE THAT HE WAS A BAPTISED JEW WHO HAD LIVED FOR SO MANY YEARS IN THE WILD THAT HE NO LONGER MAINTAINED ANY RELIGIOUS AFFILIATIONS.
WOULD YOU CARE FOR SOME OYSTERS ON THE HALF-SHELL?

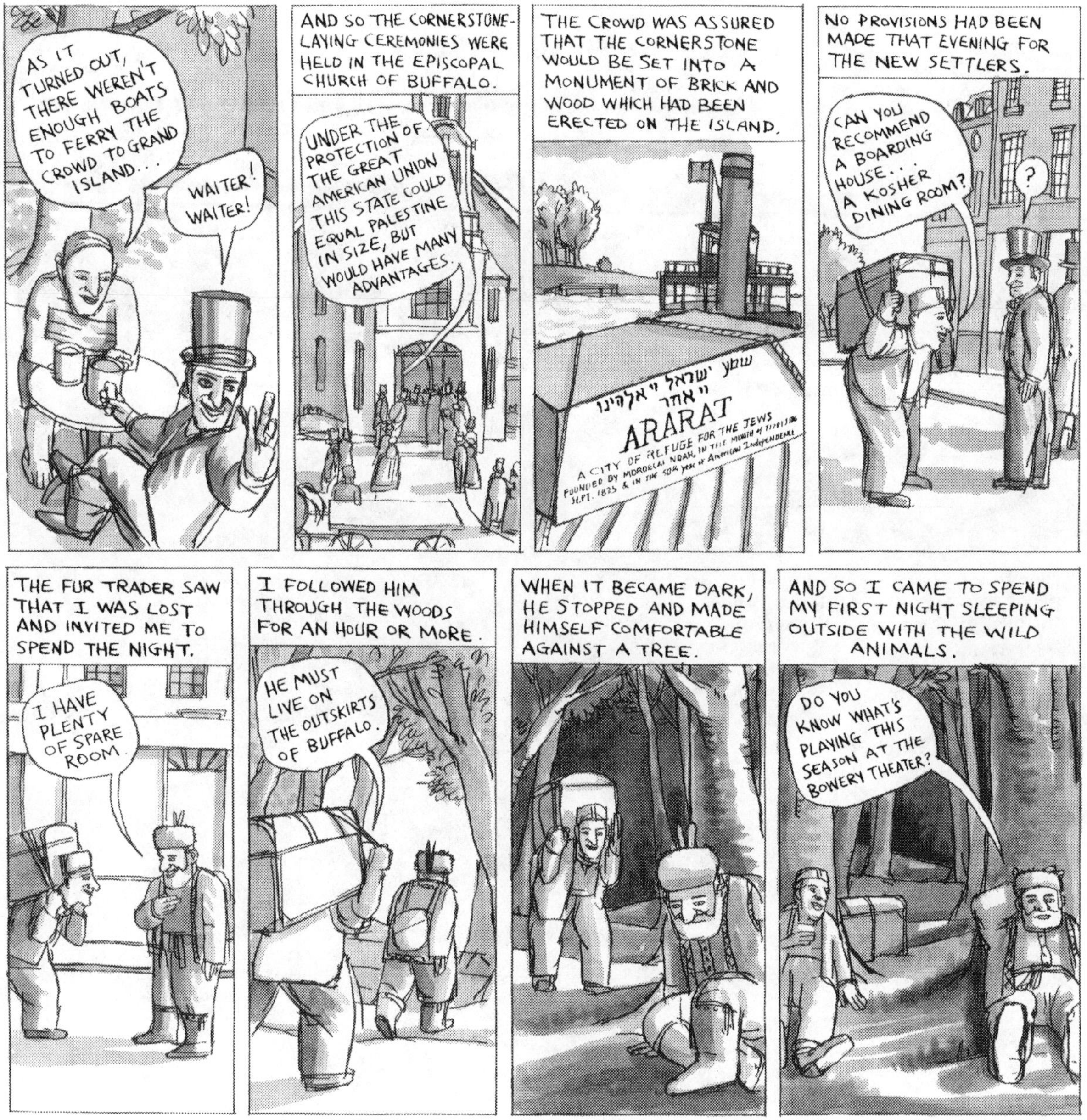
AS IT TURNED OUT, THERE WEREN'T ENOUGH BOATS TO FERRY THE CROWD TO GRAND ISLAND . . .
WAITER! WAITER!
AND SO THE CORNERSTONE-LAYING CEREMONIES WERE HELD IN THE EPISCOPAL CHURCH OF BUFFALO.
UNDER THE PROTECTION OF THE GREAT AMERICAN UNION THIS STATE COULD EQUAL PALESTINE IN SIZE, BUT WOULD HAVE MANY ADVANTAGES.
THE CROWD WAS ASSURED THAT THE CORNERSTONE WOULD BE SET INTO A MONUMENT OF BRICK AND WOOD WHICH HAD BEEN ERECTED ON THE ISLAND.
שמע ישראל יי אלהינו יי אחר
ARARAT
A CITY OF REFUGE FOR THE JEWS
FOUNDED BY MORDECAI NOAH, IN THE MONTH of
SEPT. 1825 & IN THE 50th year of American Independence
NO PROVISIONS HAD BEEN MADE THAT EVENING FOR THE NEW SETTLERS.
CAN YOU RECOMMEND A BOARDING HOUSE . . . A KOSHER DINING ROOM?
?
THE FUR TRADER SAW THAT I WAS LOST AND INVITED ME TO SPEND THE NIGHT.
I HAVE PLENTY OF SPARE ROOM.
I FOLLOWED HIM THROUGH THE WOODS FOR AN HOUR OR MORE.
HE MUST LIVE ON THE OUTSKIRTS OF BUFFALO.
WHEN IT BECAME DARK, HE STOPPED AND MADE HIMSELF COMFORTABLE AGAINST A TREE.
AND SO I CAME TO SPEND MY FIRST NIGHT SLEEPING OUTSIDE WITH THE WILD ANIMALS.
DO YOU KNOW WHAT'S PLAYING THIS SEASON AT THE BOWERY THEATER?

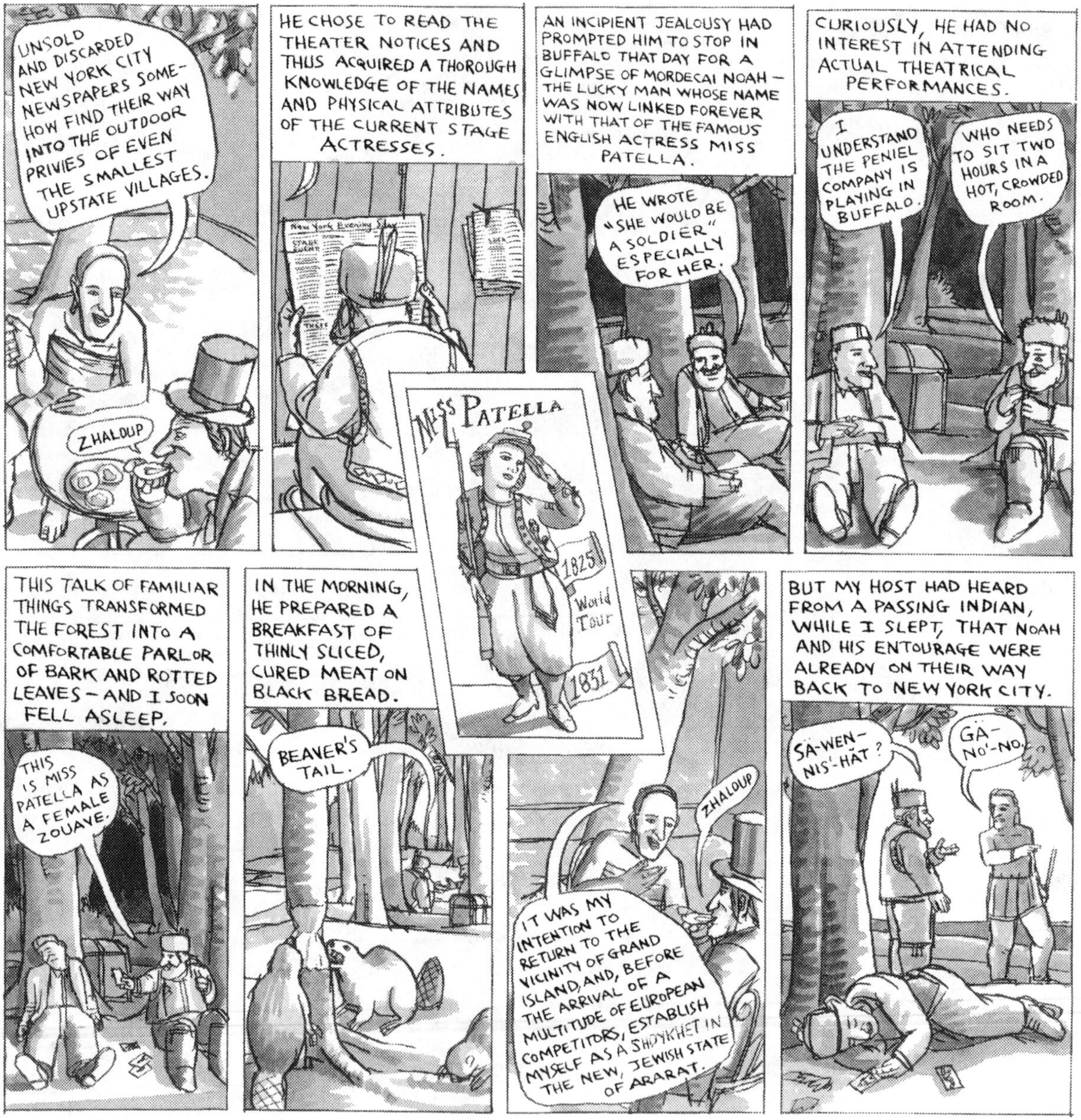
UNSOLD AND DISCARDED NEW YORK CITY NEWSPAPERS SOME-HOW FIND THEIR WAY INTO THE OUTDOOR PRIVIES OF EVEN THE SMALLEST UPSTATE VILLAGES.
ZHALOUP
HE CHOSE TO READ THE THEATER NOTICES AND THUS ACQUIRED A THOROUGH KNOWLEDGE OF THE NAMES AND PHYSICAL ATTRIBUTES OF THE CURRENT STAGE ACTRESSES.
AN INCIPIENT JEALOUSY HAD PROMPTED HIM TO STOP IN BUFFALO THAT DAY FOR A GLIMPSE OF MORDECAI NOAH — THE LUCKY MAN WHOSE NAME WAS NOW LINKED FOREVER WITH THAT OF THE FAMOUS ENGLISH ACTRESS MISS PATELLA.
HE WROTE "SHE WOULD BE A SOLDIER" ESPECIALLY FOR HER.
CURIOUSLY, HE HAD NO INTEREST IN ATTENDING ACTUAL THEATRICAL PERFORMANCES.
I UNDERSTAND THE PENIEL COMPANY IS PLAYING IN BUFFALO.
WHO NEEDS TO SIT TWO HOURS IN A HOT, CROWDED ROOM.
MISS PATELLA
1825
World Tour
1831
THIS TALK OF FAMILIAR THINGS TRANSFORMED THE FOREST INTO A COMFORTABLE PARLOR OF BARK AND ROTTED LEAVES — AND I SOON FELL ASLEEP.
THIS IS MISS PATELLA AS A FEMALE ZOUAVE.
IN THE MORNING, HE PREPARED A BREAKFAST OF THINLY SLICED, CURED MEAT ON BLACK BREAD.
BEAVER'S TAIL.
ZHALOUP
IT WAS MY INTENTION TO RETURN TO THE VICINITY OF GRAND ISLAND, AND, BEFORE THE ARRIVAL OF A MULTITUDE OF EUROPEAN COMPETITORS, ESTABLISH MYSELF AS A SHOYKHET IN THE NEW, JEWISH STATE OF ARARAT.
BUT MY HOST HAD HEARD FROM A PASSING INDIAN, WHILE I SLEPT, THAT NOAH AND HIS ENTOURAGE WERE ALREADY ON THEIR WAY BACK TO NEW YORK CITY.
SÄ-WEN-NIS'-HÄT?
GÄ-NO'-NO.

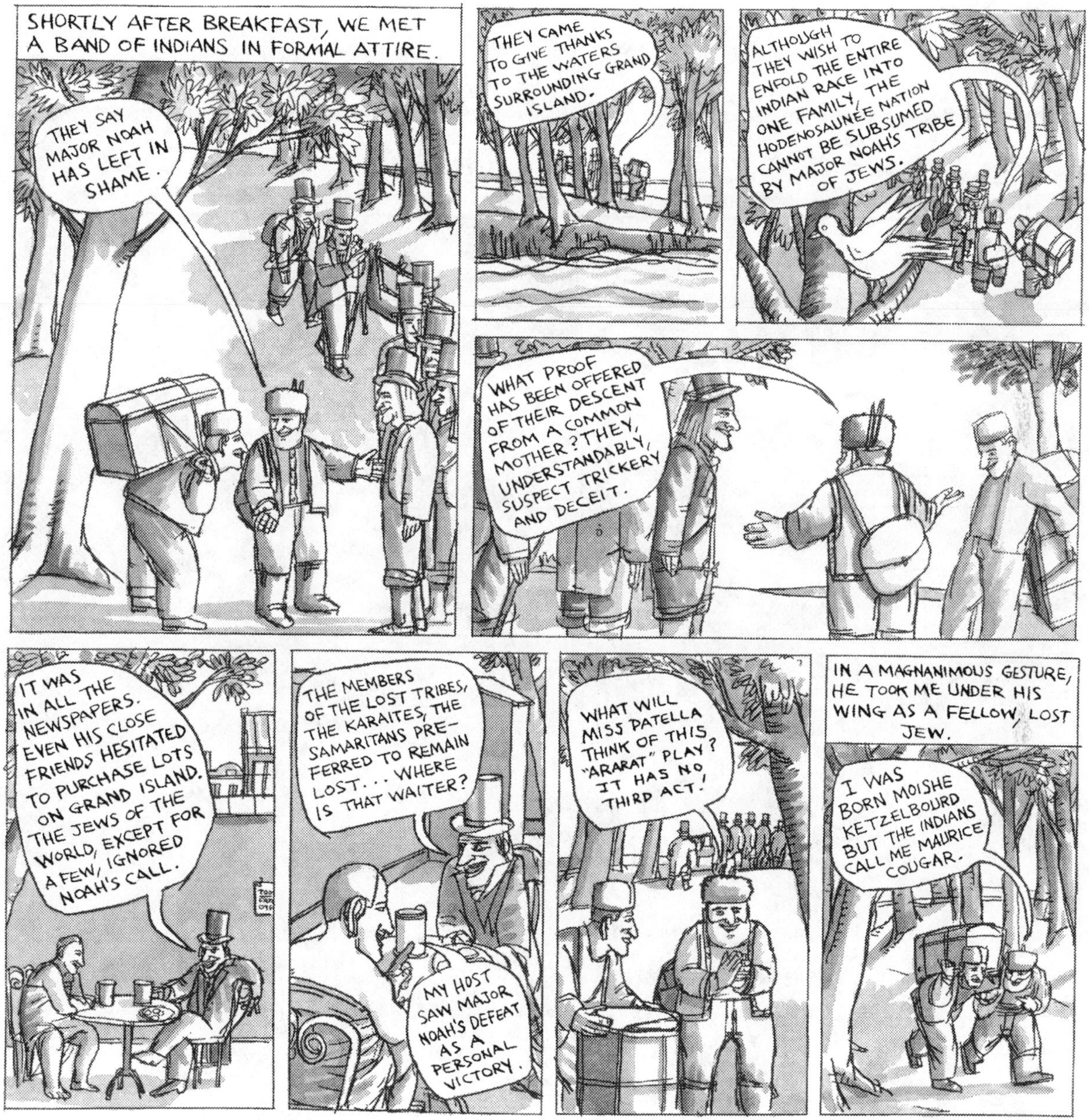
SHORTLY AFTER BREAKFAST, WE MET A BAND OF INDIANS IN FORMAL ATTIRE.
THEY SAY MAJOR NOAH HAS LEFT IN SHAME.
THEY CAME TO GIVE THANKS TO THE WATERS SURROUNDING GRAND ISLAND.
ALTHOUGH THEY WISH TO ENFOLD THE ENTIRE INDIAN RACE INTO ONE FAMILY, THE HODENOSAUNÉE NATION CANNOT BE SUBSUMED BY MAJOR NOAH'S TRIBE OF JEWS.
WHAT PROOF HAS BEEN OFFERED OF THEIR DESCENT FROM A COMMON MOTHER? THEY, UNDERSTANDABLY, SUSPECT TRICKERY AND DECEIT.
IT WAS IN ALL THE NEWSPAPERS. EVEN HIS CLOSE FRIENDS HESITATED TO PURCHASE LOTS ON GRAND ISLAND. THE JEWS OF THE WORLD, EXCEPT FOR A FEW, IGNORED NOAH'S CALL.
THE MEMBERS OF THE LOST TRIBES, THE KARAITES, THE SAMARITANS PRE-FERRED TO REMAIN LOST. . . WHERE IS THAT WAITER?
MY HOST SAW MAJOR NOAH'S DEFEAT AS A PERSONAL VICTORY.
WHAT WILL MISS PATELLA THINK OF THIS "ARARAT" PLAY? IT HAS NO THIRD ACT!
IN A MAGNANIMOUS GESTURE, HE TOOK ME UNDER HIS WING AS A FELLOW, LOST JEW.
I WAS BORN MOISHE KETZELBOURD BUT THE INDIANS CALL ME MAURICE COUGAR.

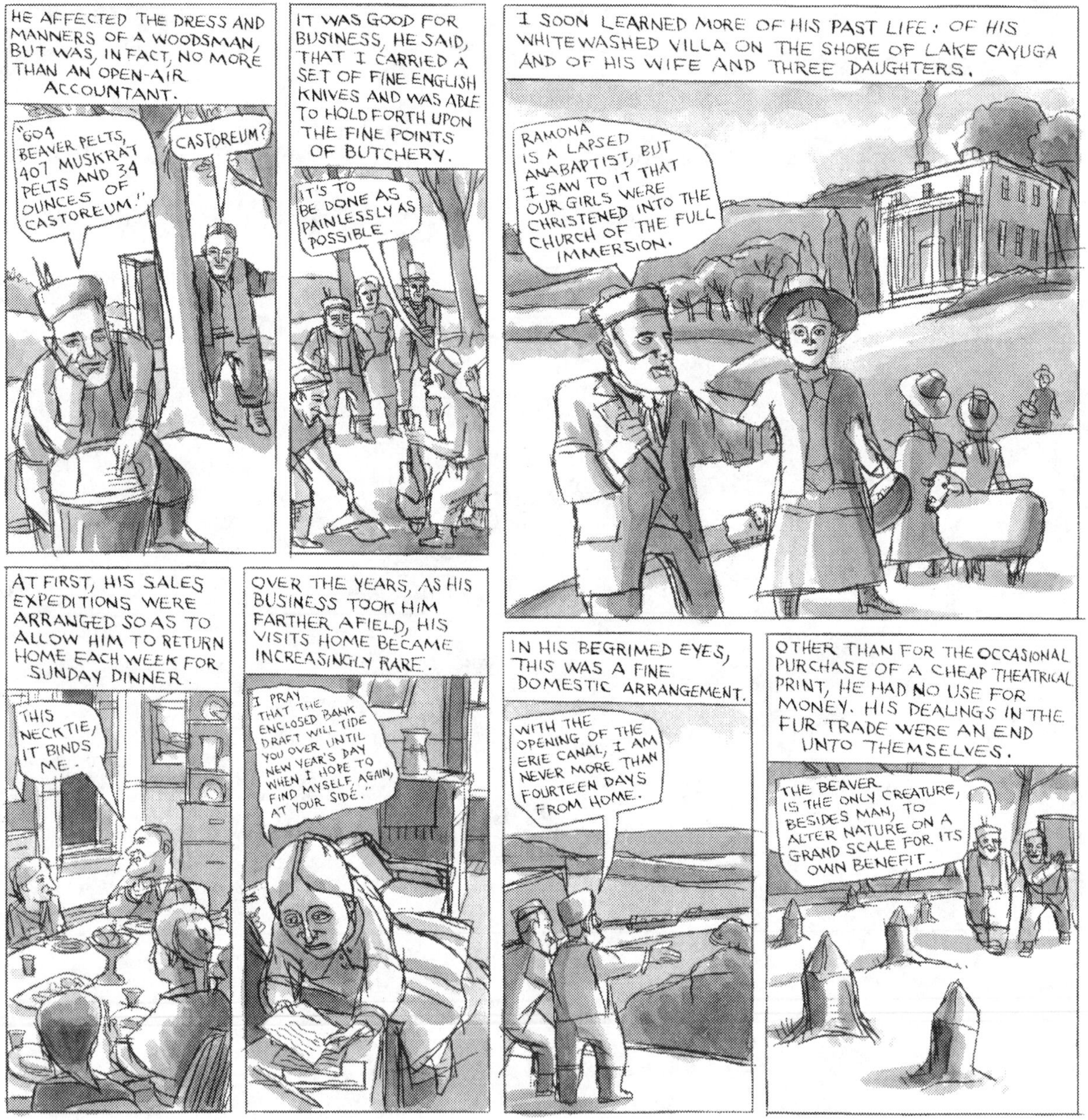
HE AFFECTED THE DRESS AND MANNERS OF A WOODSMAN, BUT WAS, IN FACT, NO MORE THAN AN OPEN-AIR ACCOUNTANT.
"604 BEAVER PELTS, 407 MUSKRAT PELTS AND 34 OUNCES OF CASTOREUM."
CASTOREUM?
IT WAS GOOD FOR BUSINESS, HE SAID, THAT I CARRIED A SET OF FINE ENGLISH KNIVES AND WAS ABLE TO HOLD FORTH UPON THE FINE POINTS OF BUTCHERY.
IT'S TO BE DONE AS PAINLESSLY AS POSSIBLE.
I SOON LEARNED MORE OF HIS PAST LIFE: OF HIS WHITEWASHED VILLA ON THE SHORE OF LAKE CAYUGA AND OF HIS WIFE AND THREE DAUGHTERS.
RAMONA IS A LAPSED ANABAPTIST, BUT I SAW TO IT THAT OUR GIRLS WERE CHRISTENED INTO THE CHURCH OF THE FULL IMMERSION.
AT FIRST, HIS SALES EXPEDITIONS WERE ARRANGED SO AS TO ALLOW HIM TO RETURN HOME EACH WEEK FOR SUNDAY DINNER.
THIS NECKTIE, IT BINDS ME.
OVER THE YEARS, AS HIS BUSINESS TOOK HIM FARTHER AFIELD, HIS VISITS HOME BECAME INCREASINGLY RARE.
"I PRAY THAT THE ENCLOSED BANK DRAFT WILL TIDE YOU OVER UNTIL NEW YEAR'S DAY WHEN I HOPE TO FIND MYSELF, AGAIN, AT YOUR SIDE."
IN HIS BEGRIMED EYES, THIS WAS A FINE DOMESTIC ARRANGEMENT.
WITH THE OPENING OF THE ERIE CANAL, I AM NEVER MORE THAN FOURTEEN DAYS FROM HOME.
OTHER THAN FOR THE OCCASIONAL PURCHASE OF A CHEAP THEATRICAL PRINT, HE HAD NO USE FOR MONEY. HIS DEALINGS IN THE FUR TRADE WERE AN END UNTO THEMSELVES.
THE BEAVER IS THE ONLY CREATURE, BESIDES MAN, TO ALTER NATURE ON A GRAND SCALE FOR ITS OWN BENEFIT.

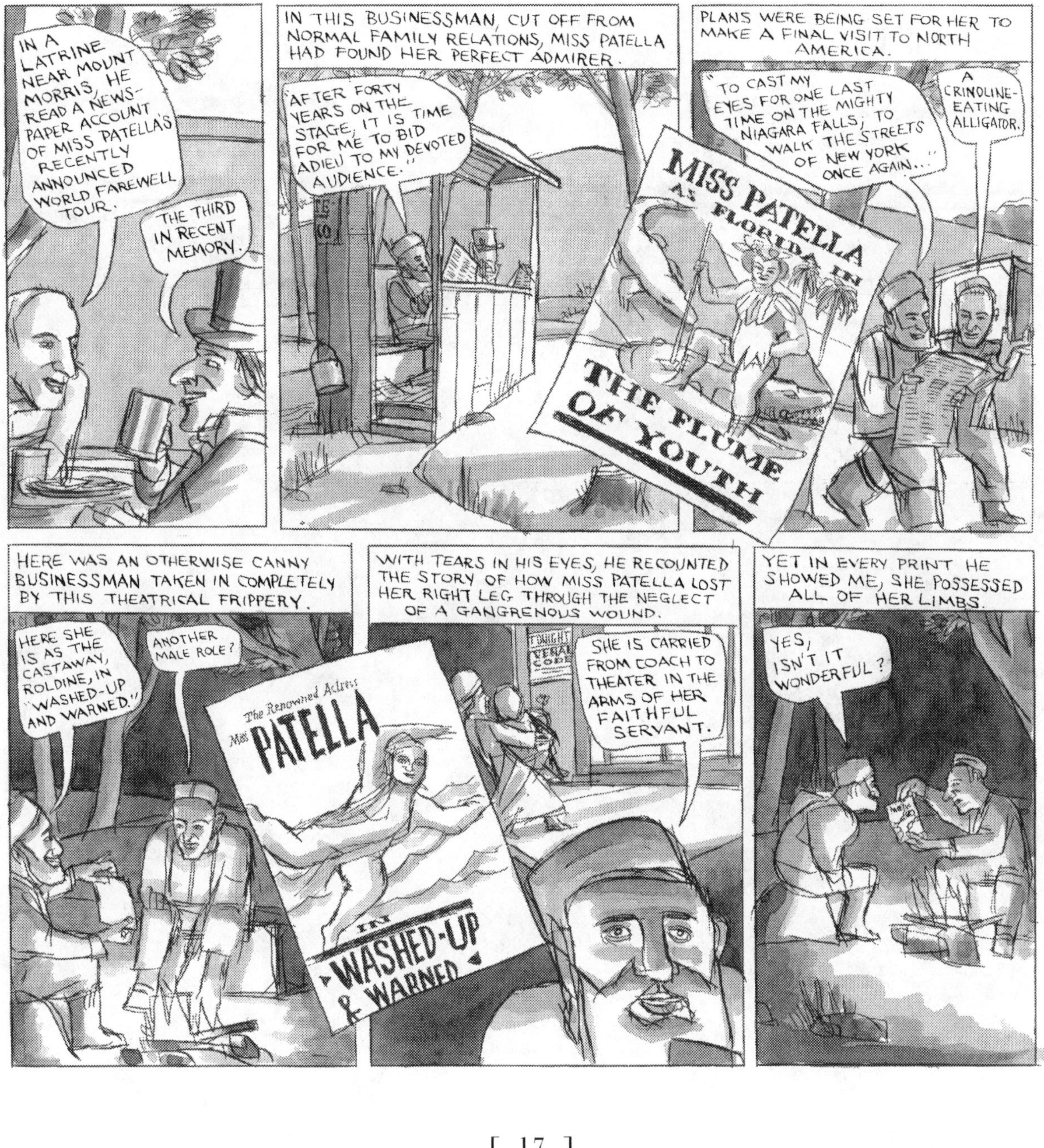
IN A LATRINE NEAR MOUNT MORRIS, HE READ A NEWSPAPER ACCOUNT OF MISS PATELLA'S RECENTLY ANNOUNCED WORLD FAREWELL TOUR.
THE THIRD IN RECENT MEMORY.
IN THIS BUSINESSMAN, CUT OFF FROM NORMAL FAMILY RELATIONS, MISS PATELLA HAD FOUND HER PERFECT ADMIRER.
"AFTER FORTY YEARS ON THE STAGE, IT IS TIME FOR ME TO BID ADIEU TO MY DEVOTED AUDIENCE."
PLANS WERE BEING SET FOR HER TO MAKE A FINAL VISIT TO NORTH AMERICA.
"TO CAST MY EYES FOR ONE LAST TIME ON THE MIGHTY NIAGARA FALLS, TO WALK THE STREETS OF NEW YORK ONCE AGAIN..."
A CRINOLINE-EATING ALLIGATOR.
MISS PATELLA AS FLORIDA IN THE FLUME OF YOUTH
HERE WAS AN OTHERWISE CANNY BUSINESSMAN TAKEN IN COMPLETELY BY THIS THEATRICAL FRIPPERY.
HERE SHE IS AS THE CASTAWAY, ROLDINE, IN "WASHED-UP AND WARNED."
ANOTHER MALE ROLE?
The Renowned Actress Miss PATELLA IN WASHED-UP & WARNED
WITH TEARS IN HIS EYES, HE RECOUNTED THE STORY OF HOW MISS PATELLA LOST HER RIGHT LEG THROUGH THE NEGLECT OF A GANGRENOUS WOUND.
TONIGHT
SHE IS CARRIED FROM COACH TO THEATER IN THE ARMS OF HER FAITHFUL SERVANT.
YET IN EVERY PRINT HE SHOWED ME, SHE POSSESSED ALL OF HER LIMBS.
YES, ISN'T IT WONDERFUL?

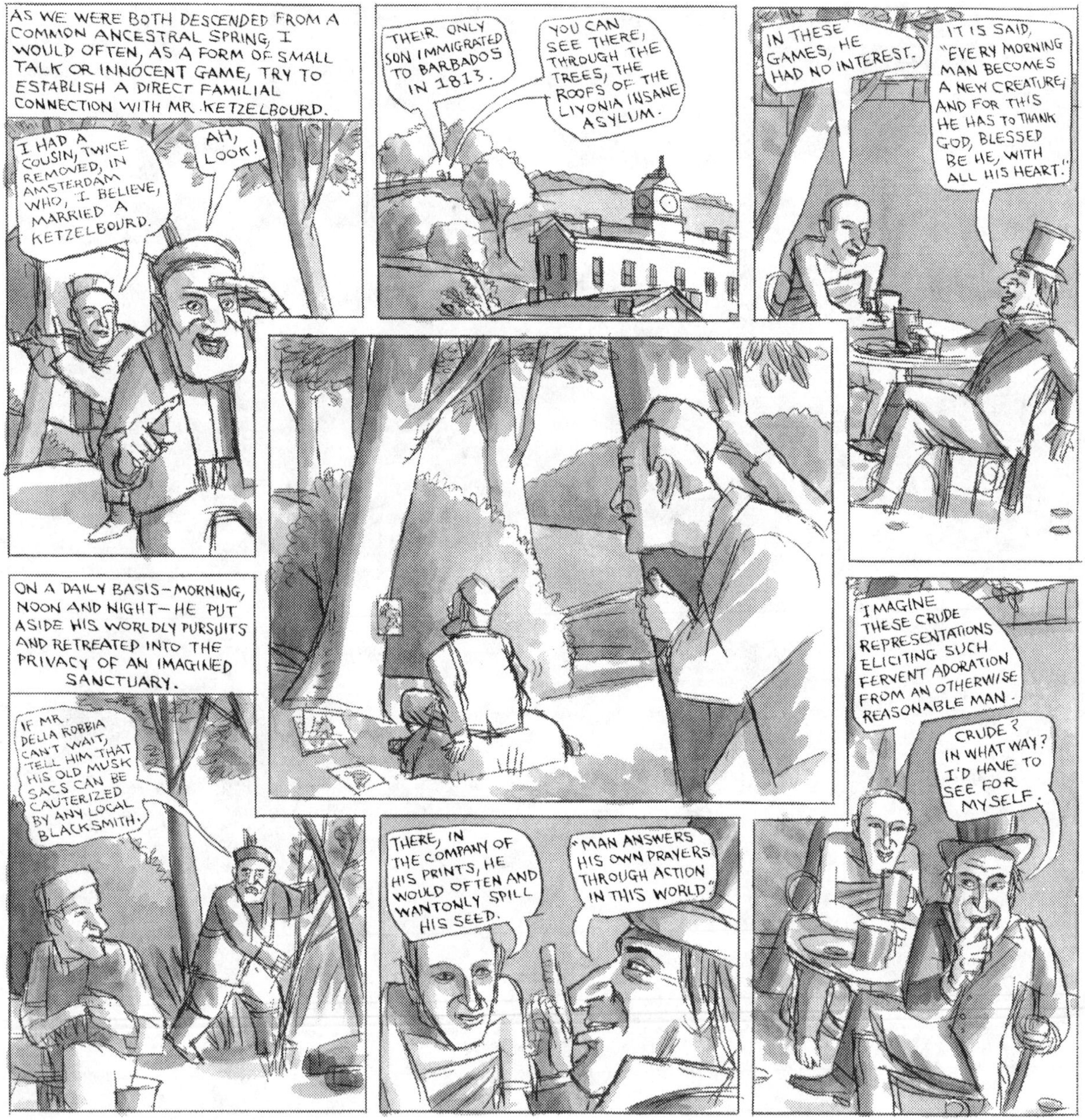
AS WE WERE BOTH DESCENDED FROM A COMMON ANCESTRAL SPRING, I WOULD OFTEN, AS A FORM OF SMALL TALK OR INNOCENT GAME, TRY TO ESTABLISH A DIRECT FAMILIAL CONNECTION WITH MR. KETZELBOURD.
I HAD A COUSIN, TWICE REMOVED, IN AMSTERDAM WHO, I BELIEVE, MARRIED A KETZELBOURD.
AH, LOOK!
THEIR ONLY SON IMMIGRATED TO BARBADOS IN 1813.
YOU CAN SEE THERE, THROUGH THE TREES, THE ROOFS OF THE LIVONIA INSANE ASYLUM.
IN THESE GAMES, HE HAD NO INTEREST.
IT IS SAID, "EVERY MORNING MAN BECOMES A NEW CREATURE; AND FOR THIS HE HAS TO THANK GOD, BLESSED BE HE, WITH ALL HIS HEART."
ON A DAILY BASIS—MORNING, NOON AND NIGHT—HE PUT ASIDE HIS WORLDLY PURSUITS AND RETREATED INTO THE PRIVACY OF AN IMAGINED SANCTUARY.
IF MR. DELLA ROBBIA CAN'T WAIT, TELL HIM THAT HIS OLD MUSK SACS CAN BE CAUTERIZED BY ANY LOCAL BLACKSMITH.
THERE, IN THE COMPANY OF HIS PRINTS, HE WOULD OFTEN AND WANTONLY SPILL HIS SEED.
"MAN ANSWERS HIS OWN PRAYERS THROUGH ACTION IN THIS WORLD."
IMAGINE THESE CRUDE REPRESENTATIONS ELICITING SUCH FERVENT ADORATION FROM AN OTHERWISE REASONABLE MAN.
CRUDE? IN WHAT WAY? I'D HAVE TO SEE FOR MYSELF.

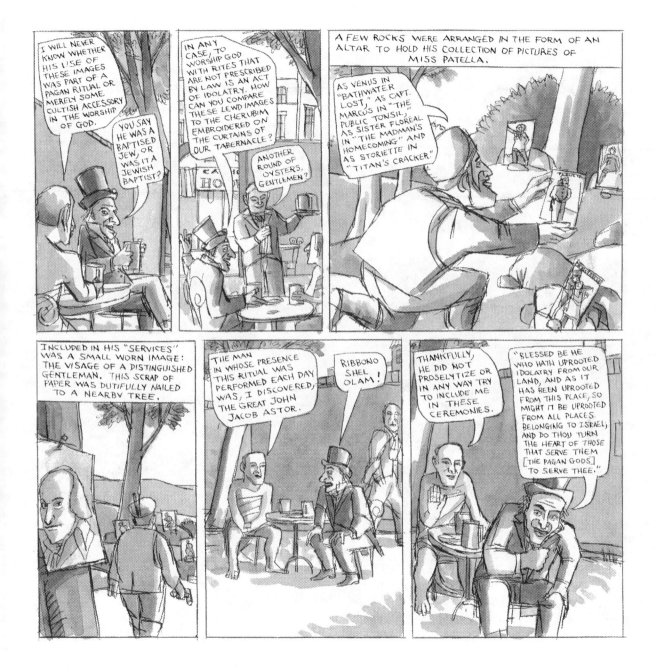

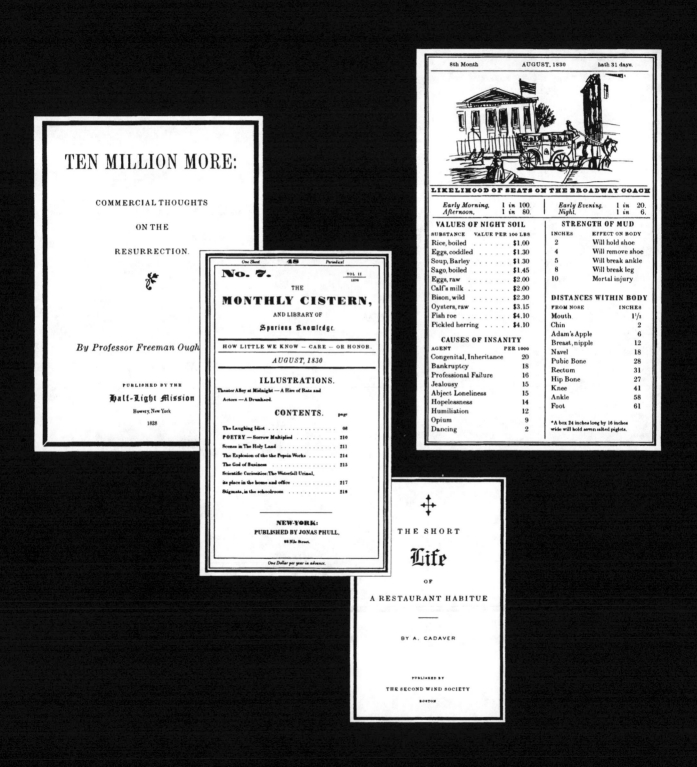

TEN MILLION MORE:

COMMERCIAL THOUGHTS

ON THE

RESURRECTION.

By Professor Freeman Ough

PUBLISHED BY THE

Half-Light Mission

Bowery New York

1828

One Sheet   48   Periodical

No. 7.

THE

MONTHLY CISTERN,

AND LIBRARY OF

Spurious Knowledge.

HOW LITTLE WE KNOW — CARE — OR HONOR.

AUGUST, 1830

VOL. II 1830

ILLUSTRATIONS.

Theater Alley at Midnight — A Hive of Rats and Actors — A Drunkard.

CONTENTS.

NEW-YORK:
PUBLISHED BY JONAS PHULL,
98 Nile Street.

One Dollar per year in advance.

8th Month	AUGUST, 1830	hath 31 days.

LIKELIHOOD OF SEATS ON THE BROADWAY COACH

Early Morning,	1 in 100.		Early Evening,	1 in 20.
Afternoon,	1 in 80.		Night,	1 in 6.

VALUES OF NIGHT SOIL

SUBSTANCE	VALUE PER 100 LBS
Rice, boiled	$1.00
Eggs, coddled	$1.30
Soup, Barley	$1.30
Sago, boiled	$1.45
Eggs, raw	$2.00
Calf's milk	$2.00
Bison, wild	$2.30
Oysters, raw	$3.15
Fish roe	$4.10
Pickled herring	$4.10

CAUSES OF INSANITY

AGENT	PER 1000
Congenital, Inheritance	20
Bankruptcy	18
Professional Failure	16
Jealousy	15
Abject Loneliness	15
Hopelessness	14
Humiliation	12
Opium	9
Dancing	2

STRENGTH OF MUD

INCHES	EFFECT ON BODY
2	Will hold shoe
4	Will remove shoe
5	Will break ankle
8	Will break leg
10	Mortal injury

DISTANCES WITHIN BODY

FROM NOSE	INCHES
Mouth	1½
Chin	2
Adam's Apple	6
Breast, nipple	12
Navel	18
Pubic Bone	28
Rectum	31
Hip Bone	27
Knee	41
Ankle	58
Foot	61

*A box 24 inches long by 16 inches wide will hold seven salted piglets.

THE SHORT

Life

OF

A RESTAURANT HABITUE

BY A. CADAVER

PUBLISHED BY

THE SECOND WIND SOCIETY

BOSTON

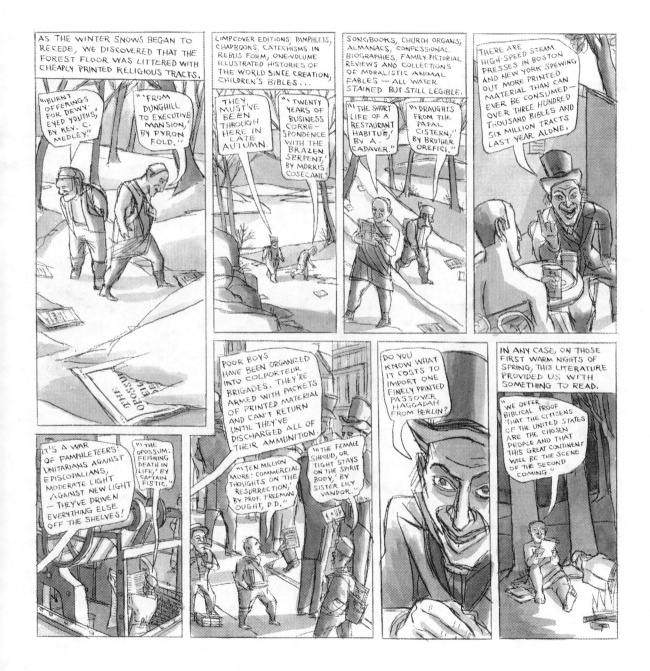

AS THE WINTER SNOWS BEGAN TO RECEDE, WE DISCOVERED THAT THE FOREST FLOOR WAS LITTERED WITH CHEAPLY PRINTED RELIGIOUS TRACTS.

"'BURNT OFFERINGS FOR DEWY-EYED YOUTHS,' BY REV. C. MEDLEY."

"'FROM DUNGHILL TO EXECUTIVE MANSION,' BY PYRON FOLD.'"

LIMPCOVER EDITIONS, PAMPHLETS, CHAPBOOKS, CATECHISMS IN REBUS FORM, ONE-VOLUME ILLUSTRATED HISTORIES OF THE WORLD SINCE CREATION, CHILDREN'S BIBLES...

THEY MUST'VE BEEN THROUGH HERE IN LATE AUTUMN.

"'TWENTY YEARS OF BUSINESS CORRE-SPONDENCE WITH THE BRAZEN SERPENT,' BY MORRIS COSECANE.'"

SONGBOOKS, CHURCH ORGANS, ALMANACS, CONFESSIONAL BIOGRAPHIES, FAMILY PICTORIAL REVIEWS AND COLLECTIONS OF MORALISTIC ANIMAL FABLES — ALL WATER-STAINED BUT STILL LEGIBLE.

"'THE SHORT LIFE OF A RESTAURANT HABITUÉ,' BY A. CADAVER."

"'DRAUGHTS FROM THE PAPAL CISTERN,' BY BROTHER OREFICI.'"

THERE ARE HIGH-SPEED STEAM PRESSES IN BOSTON AND NEW YORK SPEWING OUT MORE PRINTED MATERIAL THAN CAN EVER BE CONSUMED — OVER THREE HUNDRED THOUSAND BIBLES AND SIX MILLION TRACTS LAST YEAR ALONE.

IT'S A WAR OF PAMPHLETEERS: UNITARIANS AGAINST EPISCOPALIANS, MODERATE LIGHT AGAINST NEW LIGHT — THEY'VE DRIVEN EVERYTHING ELSE OFF THE SHELVES!

"'THE OPOSSUM: FEIGNING DEATH IN LIFE,' BY CAPTAIN FISTIC.'"

POOR BOYS HAVE BEEN ORGANIZED INTO COLPORTEUR BRIGADES. THEY'RE ARMED WITH PACKETS OF PRINTED MATERIAL AND CAN'T RETURN UNTIL THEY'VE DISCHARGED ALL OF THEIR AMMUNITION.

"'TEN MILLION MORE: COMMERCIAL THOUGHTS ON THE RESURRECTION,' BY PROF. FREEMAN OUGHT, D.D.'"

"'THE FEMALE SHROUD, OR TIGHT STAYS ON THE SPIRIT BODY,' BY SISTER LILY VANDOR.'"

DO YOU KNOW WHAT IT COSTS TO IMPORT ONE FINELY PRINTED PASSOVER HAGGADAH FROM BERLIN?

IN ANY CASE, ON THOSE FIRST WARM NIGHTS OF SPRING, THIS LITERATURE PROVIDED US WITH SOMETHING TO READ.

"'WE OFFER BIBLICAL PROOF THAT THE CITIZENS OF THE UNITED STATES ARE THE CHOSEN PEOPLE AND THAT THIS GREAT CONTINENT WILL BE THE SCENE OF THE SECOND COMING.'"

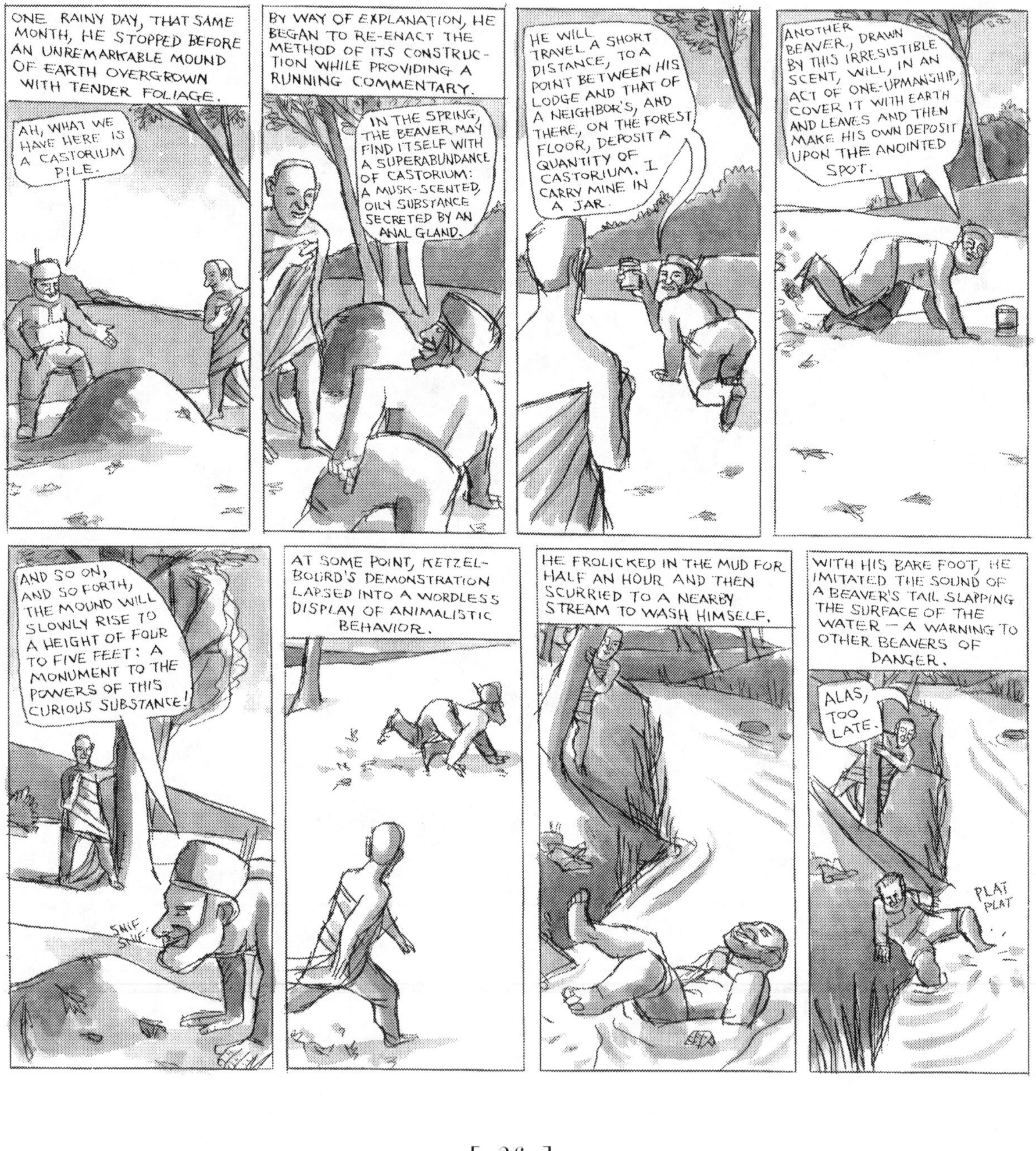
ONE RAINY DAY, THAT SAME MONTH, HE STOPPED BEFORE AN UNREMARKABLE MOUND OF EARTH OVERGROWN WITH TENDER FOLIAGE.
AH, WHAT WE HAVE HERE IS A CASTORIUM PILE.
BY WAY OF EXPLANATION, HE BEGAN TO RE-ENACT THE METHOD OF ITS CONSTRUCTION WHILE PROVIDING A RUNNING COMMENTARY.
IN THE SPRING, THE BEAVER MAY FIND ITSELF WITH A SUPERABUNDANCE OF CASTORIUM: A MUSK-SCENTED, OILY SUBSTANCE SECRETED BY AN ANAL GLAND.
HE WILL TRAVEL A SHORT DISTANCE, TO A POINT BETWEEN HIS LODGE AND THAT OF A NEIGHBOR'S, AND THERE, ON THE FOREST FLOOR, DEPOSIT A QUANTITY OF CASTORIUM. I CARRY MINE IN A JAR.
ANOTHER BEAVER, DRAWN BY THIS IRRESISTIBLE SCENT, WILL, IN AN ACT OF ONE-UPMANSHIP, COVER IT WITH EARTH AND LEAVES AND THEN MAKE HIS OWN DEPOSIT UPON THE ANOINTED SPOT.
AND SO ON, AND SO FORTH, THE MOUND WILL SLOWLY RISE TO A HEIGHT OF FOUR TO FIVE FEET: A MONUMENT TO THE POWERS OF THIS CURIOUS SUBSTANCE!
SNIF SNIF
AT SOME POINT, KETZELBOURD'S DEMONSTRATION LAPSED INTO A WORDLESS DISPLAY OF ANIMALISTIC BEHAVIOR.
HE FROLICKED IN THE MUD FOR HALF AN HOUR AND THEN SCURRIED TO A NEARBY STREAM TO WASH HIMSELF.
WITH HIS BARE FOOT, HE IMITATED THE SOUND OF A BEAVER'S TAIL SLAPPING THE SURFACE OF THE WATER — A WARNING TO OTHER BEAVERS OF DANGER.
ALAS, TOO LATE.
PLAT PLAT

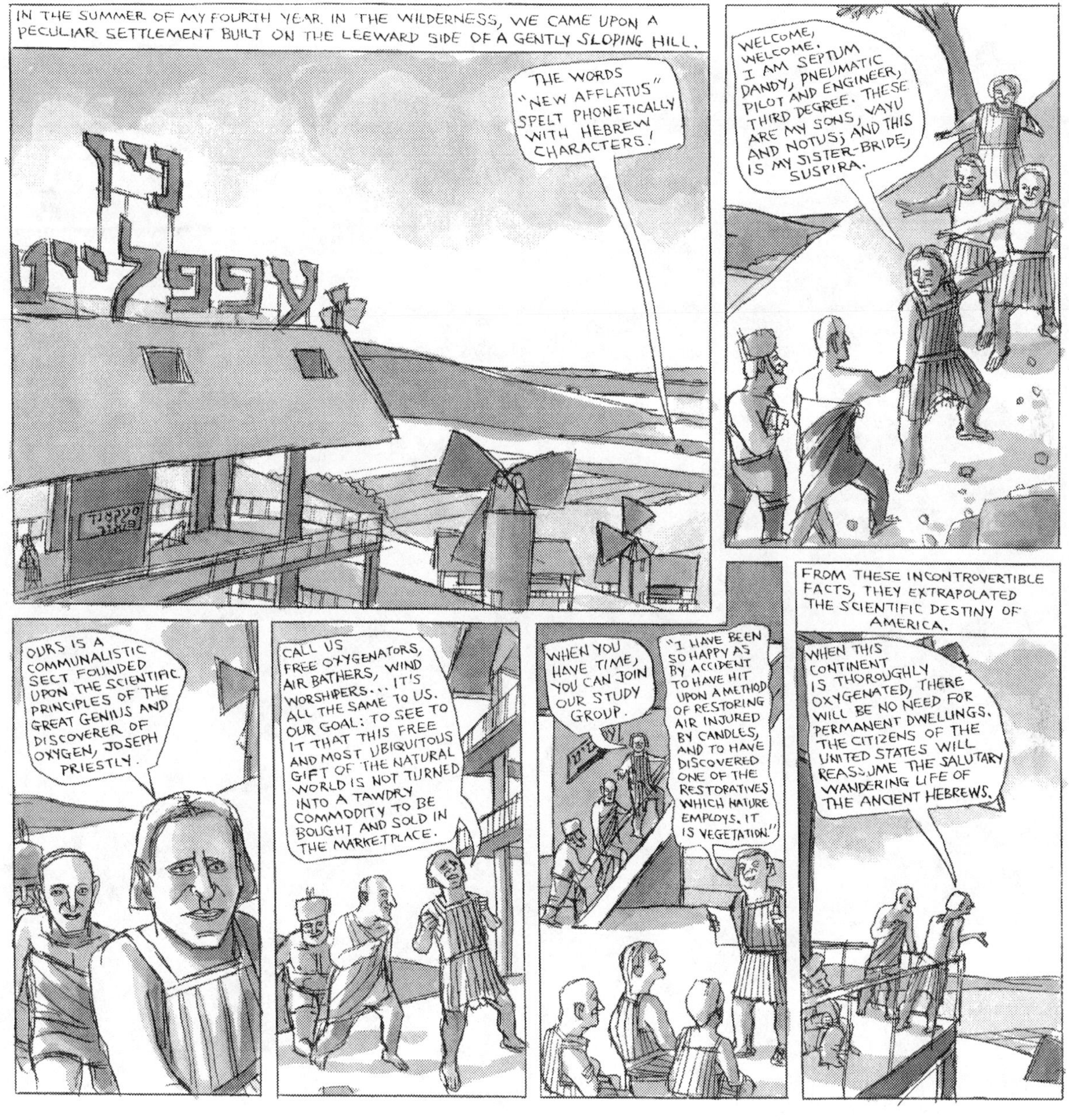
IN THE SUMMER OF MY FOURTH YEAR IN THE WILDERNESS, WE CAME UPON A PECULIAR SETTLEMENT BUILT ON THE LEEWARD SIDE OF A GENTLY SLOPING HILL.
THE WORDS "NEW AFFLATUS" SPELT PHONETICALLY WITH HEBREW CHARACTERS!
WELCOME, WELCOME. I AM SEPTUM DANDY, PNEUMATIC PILOT AND ENGINEER, THIRD DEGREE. THESE ARE MY SONS, VAYU AND NOTUS; AND THIS IS MY SISTER-BRIDE, SUSPIRA.
OURS IS A COMMUNALISTIC SECT FOUNDED UPON THE SCIENTIFIC PRINCIPLES OF THE GREAT GENIUS AND DISCOVERER OF OXYGEN, JOSEPH PRIESTLY.
CALL US FREE OXYGENATORS, AIR BATHERS, WIND WORSHIPERS... IT'S ALL THE SAME TO US. OUR GOAL: TO SEE TO IT THAT THIS FREE AND MOST UBIQUITOUS GIFT OF THE NATURAL WORLD IS NOT TURNED INTO A TAWDRY COMMODITY TO BE BOUGHT AND SOLD IN THE MARKETPLACE.
WHEN YOU HAVE TIME, YOU CAN JOIN OUR STUDY GROUP.
"I HAVE BEEN SO HAPPY AS BY ACCIDENT TO HAVE HIT UPON A METHOD OF RESTORING AIR INJURED BY CANDLES, AND TO HAVE DISCOVERED ONE OF THE RESTORATIVES WHICH NATURE EMPLOYS. IT IS VEGETATION."
FROM THESE INCONTROVERTIBLE FACTS, THEY EXTRAPOLATED THE SCIENTIFIC DESTINY OF AMERICA.
WHEN THIS CONTINENT IS THOROUGHLY OXYGENATED, THERE WILL BE NO NEED FOR PERMANENT DWELLINGS. THE CITIZENS OF THE UNITED STATES WILL REASSUME THE SALUTARY WANDERING LIFE OF THE ANCIENT HEBREWS.

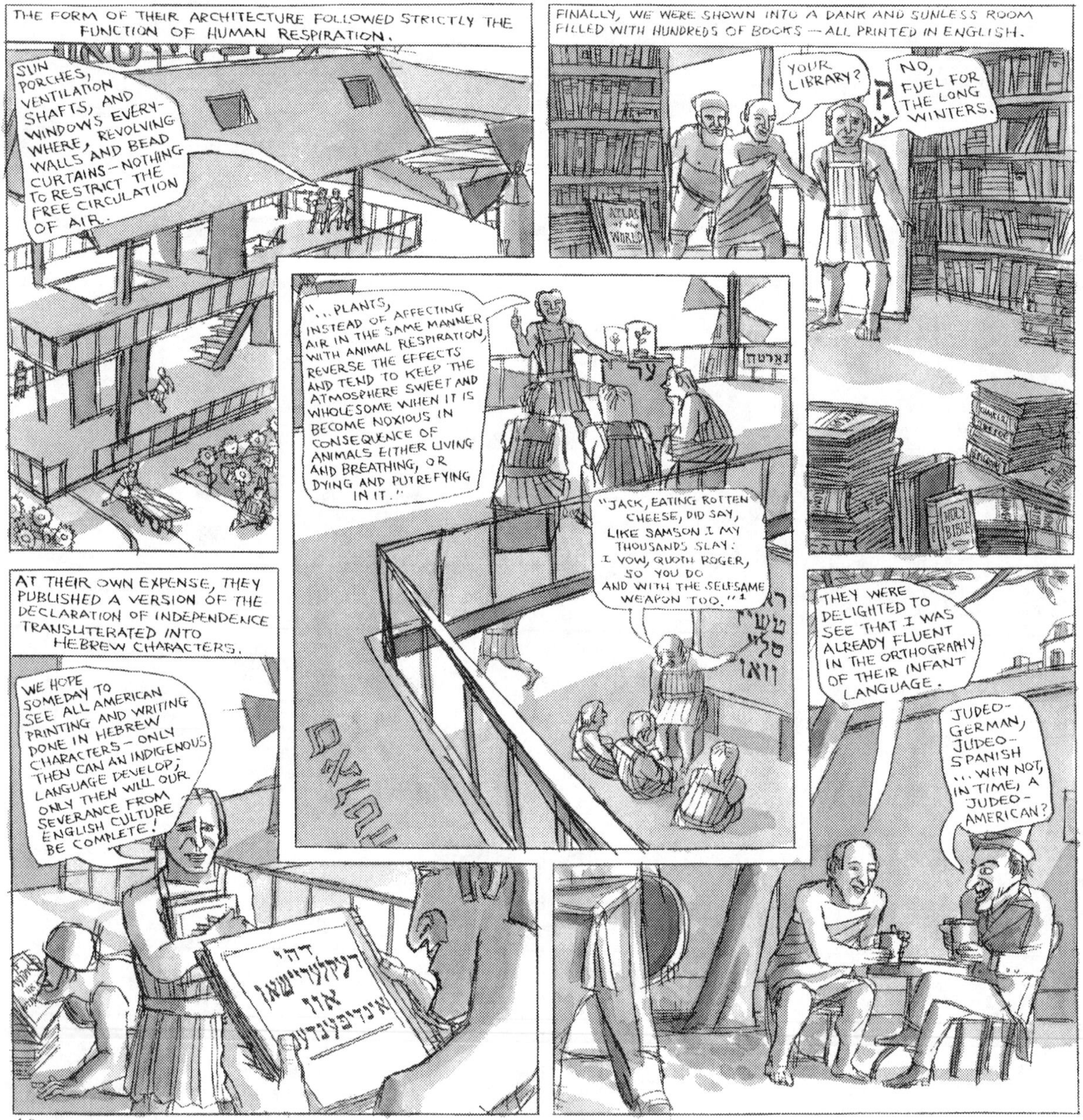
THE FORM OF THEIR ARCHITECTURE FOLLOWED STRICTLY THE FUNCTION OF HUMAN RESPIRATION.
SUN PORCHES, VENTILATION SHAFTS, AND WINDOWS EVERYWHERE, REVOLVING WALLS AND BEAD CURTAINS — NOTHING TO RESTRICT THE FREE CIRCULATION OF AIR.
FINALLY, WE WERE SHOWN INTO A DANK AND SUNLESS ROOM FILLED WITH HUNDREDS OF BOOKS — ALL PRINTED IN ENGLISH.
YOUR LIBRARY?
NO, FUEL FOR THE LONG WINTERS.
ATLAS of the WORLD
HOLY BIBLE
"...PLANTS, INSTEAD OF AFFECTING AIR IN THE SAME MANNER WITH ANIMAL RESPIRATION, REVERSE THE EFFECTS AND TEND TO KEEP THE ATMOSPHERE SWEET AND WHOLESOME WHEN IT IS BECOME NOXIOUS IN CONSEQUENCE OF ANIMALS EITHER LIVING AND BREATHING, OR DYING AND PUTREFYING IN IT."
"JACK, EATING ROTTEN CHEESE, DID SAY, LIKE SAMSON I MY THOUSANDS SLAY: I VOW, QUOTH ROGER, SO YOU DO AND WITH THE SELFSAME WEAPON TOO."[1]
AT THEIR OWN EXPENSE, THEY PUBLISHED A VERSION OF THE DECLARATION OF INDEPENDENCE TRANSLITERATED INTO HEBREW CHARACTERS.
WE HOPE SOMEDAY TO SEE ALL AMERICAN PRINTING AND WRITING DONE IN HEBREW CHARACTERS — ONLY THEN CAN AN INDIGENOUS LANGUAGE DEVELOP; ONLY THEN WILL OUR SEVERANCE FROM ENGLISH CULTURE BE COMPLETE!
THEY WERE DELIGHTED TO SEE THAT I WAS ALREADY FLUENT IN THE ORTHOGRAPHY OF THEIR INFANT LANGUAGE.
JUDEO-GERMAN, JUDEO-SPANISH ... WHY NOT, IN TIME, A JUDEO-AMERICAN?

1 BENJAMIN FRANKLIN

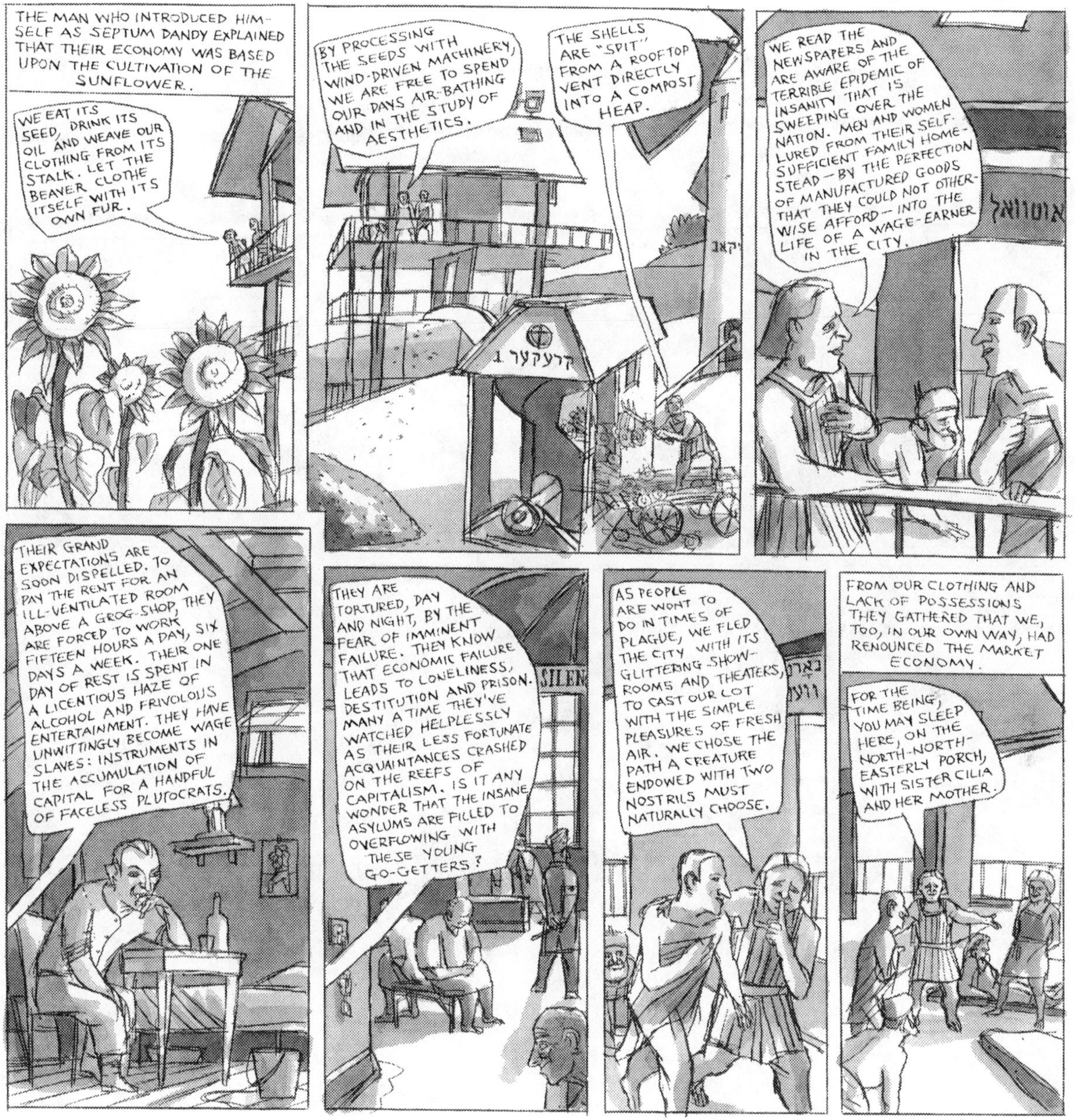
THE MAN WHO INTRODUCED HIMSELF AS SEPTUM DANDY EXPLAINED THAT THEIR ECONOMY WAS BASED UPON THE CULTIVATION OF THE SUNFLOWER.
WE EAT ITS SEED, DRINK ITS OIL AND WEAVE OUR CLOTHING FROM ITS STALK. LET THE BEAVER CLOTHE ITSELF WITH ITS OWN FUR.
BY PROCESSING THE SEEDS WITH WIND-DRIVEN MACHINERY, WE ARE FREE TO SPEND OUR DAYS AIR-BATHING AND IN THE STUDY OF AESTHETICS.
THE SHELLS ARE "SPIT" FROM A ROOFTOP VENT DIRECTLY INTO A COMPOST HEAP.
WE READ THE NEWSPAPERS AND ARE AWARE OF THE TERRIBLE EPIDEMIC OF INSANITY THAT IS SWEEPING OVER THE NATION. MEN AND WOMEN LURED FROM THEIR SELF-SUFFICIENT FAMILY HOMESTEAD -- BY THE PERFECTION OF MANUFACTURED GOODS THAT THEY COULD NOT OTHERWISE AFFORD -- INTO THE LIFE OF A WAGE-EARNER IN THE CITY.
THEIR GRAND EXPECTATIONS ARE SOON DISPELLED. TO PAY THE RENT FOR AN ILL-VENTILATED ROOM ABOVE A GROG-SHOP, THEY ARE FORCED TO WORK FIFTEEN HOURS A DAY, SIX DAYS A WEEK. THEIR ONE DAY OF REST IS SPENT IN A LICENTIOUS HAZE OF ALCOHOL AND FRIVOLOUS ENTERTAINMENT. THEY HAVE UNWITTINGLY BECOME WAGE SLAVES: INSTRUMENTS IN THE ACCUMULATION OF CAPITAL FOR A HANDFUL OF FACELESS PLUTOCRATS.
THEY ARE TORTURED, DAY AND NIGHT, BY THE FEAR OF IMMINENT FAILURE. THEY KNOW THAT ECONOMIC FAILURE LEADS TO LONELINESS, DESTITUTION AND PRISON. MANY A TIME THEY'VE WATCHED HELPLESSLY AS THEIR LESS FORTUNATE ACQUAINTANCES CRASHED ON THE REEFS OF CAPITALISM. IS IT ANY WONDER THAT THE INSANE ASYLUMS ARE FILLED TO OVERFLOWING WITH THESE YOUNG GO-GETTERS?
AS PEOPLE ARE WONT TO DO IN TIMES OF PLAGUE, WE FLED THE CITY WITH ITS GLITTERING SHOW-ROOMS AND THEATERS, TO CAST OUR LOT WITH THE SIMPLE PLEASURES OF FRESH AIR. WE CHOSE THE PATH A CREATURE ENDOWED WITH TWO NOSTRILS MUST NATURALLY CHOOSE.
FROM OUR CLOTHING AND LACK OF POSSESSIONS THEY GATHERED THAT WE, TOO, IN OUR OWN WAY, HAD RENOUNCED THE MARKET ECONOMY.
FOR THE TIME BEING, YOU MAY SLEEP HERE, ON THE NORTH-NORTH-EASTERLY PORCH, WITH SISTER CILIA AND HER MOTHER.

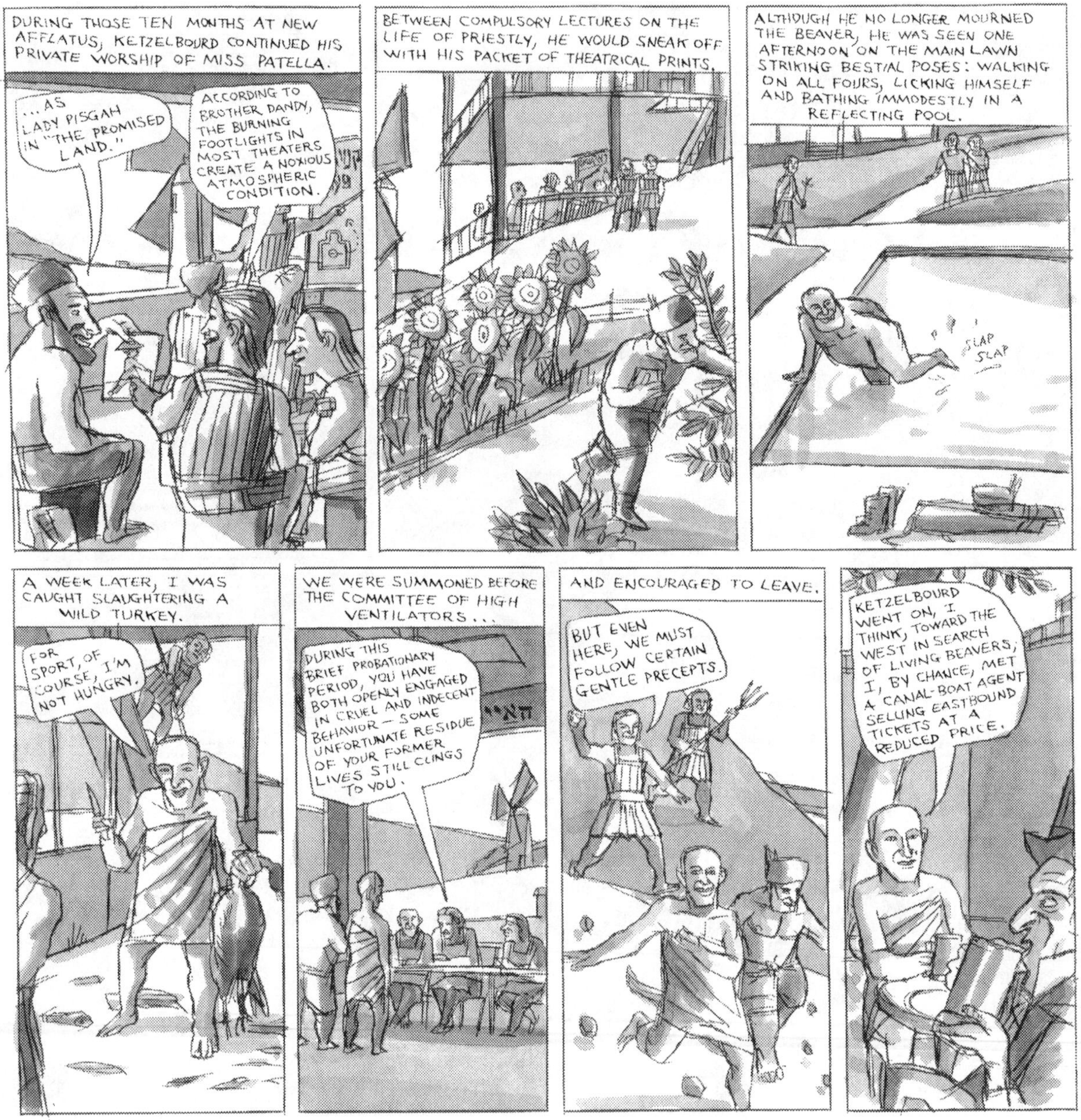
DURING THOSE TEN MONTHS AT NEW AFFLATUS, KETZELBOURD CONTINUED HIS PRIVATE WORSHIP OF MISS PATELLA.
...AS LADY PISGAH IN "THE PROMISED LAND."
ACCORDING TO BROTHER DANDY, THE BURNING FOOTLIGHTS IN MOST THEATERS CREATE A NOXIOUS ATMOSPHERIC CONDITION.
BETWEEN COMPULSORY LECTURES ON THE LIFE OF PRIESTLY, HE WOULD SNEAK OFF WITH HIS PACKET OF THEATRICAL PRINTS.
ALTHOUGH HE NO LONGER MOURNED THE BEAVER, HE WAS SEEN ONE AFTERNOON ON THE MAIN LAWN STRIKING BESTIAL POSES: WALKING ON ALL FOURS, LICKING HIMSELF AND BATHING IMMODESTLY IN A REFLECTING POOL.
SLAP SLAP
A WEEK LATER, I WAS CAUGHT SLAUGHTERING A WILD TURKEY.
FOR SPORT, OF COURSE, I'M NOT HUNGRY.
WE WERE SUMMONED BEFORE THE COMMITTEE OF HIGH VENTILATORS...
DURING THIS BRIEF PROBATIONARY PERIOD, YOU HAVE BOTH OPENLY ENGAGED IN CRUEL AND INDECENT BEHAVIOR — SOME UNFORTUNATE RESIDUE OF YOUR FORMER LIVES STILL CLINGS TO YOU.
AND ENCOURAGED TO LEAVE.
BUT EVEN HERE, WE MUST FOLLOW CERTAIN GENTLE PRECEPTS.
KETZELBOURD WENT ON, I THINK, TOWARD THE WEST IN SEARCH OF LIVING BEAVERS; I, BY CHANCE, MET A CANAL-BOAT AGENT SELLING EASTBOUND TICKETS AT A REDUCED PRICE.

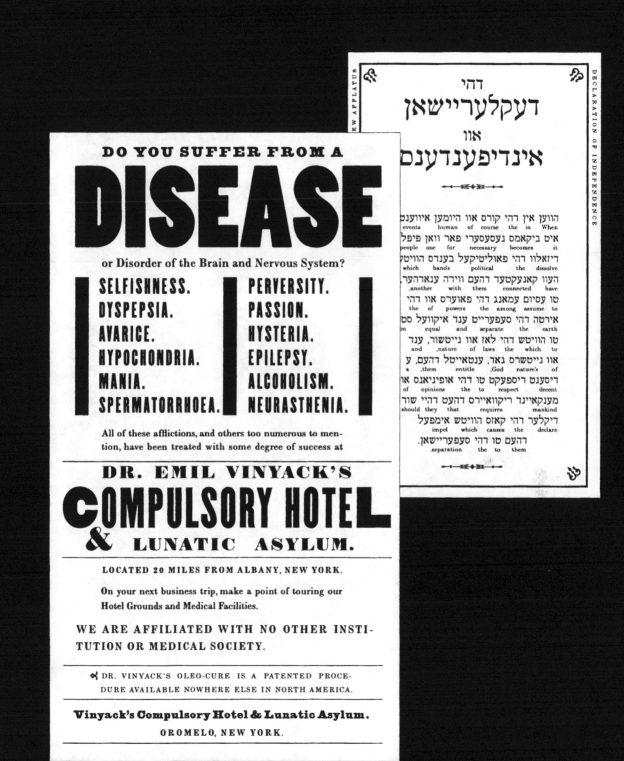

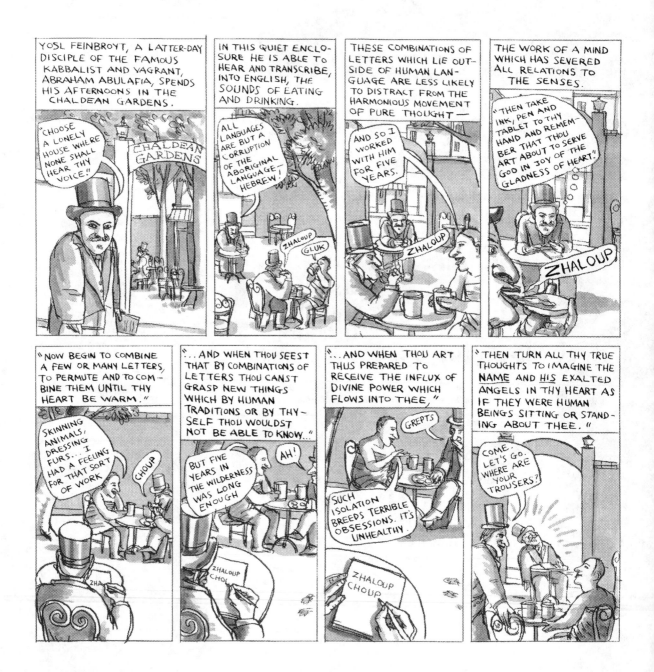

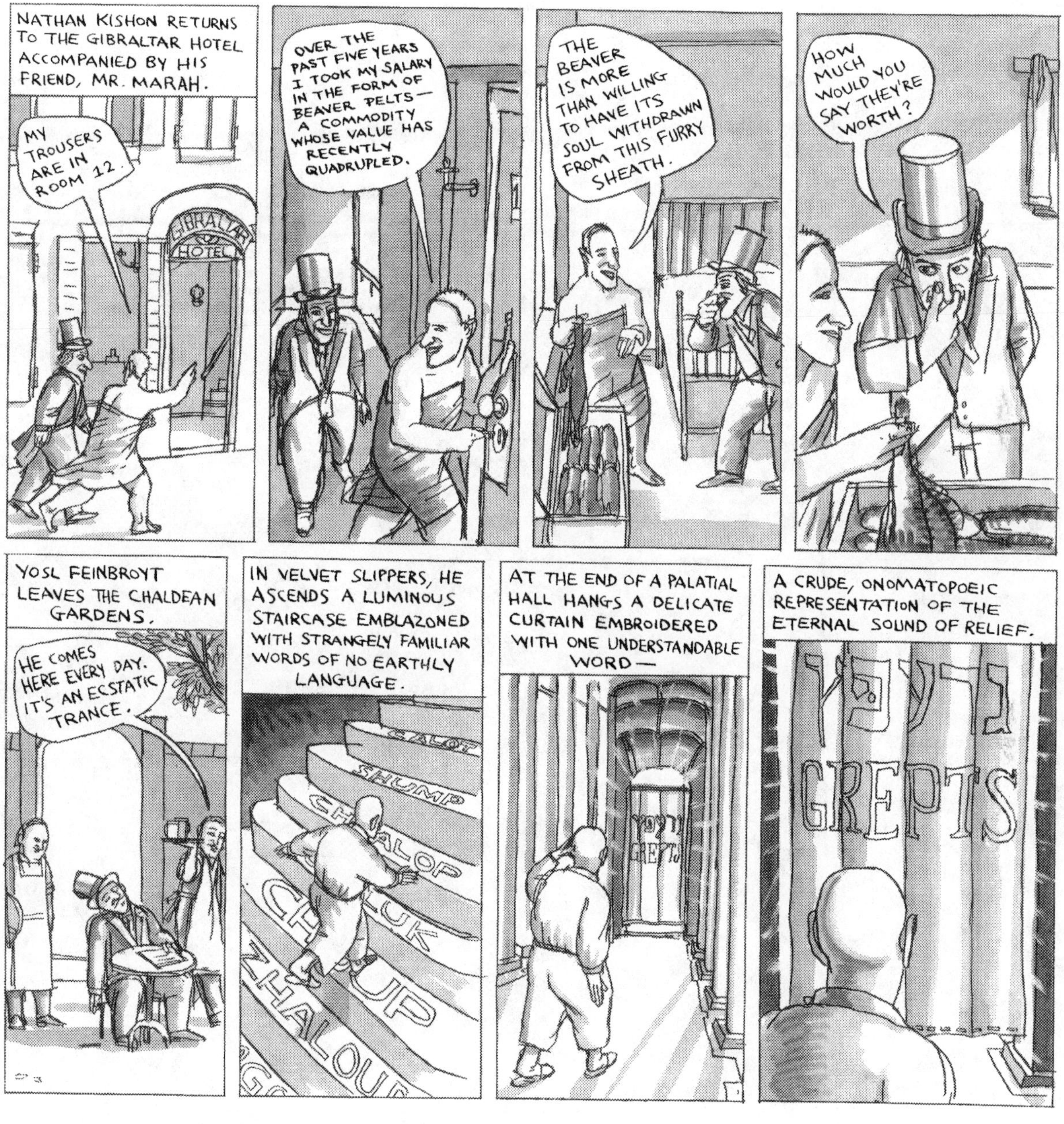
NATHAN KISHON RETURNS TO THE GIBRALTAR HOTEL ACCOMPANIED BY HIS FRIEND, MR. MARAH.
MY TROUSERS ARE IN ROOM 12.
GIBRALTAR HOTEL
OVER THE PAST FIVE YEARS I TOOK MY SALARY IN THE FORM OF BEAVER PELTS— A COMMODITY WHOSE VALUE HAS RECENTLY QUADRUPLED.
THE BEAVER IS MORE THAN WILLING TO HAVE ITS SOUL WITHDRAWN FROM THIS FURRY SHEATH.
HOW MUCH WOULD YOU SAY THEY'RE WORTH?
YOSL FEINBROYT LEAVES THE CHALDEAN GARDENS.
HE COMES HERE EVERY DAY. IT'S AN ECSTATIC TRANCE.
IN VELVET SLIPPERS, HE ASCENDS A LUMINOUS STAIRCASE EMBLAZONED WITH STRANGELY FAMILIAR WORDS OF NO EARTHLY LANGUAGE.
SHUMP
AT THE END OF A PALATIAL HALL HANGS A DELICATE CURTAIN EMBROIDERED WITH ONE UNDERSTANDABLE WORD—
A CRUDE, ONOMATOPOEIC REPRESENTATION OF THE ETERNAL SOUND OF RELIEF.
GREPTS

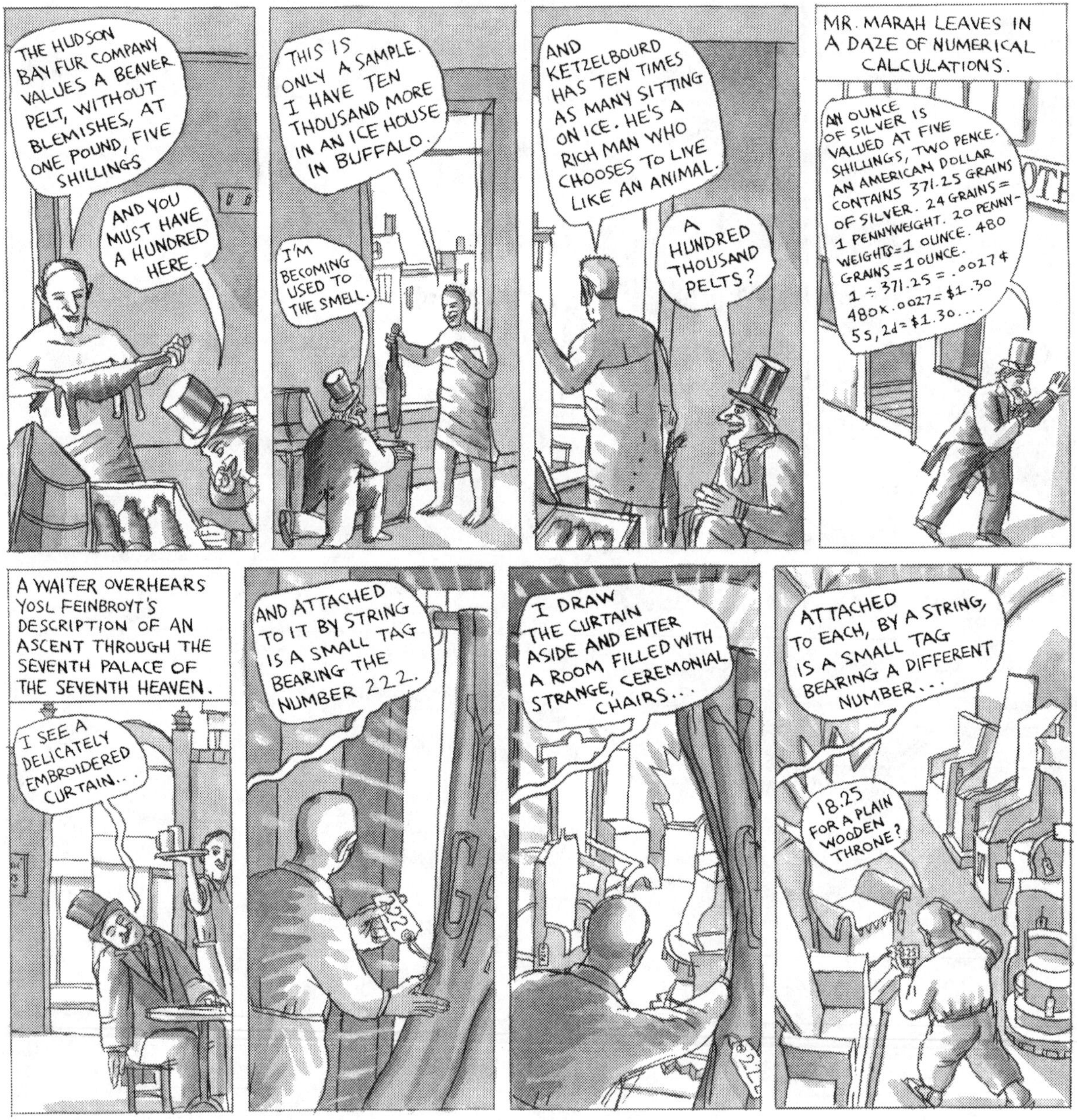

THE HUDSON BAY FUR COMPANY VALUES A BEAVER PELT, WITHOUT BLEMISHES, AT ONE POUND, FIVE SHILLINGS
AND YOU MUST HAVE A HUNDRED HERE.
THIS IS ONLY A SAMPLE. I HAVE TEN THOUSAND MORE IN AN ICE HOUSE IN BUFFALO.
I'M BECOMING USED TO THE SMELL.
AND KETZELBOURD HAS TEN TIMES AS MANY SITTING ON ICE. HE'S A RICH MAN WHO CHOOSES TO LIVE LIKE AN ANIMAL.
A HUNDRED THOUSAND PELTS?
MR. MARAH LEAVES IN A DAZE OF NUMERICAL CALCULATIONS.
AN OUNCE OF SILVER IS VALUED AT FIVE SHILLINGS, TWO PENCE. AN AMERICAN DOLLAR CONTAINS 371.25 GRAINS OF SILVER. 24 GRAINS = 1 PENNYWEIGHT. 20 PENNY-WEIGHTS = 1 OUNCE. 480 GRAINS = 1 OUNCE. 1 ÷ 371.25 = .0027¢ 480x.0027 = $1.30 5s, 2d = $1.30....
A WAITER OVERHEARS YOSL FEINBROYT'S DESCRIPTION OF AN ASCENT THROUGH THE SEVENTH PALACE OF THE SEVENTH HEAVEN.
I SEE A DELICATELY EMBROIDERED CURTAIN...
AND ATTACHED TO IT BY STRING IS A SMALL TAG BEARING THE NUMBER 222.
I DRAW THE CURTAIN ASIDE AND ENTER A ROOM FILLED WITH STRANGE, CEREMONIAL CHAIRS...
ATTACHED TO EACH, BY A STRING, IS A SMALL TAG BEARING A DIFFERENT NUMBER...
18.25 FOR A PLAIN WOODEN THRONE?

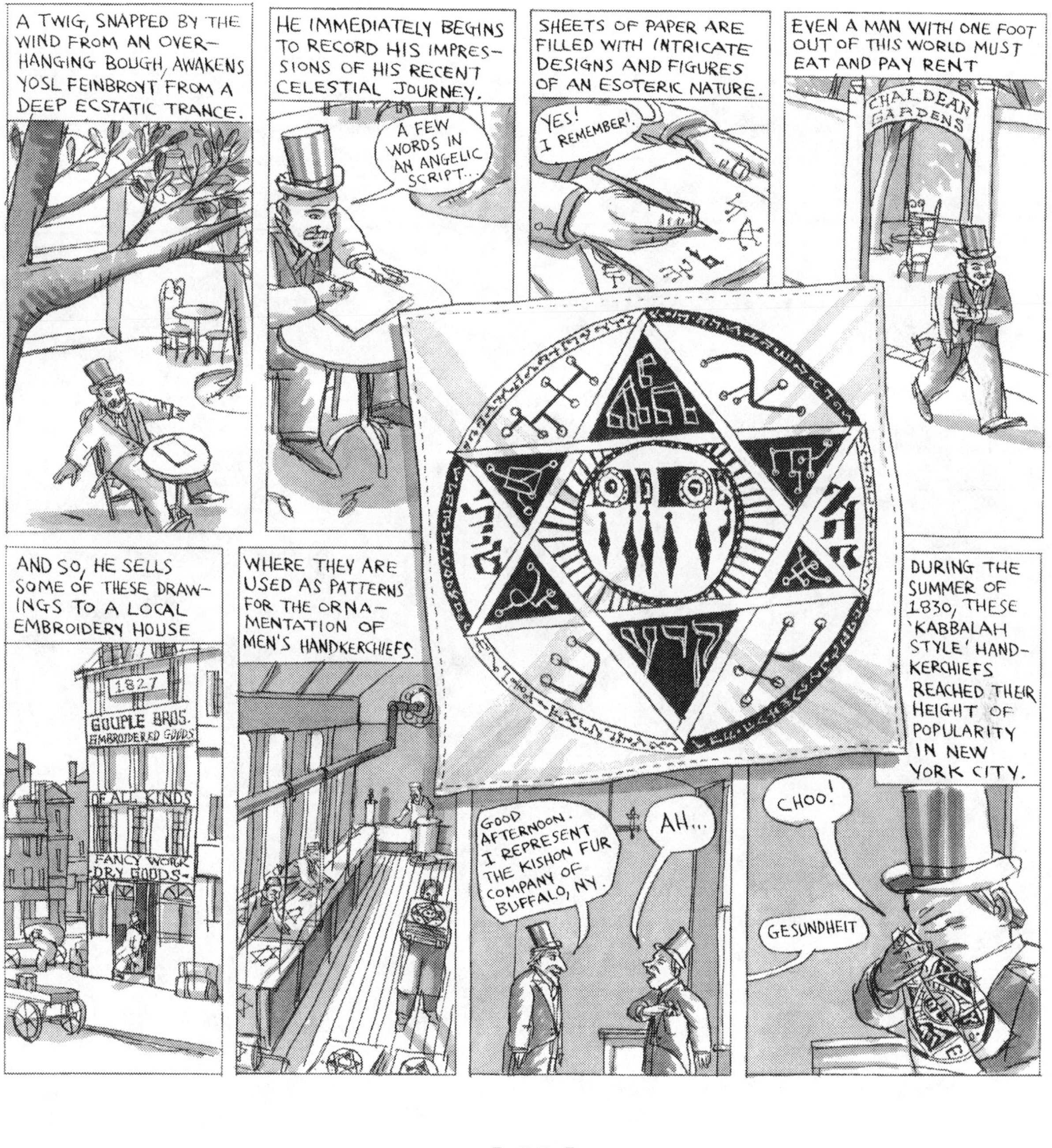
A TWIG, SNAPPED BY THE WIND FROM AN OVER-HANGING BOUGH, AWAKENS YOSL FEINBROYT FROM A DEEP ECSTATIC TRANCE.
HE IMMEDIATELY BEGINS TO RECORD HIS IMPRES-SIONS OF HIS RECENT CELESTIAL JOURNEY.
A FEW WORDS IN AN ANGELIC SCRIPT...
SHEETS OF PAPER ARE FILLED WITH INTRICATE DESIGNS AND FIGURES OF AN ESOTERIC NATURE.
YES! I REMEMBER!
EVEN A MAN WITH ONE FOOT OUT OF THIS WORLD MUST EAT AND PAY RENT
CHALDEAN GARDENS
AND SO, HE SELLS SOME OF THESE DRAW-INGS TO A LOCAL EMBROIDERY HOUSE
1827
GOUPLE BROS.
EMBROIDERED GOODS
OF ALL KINDS
FANCY WORK
DRY GOODS
WHERE THEY ARE USED AS PATTERNS FOR THE ORNA-MENTATION OF MEN'S HANDKERCHIEFS.
GOOD AFTERNOON. I REPRESENT THE KISHON FUR COMPANY OF BUFFALO, NY.
AH...
DURING THE SUMMER OF 1830, THESE 'KABBALAH STYLE' HAND-KERCHIEFS REACHED THEIR HEIGHT OF POPULARITY IN NEW YORK CITY.
CHOO!
GESUNDHEIT

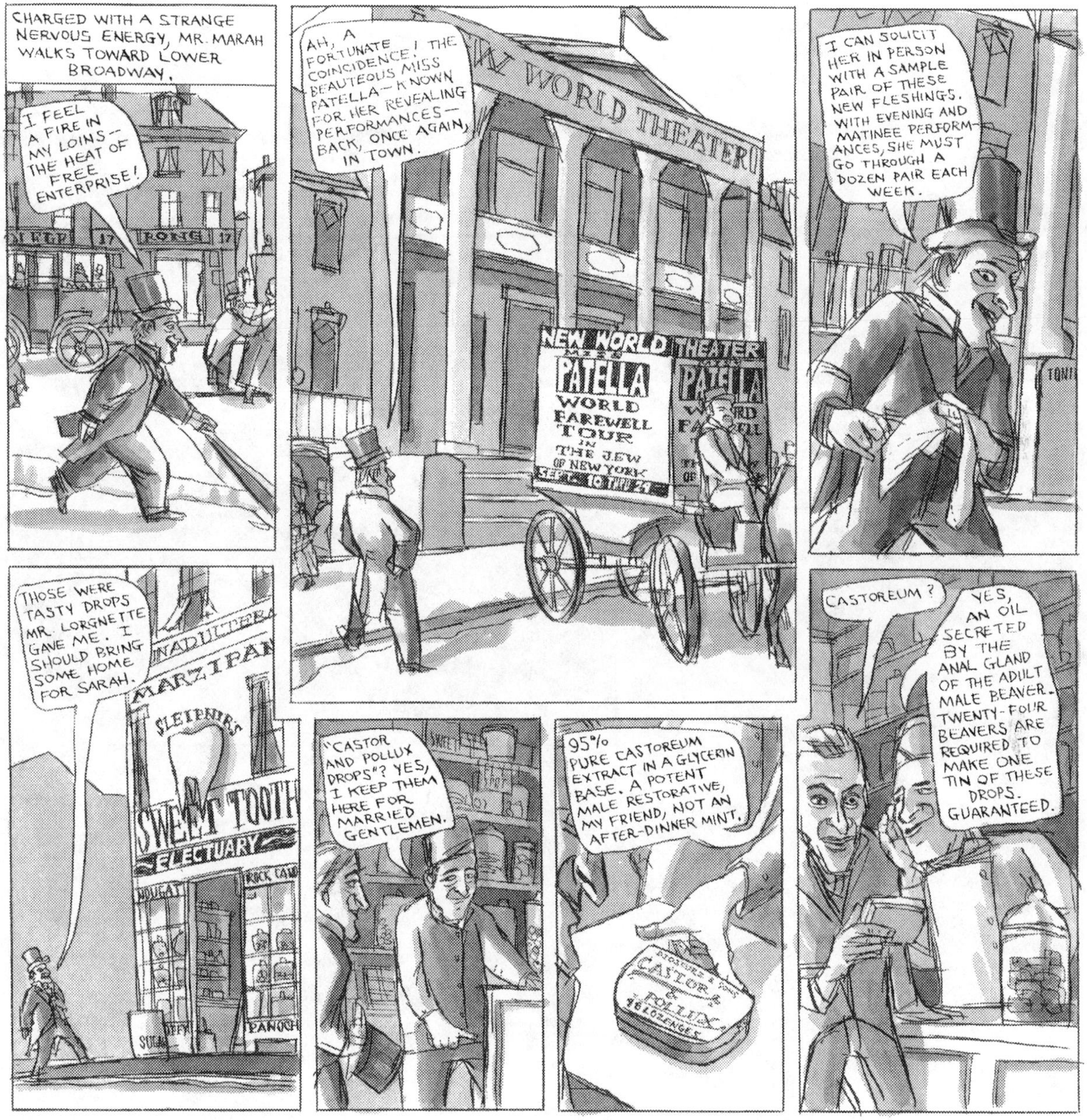

CHARGED WITH A STRANGE NERVOUS ENERGY, MR. MARAH WALKS TOWARD LOWER BROADWAY.
I FEEL A FIRE IN MY LOINS-- THE HEAT OF FREE ENTERPRISE!
AH, A FORTUNATE COINCIDENCE! THE BEAUTEOUS MISS PATELLA-- KNOWN FOR HER REVEALING PERFORMANCES-- BACK, ONCE AGAIN, IN TOWN.
NEW WORLD THEATER
NEW WORLD THEATER
MISS
PATELLA
WORLD
FAREWELL
TOUR
IN
THE JEW
OF NEW YORK
SEPT. 10 THRU 24
I CAN SOLICIT HER IN PERSON WITH A SAMPLE PAIR OF THESE NEW FLESHINGS. WITH EVENING AND MATINEE PERFORMANCES, SHE MUST GO THROUGH A DOZEN PAIR EACH WEEK.
THOSE WERE TASTY DROPS MR. LORGNETTE GAVE ME. I SHOULD BRING SOME HOME FOR SARAH.
MARZIPAN
SLEIPNIR'S
SWEET TOOTH
ELECTUARY
NOUGAT
"CASTOR AND POLLUX DROPS"? YES, I KEEP THEM HERE FOR MARRIED GENTLEMEN.
95% PURE CASTOREUM EXTRACT IN A GLYCERIN BASE. A POTENT MALE RESTORATIVE, MY FRIEND, NOT AN AFTER-DINNER MINT.
CASTOR
&
POLLUX
CASTOREUM?
YES, AN OIL SECRETED BY THE ANAL GLAND OF THE ADULT MALE BEAVER. TWENTY-FOUR BEAVERS ARE REQUIRED TO MAKE ONE TIN OF THESE DROPS. GUARANTEED.

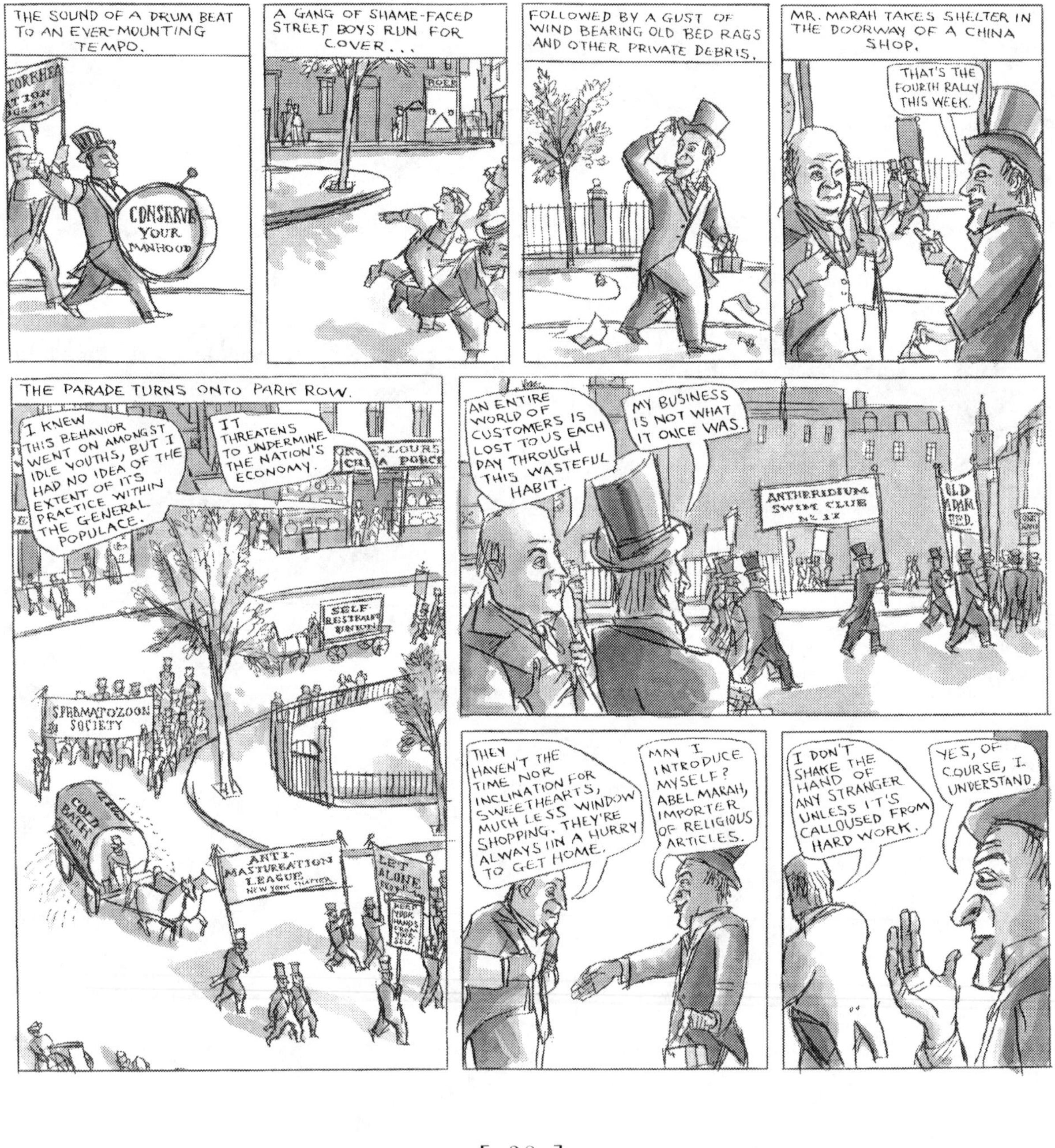
THE SOUND OF A DRUM BEAT TO AN EVER-MOUNTING TEMPO.
CONSERVE YOUR MANHOOD
A GANG OF SHAME-FACED STREET BOYS RUN FOR COVER...
FOLLOWED BY A GUST OF WIND BEARING OLD BED RAGS AND OTHER PRIVATE DEBRIS.
MR. MARAH TAKES SHELTER IN THE DOORWAY OF A CHINA SHOP.
THAT'S THE FOURTH RALLY THIS WEEK.
THE PARADE TURNS ONTO PARK ROW.
I KNEW THIS BEHAVIOR WENT ON AMONGST IDLE YOUTHS, BUT I HAD NO IDEA OF THE EXTENT OF ITS PRACTICE WITHIN THE GENERAL POPULACE.
IT THREATENS TO UNDERMINE THE NATION'S ECONOMY.
SELF RESTRAINT UNION
SPERMATOZOON SOCIETY
COLD BATHS
ANTI-MASTURBATION LEAGUE New York Chapter
LET ALONE
KEEP YOUR HANDS FROM YOUR SELF
AN ENTIRE WORLD OF CUSTOMERS IS LOST TO US EACH DAY THROUGH THIS WASTEFUL HABIT.
MY BUSINESS IS NOT WHAT IT ONCE WAS.
ANTHERIDIUM SWIM CLUB
THEY HAVEN'T THE TIME NOR INCLINATION FOR SWEETHEARTS, MUCH LESS WINDOW SHOPPING. THEY'RE ALWAYS IN A HURRY TO GET HOME.
MAY I INTRODUCE MYSELF? ABEL MARAH, IMPORTER OF RELIGIOUS ARTICLES.
I DON'T SHAKE THE HAND OF ANY STRANGER UNLESS IT'S CALLOUSED FROM HARD WORK.
YES, OF COURSE, I UNDERSTAND.

[40]

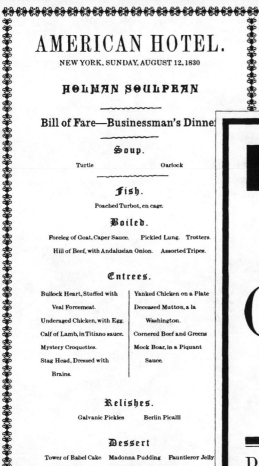

AMERICAN HOTEL.

NEW YORK, SUNDAY, AUGUST 12, 1830

HOLMAN SOULPEAN

Bill of Fare—Businessman's Dinner

Soup.

Turtle   Oarlock

Fish.

Poached Turbot, en cage.

Boiled.

Foreleg of Goat, Caper Sauce.   Pickled Lung.   Trotters.

Hill of Beef, with Andalusian Onion.   Assorted Tripes.

Entrees.

Bullock Heart, Stuffed with   Yanked Chicken on a Plate

Veal Forcemeat.   Deceased Mutton, a la

Underaged Chicken, with Egg.   Washington.

Calf of Lamb, in Titiano sauce.   Cornered Beef and Greens

Mystery Croquettes.   Mock Boar, in a Piquant

Stag Head, Dressed with   Sauce.

Brains.

Relishes.

Galvanic Pickles   Berlin Picalll

Dessert

Tower of Babel Cake   Madonna Pudding   Fauntleroy Jelly

REFRAIN.

Whereas, it is admitted that the Practice of

ONANISM

IN PRIVATE HOUSES,

Is Engaged in on a Nightly Basis,

Its Effect is Underestimated.

Dr. Pettersham and The Mutual Intercourse Union, Hereby Stand and GIVE NOTICE that this practice be considered a form of TREASON, a crime punishable by DEATH.

Dated this 10th August, 1830,

DR. V. PETTERSHAM,

President and Acting Physician-in-Residence

G. VILLOTINAS, PRINTER AND SELLER OF GUMMED PAPERS, Queen St.

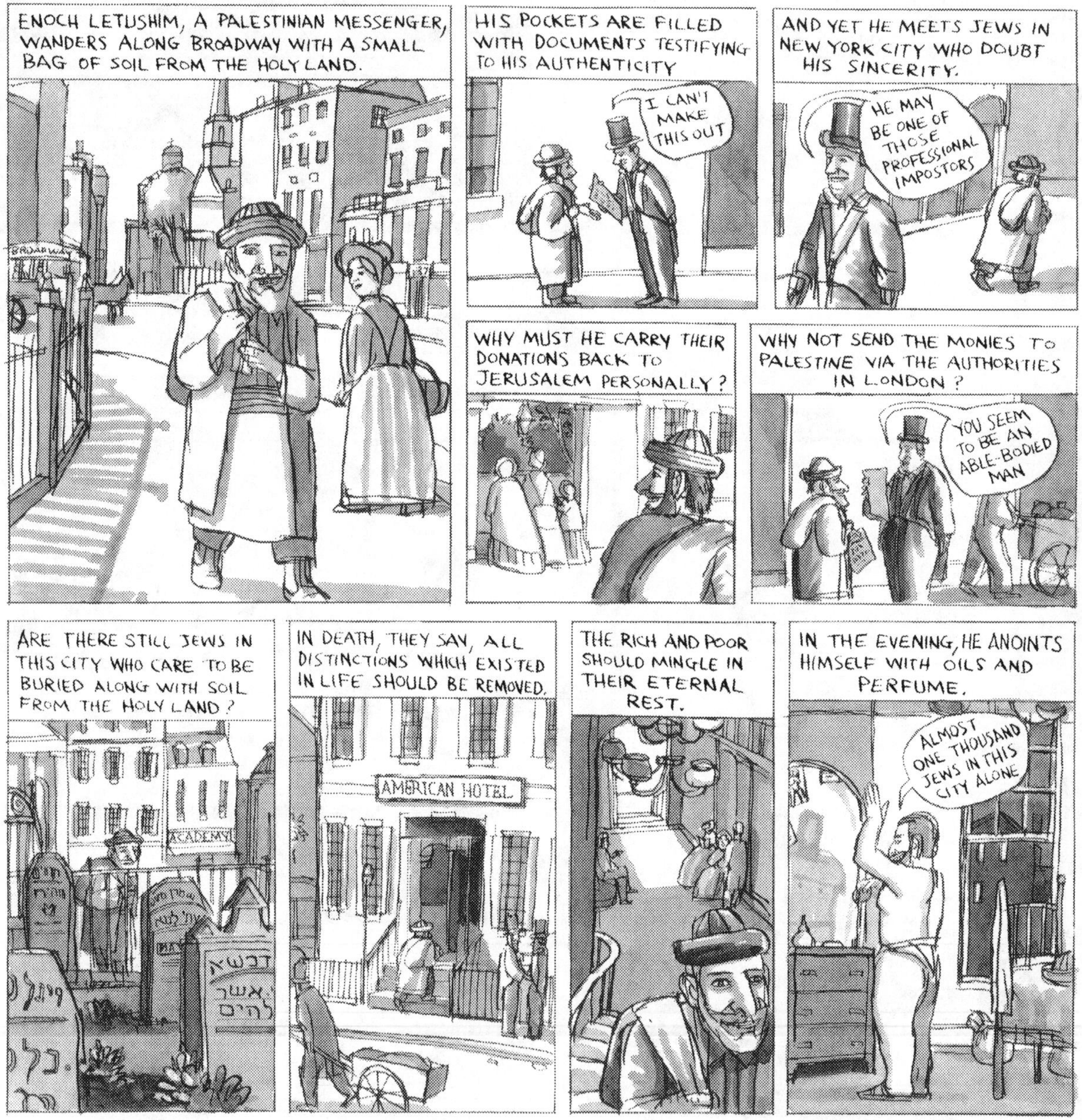
ENOCH LETUSHIM, A PALESTINIAN MESSENGER, WANDERS ALONG BROADWAY WITH A SMALL BAG OF SOIL FROM THE HOLY LAND.
BROADWAY
HIS POCKETS ARE FILLED WITH DOCUMENTS TESTIFYING TO HIS AUTHENTICITY
I CAN'T MAKE THIS OUT
AND YET HE MEETS JEWS IN NEW YORK CITY WHO DOUBT HIS SINCERITY.
HE MAY BE ONE OF THOSE PROFESSIONAL IMPOSTORS
WHY MUST HE CARRY THEIR DONATIONS BACK TO JERUSALEM PERSONALLY?
WHY NOT SEND THE MONIES TO PALESTINE VIA THE AUTHORITIES IN LONDON?
YOU SEEM TO BE AN ABLE-BODIED MAN
ARE THERE STILL JEWS IN THIS CITY WHO CARE TO BE BURIED ALONG WITH SOIL FROM THE HOLY LAND?
ACADEMY
IN DEATH, THEY SAY, ALL DISTINCTIONS WHICH EXISTED IN LIFE SHOULD BE REMOVED.
AMERICAN HOTEL
THE RICH AND POOR SHOULD MINGLE IN THEIR ETERNAL REST.
IN THE EVENING, HE ANOINTS HIMSELF WITH OILS AND PERFUME.
ALMOST ONE THOUSAND JEWS IN THIS CITY ALONE

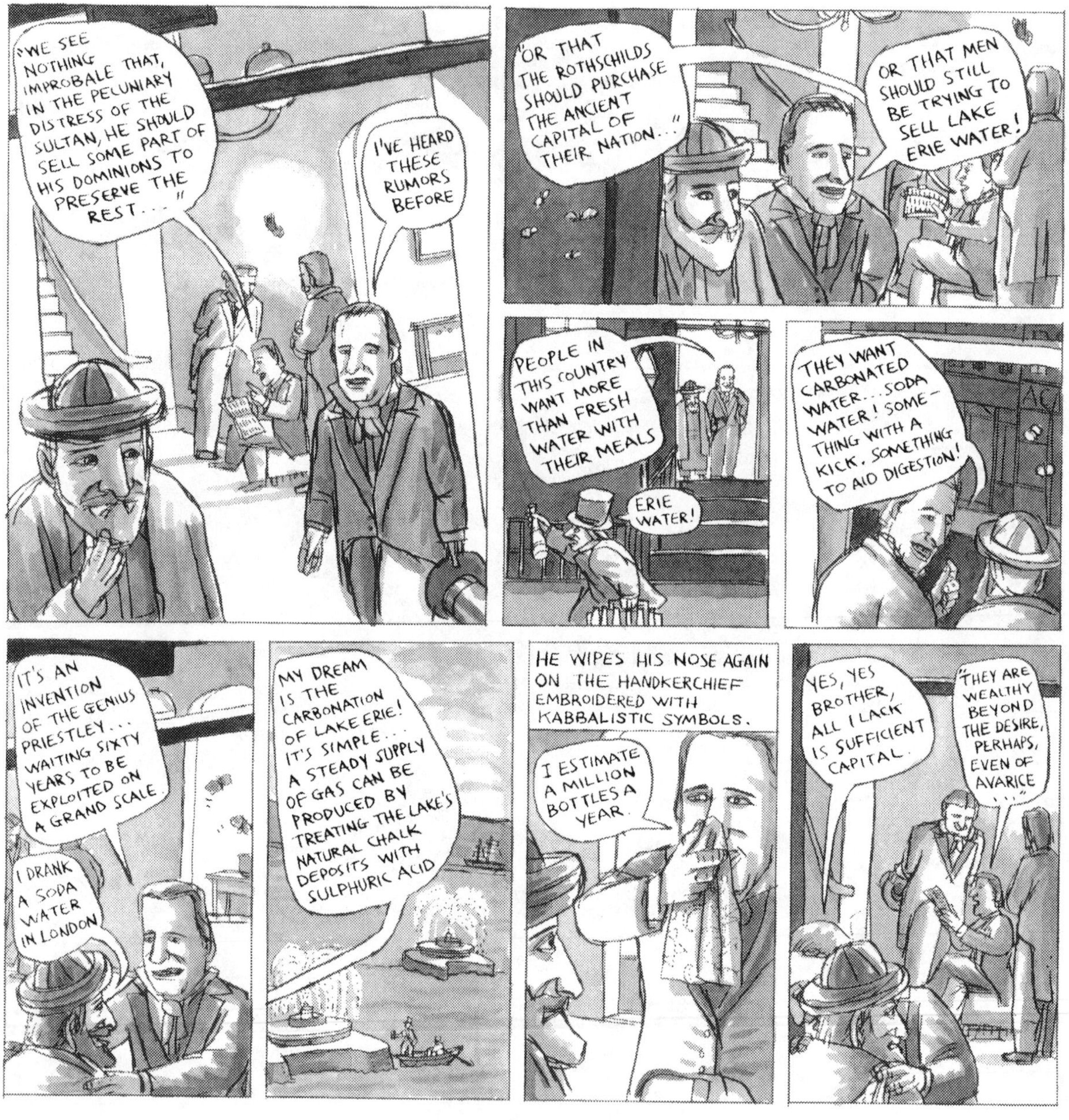
"WE SEE NOTHING IMPROBALE THAT, IN THE PECUNIARY DISTRESS OF THE SULTAN, HE SHOULD SELL SOME PART OF HIS DOMINIONS TO PRESERVE THE REST. . . ."
I'VE HEARD THESE RUMORS BEFORE
"OR THAT THE ROTHSCHILDS SHOULD PURCHASE THE ANCIENT CAPITAL OF THEIR NATION. . ."
OR THAT MEN SHOULD STILL BE TRYING TO SELL LAKE ERIE WATER!
PEOPLE IN THIS COUNTRY WANT MORE THAN FRESH WATER WITH THEIR MEALS
ERIE WATER!
THEY WANT CARBONATED WATER. . . SODA WATER! SOME-THING WITH A KICK. SOMETHING TO AID DIGESTION!
IT'S AN INVENTION OF THE GENIUS PRIESTLEY. . . WAITING SIXTY YEARS TO BE EXPLOITED ON A GRAND SCALE
I DRANK A SODA WATER IN LONDON
MY DREAM IS THE CARBONATION OF LAKE ERIE! IT'S SIMPLE. . . A STEADY SUPPLY OF GAS CAN BE PRODUCED BY TREATING THE LAKE'S NATURAL CHALK DEPOSITS WITH SULPHURIC ACID
HE WIPES HIS NOSE AGAIN ON THE HANDKERCHIEF EMBROIDERED WITH KABBALISTIC SYMBOLS.
I ESTIMATE A MILLION BOTTLES A YEAR.
YES, YES BROTHER, ALL I LACK IS SUFFICIENT CAPITAL.
"THEY ARE WEALTHY BEYOND THE DESIRE, PERHAPS, EVEN OF AVARICE . . ."

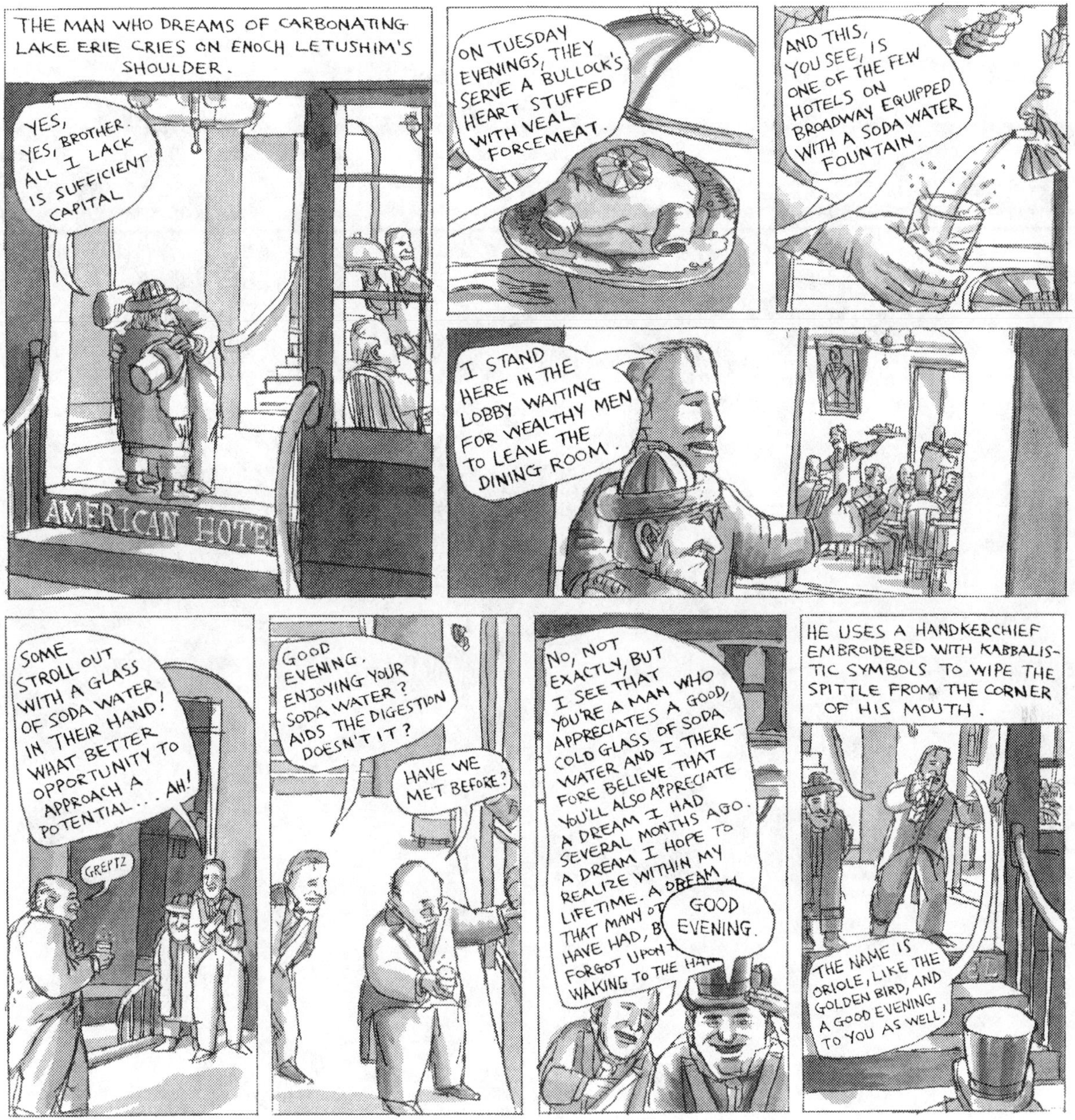
THE MAN WHO DREAMS OF CARBONATING LAKE ERIE CRIES ON ENOCH LETUSHIM'S SHOULDER.
YES, YES, BROTHER. ALL I LACK IS SUFFICIENT CAPITAL
AMERICAN HOTE
ON TUESDAY EVENINGS, THEY SERVE A BULLOCK'S HEART STUFFED WITH VEAL FORCEMEAT.
AND THIS, YOU SEE, IS ONE OF THE FEW HOTELS ON BROADWAY EQUIPPED WITH A SODA WATER FOUNTAIN.
I STAND HERE IN THE LOBBY WAITING FOR WEALTHY MEN TO LEAVE THE DINING ROOM.
SOME STROLL OUT WITH A GLASS OF SODA WATER IN THEIR HAND! WHAT BETTER OPPORTUNITY TO APPROACH A POTENTIAL... AH!
GREPTZ
GOOD EVENING. ENJOYING YOUR SODA WATER? SODA WATER AIDS THE DIGESTION DOESN'T IT?
HAVE WE MET BEFORE?
No, NOT EXACTLY, BUT I SEE THAT YOU'RE A MAN WHO APPRECIATES A GOOD, COLD GLASS OF SODA WATER AND I THERE-FORE BELIEVE THAT YOU'LL ALSO APPRECIATE A DREAM I HAD SEVERAL MONTHS AGO. A DREAM I HOPE TO REALIZE WITHIN MY LIFETIME. A DREAM THAT MANY HAVE HAD, FORGOT UPON WAKING TO THE
GOOD EVENING.
HE USES A HANDKERCHIEF EMBROIDERED WITH KABBALIS-TIC SYMBOLS TO WIPE THE SPITTLE FROM THE CORNER OF HIS MOUTH.
THE NAME IS ORIOLE, LIKE THE GOLDEN BIRD, AND A GOOD EVENING TO YOU AS WELL!

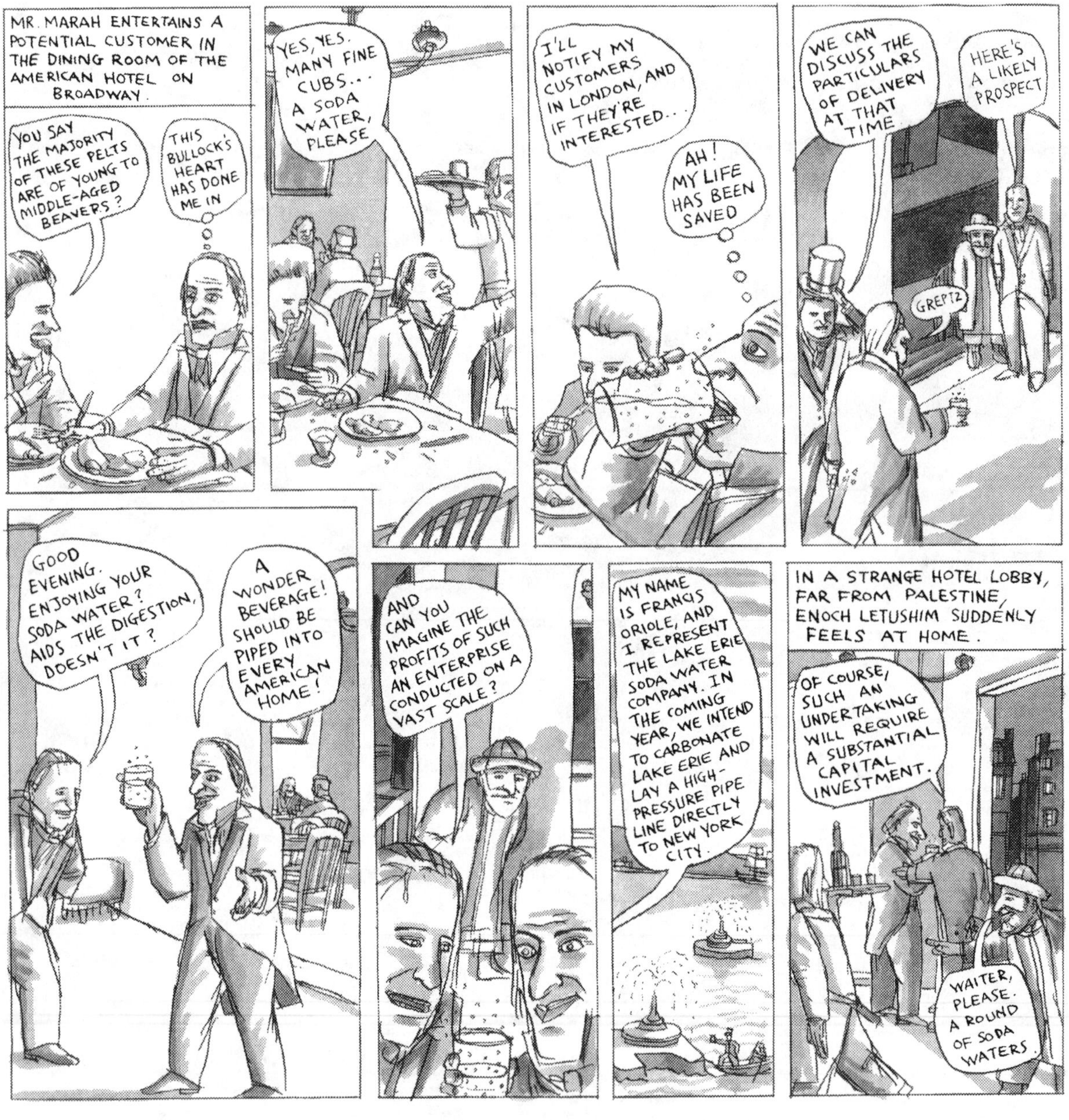
MR. MARAH ENTERTAINS A POTENTIAL CUSTOMER IN THE DINING ROOM OF THE AMERICAN HOTEL ON BROADWAY.
YOU SAY THE MAJORITY OF THESE PELTS ARE OF YOUNG TO MIDDLE-AGED BEAVERS?
THIS BULLOCK'S HEART HAS DONE ME IN
YES, YES. MANY FINE CUBS... A SODA WATER, PLEASE
I'LL NOTIFY MY CUSTOMERS IN LONDON, AND IF THEY'RE INTERESTED...
AH! MY LIFE HAS BEEN SAVED
WE CAN DISCUSS THE PARTICULARS OF DELIVERY AT THAT TIME
HERE'S A LIKELY PROSPECT
GREPTZ
GOOD EVENING. ENJOYING YOUR SODA WATER? AIDS THE DIGESTION, DOESN'T IT?
A WONDER BEVERAGE! SHOULD BE PIPED INTO EVERY AMERICAN HOME!
AND CAN YOU IMAGINE THE PROFITS OF SUCH AN ENTERPRISE CONDUCTED ON A VAST SCALE?
MY NAME IS FRANCIS ORIOLE, AND I REPRESENT THE LAKE ERIE SODA WATER COMPANY. IN THE COMING YEAR, WE INTEND TO CARBONATE LAKE ERIE AND LAY A HIGH-PRESSURE PIPE LINE DIRECTLY TO NEW YORK CITY.
IN A STRANGE HOTEL LOBBY, FAR FROM PALESTINE, ENOCH LETUSHIM SUDDENLY FEELS AT HOME.
OF COURSE, SUCH AN UNDERTAKING WILL REQUIRE A SUBSTANTIAL CAPITAL INVESTMENT.
WAITER, PLEASE. A ROUND OF SODA WATERS.

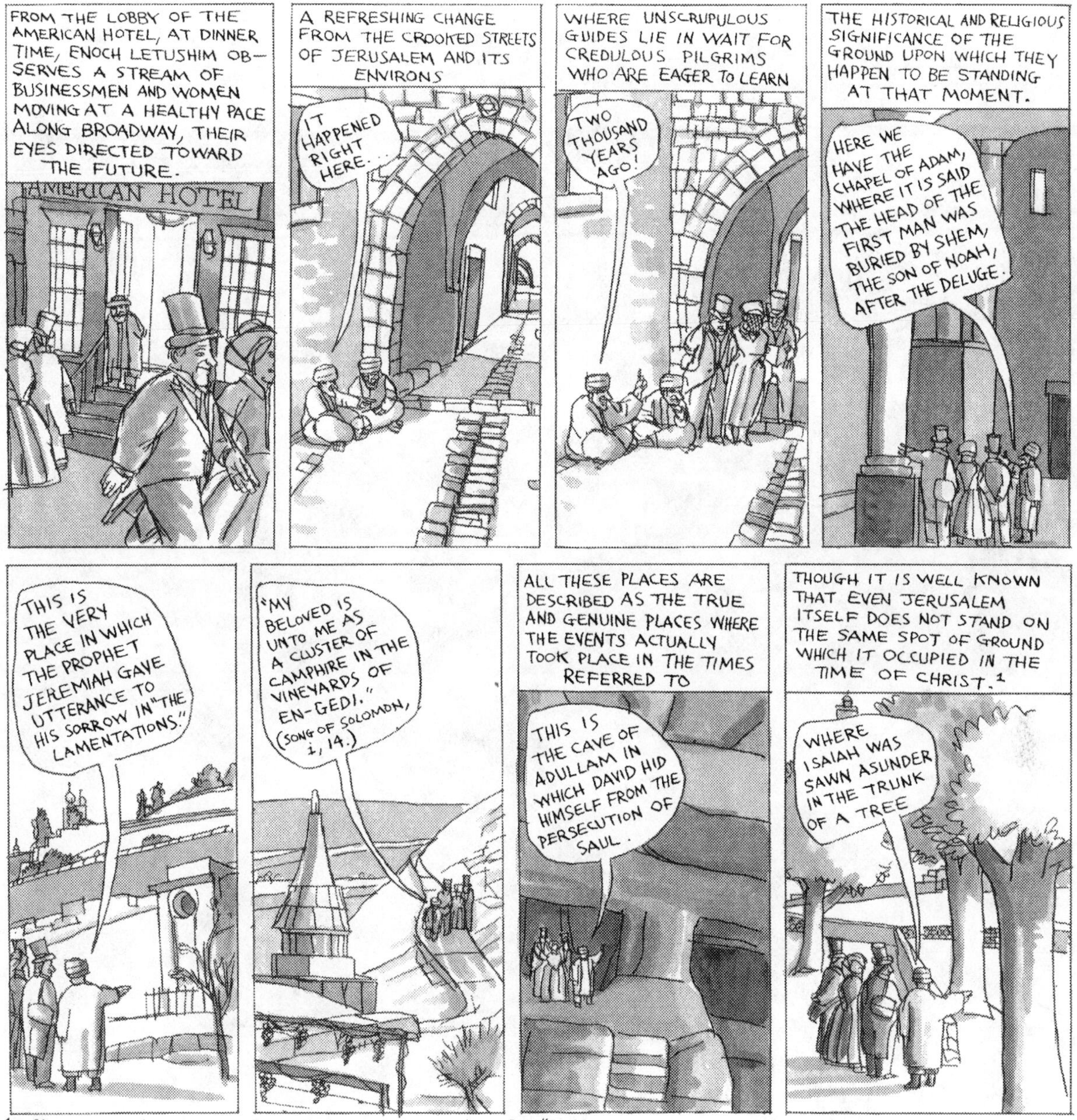
FROM THE LOBBY OF THE AMERICAN HOTEL, AT DINNER TIME, ENOCH LETUSHIM OBSERVES A STREAM OF BUSINESSMEN AND WOMEN MOVING AT A HEALTHY PACE ALONG BROADWAY, THEIR EYES DIRECTED TOWARD THE FUTURE.
AMERICAN HOTEL
A REFRESHING CHANGE FROM THE CROOKED STREETS OF JERUSALEM AND ITS ENVIRONS
IT HAPPENED RIGHT HERE...
WHERE UNSCRUPULOUS GUIDES LIE IN WAIT FOR CREDULOUS PILGRIMS WHO ARE EAGER TO LEARN
TWO THOUSAND YEARS AGO!
THE HISTORICAL AND RELIGIOUS SIGNIFICANCE OF THE GROUND UPON WHICH THEY HAPPEN TO BE STANDING AT THAT MOMENT.
HERE WE HAVE THE CHAPEL OF ADAM, WHERE IT IS SAID THE HEAD OF THE FIRST MAN WAS BURIED BY SHEM, THE SON OF NOAH, AFTER THE DELUGE.
THIS IS THE VERY PLACE IN WHICH THE PROPHET JEREMIAH GAVE UTTERANCE TO HIS SORROW IN "THE LAMENTATIONS."
"MY BELOVED IS UNTO ME AS A CLUSTER OF CAMPHIRE IN THE VINEYARDS OF EN-GEDI." (SONG OF SOLOMON, i, 14.)
ALL THESE PLACES ARE DESCRIBED AS THE TRUE AND GENUINE PLACES WHERE THE EVENTS ACTUALLY TOOK PLACE IN THE TIMES REFERRED TO
THIS IS THE CAVE OF ADULLAM IN WHICH DAVID HID HIMSELF FROM THE PERSECUTION OF SAUL.
THOUGH IT IS WELL KNOWN THAT EVEN JERUSALEM ITSELF DOES NOT STAND ON THE SAME SPOT OF GROUND WHICH IT OCCUPIED IN THE TIME OF CHRIST.[1]
WHERE ISAIAH WAS SAWN ASUNDER IN THE TRUNK OF A TREE

[1] Châteaubriand, "L'Intinéraire de Paris à Jérusalem et de Jérusalem à Paris" (1811)

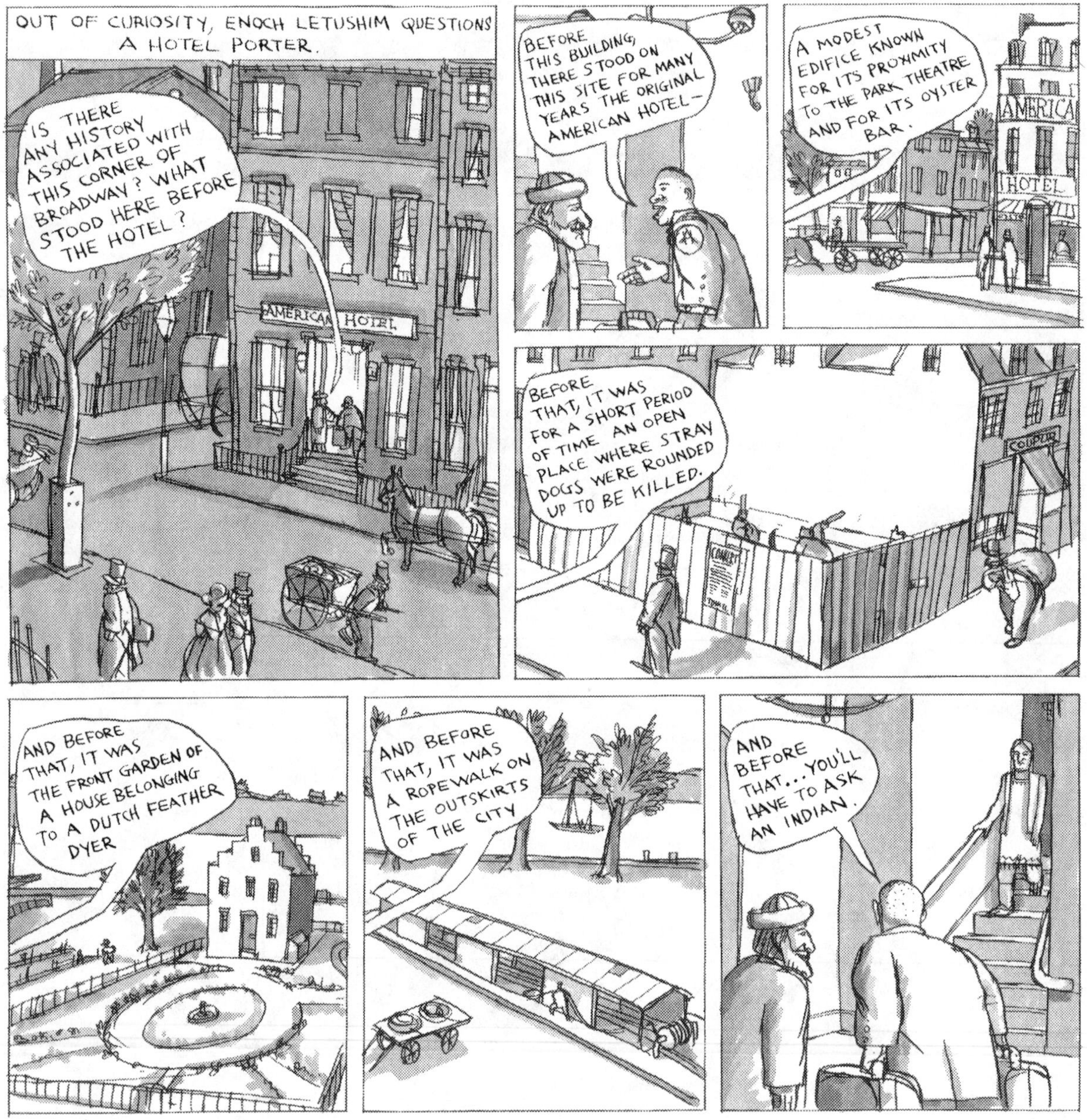
OUT OF CURIOSITY, ENOCH LETUSHIM QUESTIONS A HOTEL PORTER.
IS THERE ANY HISTORY ASSOCIATED WITH THIS CORNER OF BROADWAY? WHAT STOOD HERE BEFORE THE HOTEL?
AMERICAN HOTEL
BEFORE THIS BUILDING, THERE STOOD ON THIS SITE FOR MANY YEARS THE ORIGINAL AMERICAN HOTEL—
A MODEST EDIFICE KNOWN FOR ITS PROXIMITY TO THE PARK THEATRE AND FOR ITS OYSTER BAR.
AMERICA
HOTEL
BEFORE THAT, IT WAS FOR A SHORT PERIOD OF TIME AN OPEN PLACE WHERE STRAY DOGS WERE ROUNDED UP TO BE KILLED.
AND BEFORE THAT, IT WAS THE FRONT GARDEN OF A HOUSE BELONGING TO A DUTCH FEATHER DYER
AND BEFORE THAT, IT WAS A ROPEWALK ON THE OUTSKIRTS OF THE CITY
AND BEFORE THAT... YOU'LL HAVE TO ASK AN INDIAN.

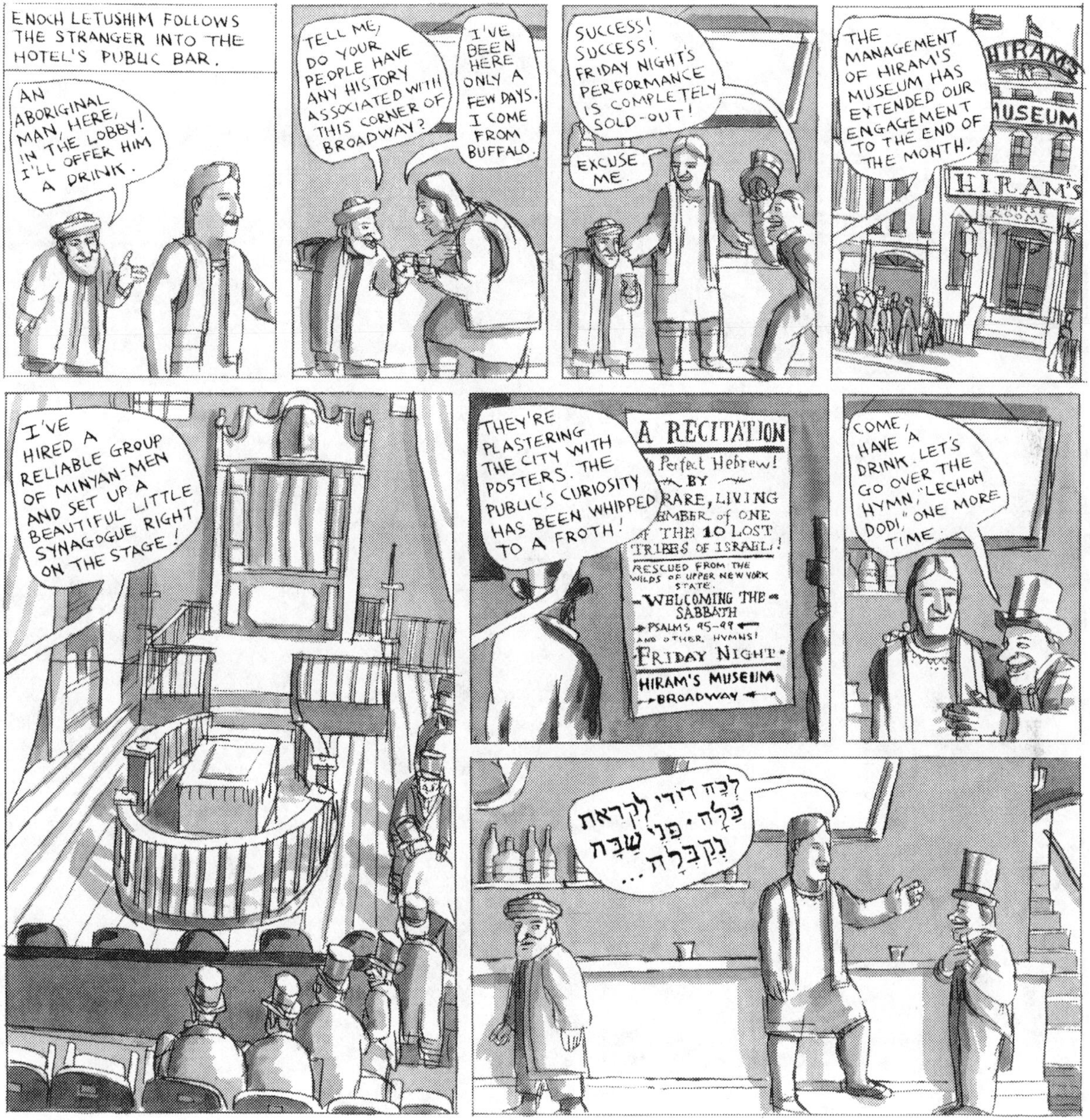
ENOCH LETUSHIM FOLLOWS THE STRANGER INTO THE HOTEL'S PUBLIC BAR.
AN ABORIGINAL MAN, HERE, IN THE LOBBY! I'LL OFFER HIM A DRINK.
TELL ME, DO YOUR PEOPLE HAVE ANY HISTORY ASSOCIATED WITH THIS CORNER OF BROADWAY?
I'VE BEEN HERE ONLY A FEW DAYS. I COME FROM BUFFALO.
SUCCESS! SUCCESS! FRIDAY NIGHT'S PERFORMANCE IS COMPLETELY SOLD-OUT!
EXCUSE ME.
THE MANAGEMENT OF HIRAM'S MUSEUM HAS EXTENDED OUR ENGAGEMENT TO THE END OF THE MONTH.
HIRAM'S
MUSEUM
HIRAM'S
CHINESE ROOMS
I'VE HIRED A RELIABLE GROUP OF MINYAN-MEN AND SET UP A BEAUTIFUL LITTLE SYNAGOGUE RIGHT ON THE STAGE!
THEY'RE PLASTERING THE CITY WITH POSTERS. THE PUBLIC'S CURIOSITY HAS BEEN WHIPPED TO A FROTH!
A RECITATION
n Perfect Hebrew!
BY
RARE, LIVING
EMBER of ONE
F THE 10 LOST
TRIBES OF ISRAEL!
RESCUED FROM THE WILDS OF UPPER NEW YORK STATE.
WELCOMING THE SABBATH
PSALMS 95-99
AND OTHER HYMNS!
FRIDAY NIGHT
HIRAM'S MUSEUM
BROADWAY
COME, HAVE A DRINK. LET'S GO OVER THE HYMN, "LECHOH DODI," ONE MORE TIME.
לכה דודי לקראת
כלה · פני שבת
נקבלה ...

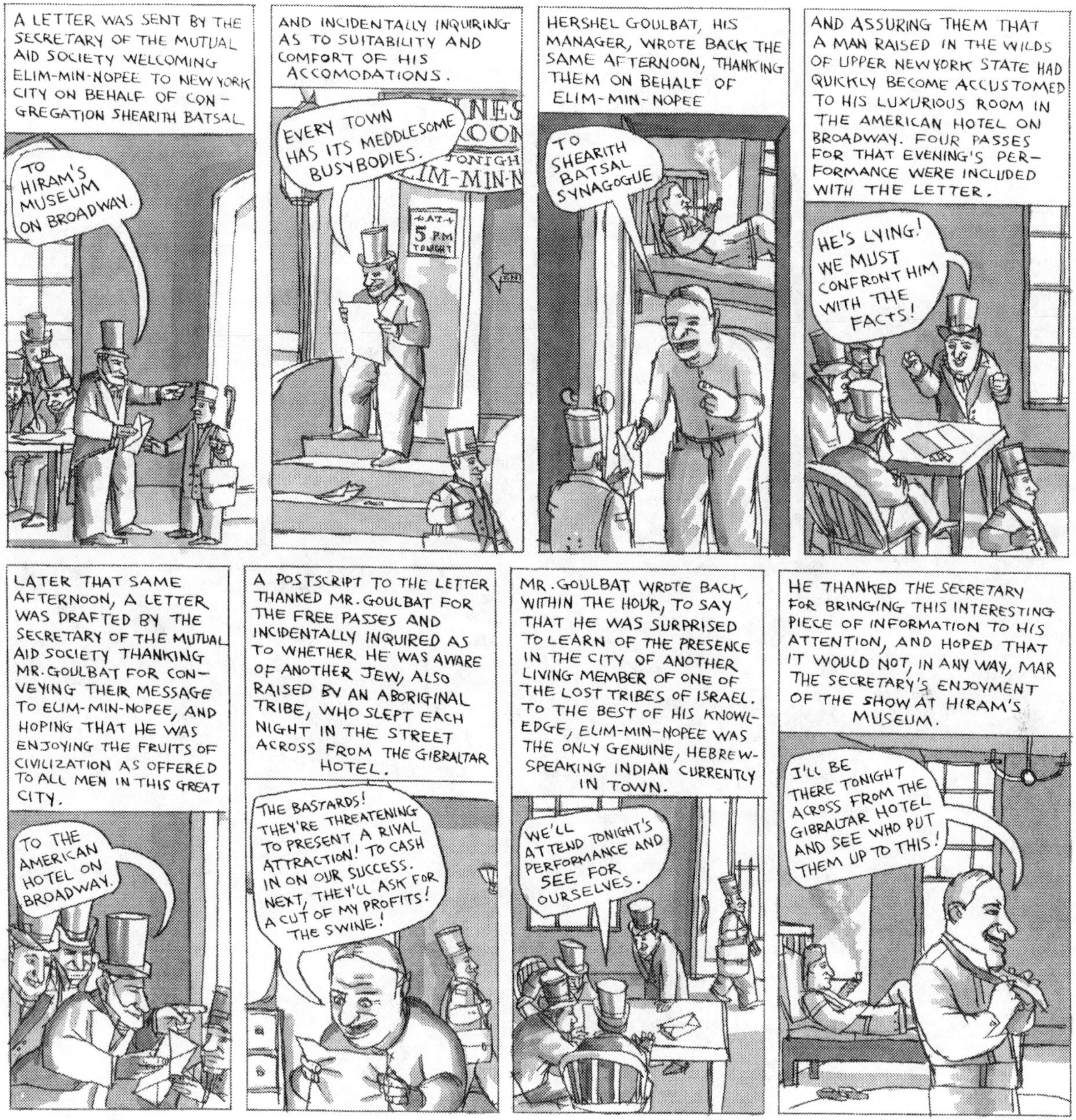
A LETTER WAS SENT BY THE SECRETARY OF THE MUTUAL AID SOCIETY WELCOMING ELIM-MIN-NOPEE TO NEW YORK CITY ON BEHALF OF CONGREGATION SHEARITH BATSAL
TO HIRAM'S MUSEUM ON BROADWAY.
AND INCIDENTALLY INQUIRING AS TO SUITABILITY AND COMFORT OF HIS ACCOMODATIONS.
EVERY TOWN HAS ITS MEDDLESOME BUSYBODIES.
SAT. 5 P.M. TONIGHT
HERSHEL GOULBAT, HIS MANAGER, WROTE BACK THE SAME AFTERNOON, THANKING THEM ON BEHALF OF ELIM-MIN-NOPEE
TO SHEARITH BATSAL SYNAGOGUE
AND ASSURING THEM THAT A MAN RAISED IN THE WILDS OF UPPER NEW YORK STATE HAD QUICKLY BECOME ACCUSTOMED TO HIS LUXURIOUS ROOM IN THE AMERICAN HOTEL ON BROADWAY. FOUR PASSES FOR THAT EVENING'S PERFORMANCE WERE INCLUDED WITH THE LETTER.
HE'S LYING! WE MUST CONFRONT HIM WITH THE FACTS!
LATER THAT SAME AFTERNOON, A LETTER WAS DRAFTED BY THE SECRETARY OF THE MUTUAL AID SOCIETY THANKING MR. GOULBAT FOR CONVEYING THEIR MESSAGE TO ELIM-MIN-NOPEE, AND HOPING THAT HE WAS ENJOYING THE FRUITS OF CIVILIZATION AS OFFERED TO ALL MEN IN THIS GREAT CITY.
TO THE AMERICAN HOTEL ON BROADWAY.
A POSTSCRIPT TO THE LETTER THANKED MR. GOULBAT FOR THE FREE PASSES AND INCIDENTALLY INQUIRED AS TO WHETHER HE WAS AWARE OF ANOTHER JEW, ALSO RAISED BY AN ABORIGINAL TRIBE, WHO SLEPT EACH NIGHT IN THE STREET ACROSS FROM THE GIBRALTAR HOTEL.
THE BASTARDS! THEY'RE THREATENING TO PRESENT A RIVAL ATTRACTION! TO CASH IN ON OUR SUCCESS. NEXT, THEY'LL ASK FOR A CUT OF MY PROFITS! THE SWINE!
MR. GOULBAT WROTE BACK, WITHIN THE HOUR, TO SAY THAT HE WAS SURPRISED TO LEARN OF THE PRESENCE IN THE CITY OF ANOTHER LIVING MEMBER OF ONE OF THE LOST TRIBES OF ISRAEL. TO THE BEST OF HIS KNOWLEDGE, ELIM-MIN-NOPEE WAS THE ONLY GENUINE, HEBREW-SPEAKING INDIAN CURRENTLY IN TOWN.
WE'LL ATTEND TONIGHT'S PERFORMANCE AND SEE FOR OURSELVES.
HE THANKED THE SECRETARY FOR BRINGING THIS INTERESTING PIECE OF INFORMATION TO HIS ATTENTION, AND HOPED THAT IT WOULD NOT, IN ANY WAY, MAR THE SECRETARY'S ENJOYMENT OF THE SHOW AT HIRAM'S MUSEUM.
I'LL BE THERE TONIGHT ACROSS FROM THE GIBRALTAR HOTEL AND SEE WHO PUT THEM UP TO THIS!

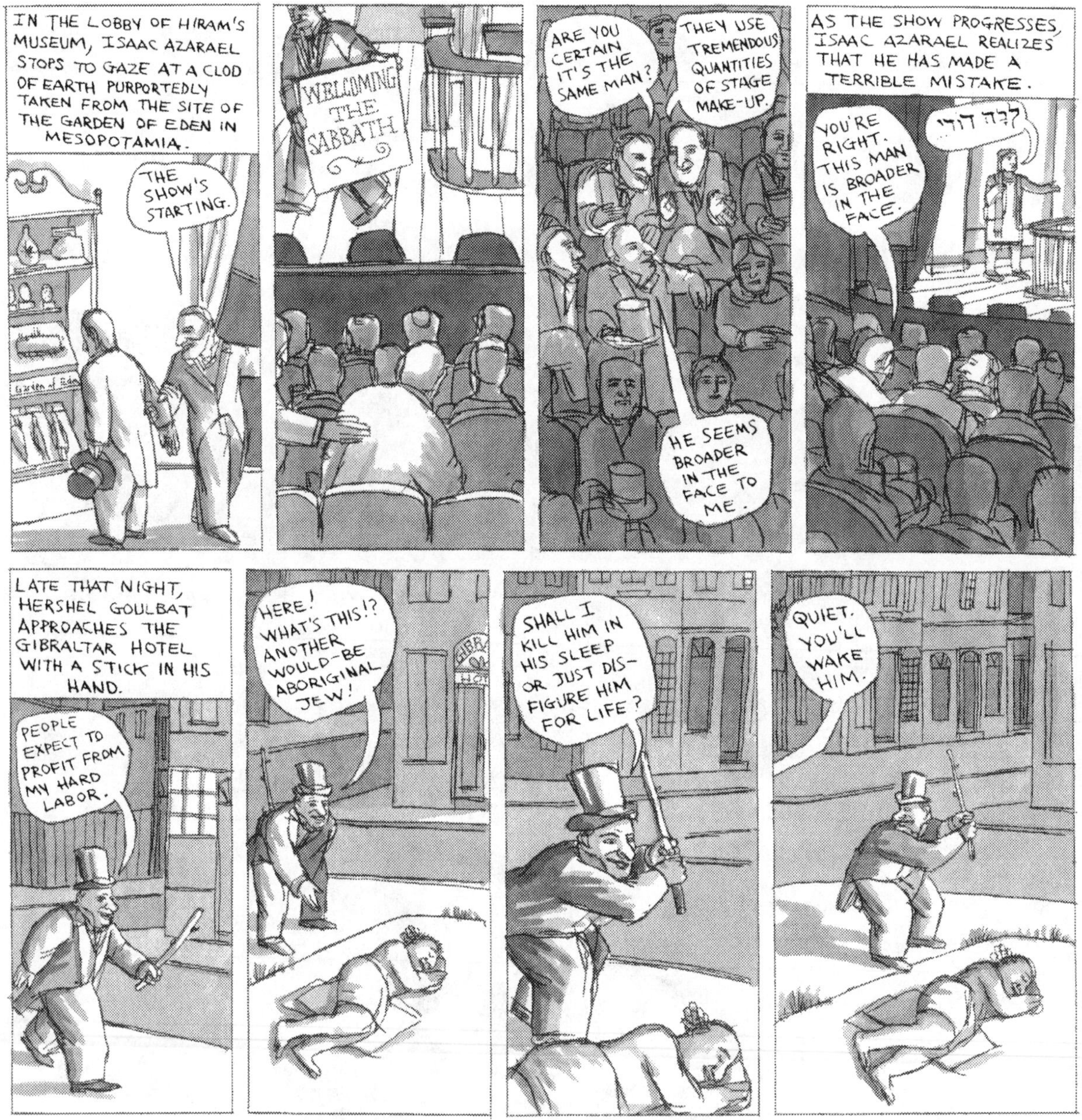
IN THE LOBBY OF HIRAM'S MUSEUM, ISAAC AZARAEL STOPS TO GAZE AT A CLOD OF EARTH PURPORTEDLY TAKEN FROM THE SITE OF THE GARDEN OF EDEN IN MESOPOTAMIA.
THE SHOW'S STARTING.
WELCOMING THE SABBATH
ARE YOU CERTAIN IT'S THE SAME MAN?
THEY USE TREMENDOUS QUANTITIES OF STAGE MAKE-UP.
HE SEEMS BROADER IN THE FACE TO ME.
AS THE SHOW PROGRESSES, ISAAC AZARAEL REALIZES THAT HE HAS MADE A TERRIBLE MISTAKE.
YOU'RE RIGHT. THIS MAN IS BROADER IN THE FACE.
לכה דודי
LATE THAT NIGHT, HERSHEL GOULBAT APPROACHES THE GIBRALTAR HOTEL WITH A STICK IN HIS HAND.
PEOPLE EXPECT TO PROFIT FROM MY HARD LABOR.
HERE! WHAT'S THIS!? ANOTHER WOULD-BE ABORIGINAL JEW!
SHALL I KILL HIM IN HIS SLEEP OR JUST DIS-FIGURE HIM FOR LIFE?
QUIET. YOU'LL WAKE HIM.

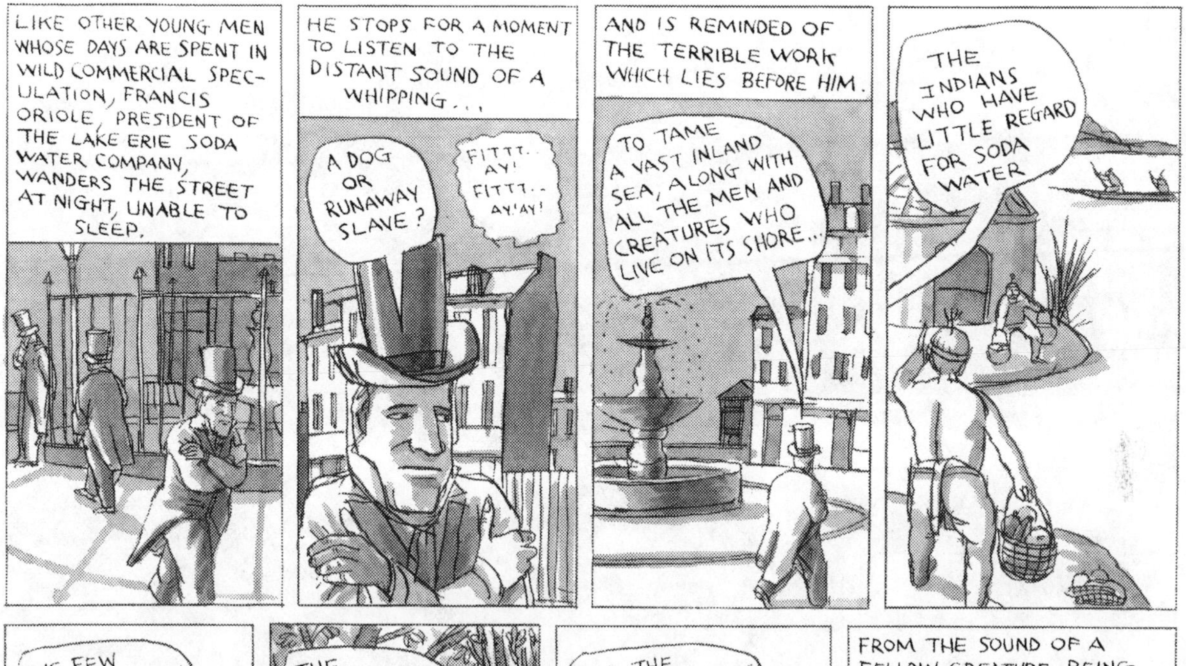
LIKE OTHER YOUNG MEN WHOSE DAYS ARE SPENT IN WILD COMMERCIAL SPECULATION, FRANCIS ORIOLE, PRESIDENT OF THE LAKE ERIE SODA WATER COMPANY, WANDERS THE STREET AT NIGHT, UNABLE TO SLEEP.
HE STOPS FOR A MOMENT TO LISTEN TO THE DISTANT SOUND OF A WHIPPING...
A DOG OR RUNAWAY SLAVE?
FITTT.. AY! FITTT.. AY! AY!
AND IS REMINDED OF THE TERRIBLE WORK WHICH LIES BEFORE HIM.
TO TAME A VAST INLAND SEA, ALONG WITH ALL THE MEN AND CREATURES WHO LIVE ON ITS SHORE...
THE INDIANS WHO HAVE LITTLE REGARD FOR SODA WATER
THE FEW NORTH AMERICAN DISCIPLES OF COMTE DE SAINT-SIMON WHO HAIL SODA WATER AS THE SACRAMENTAL BEVERAGE OF THEIR NEW RELIGION OF THE FLESH.
META
THE FUR TRADERS WHO BLAME CARBONATION FOR THE BEAVER'S FLAGGING DESIRE TO PROCREATE.
AND THE AQUATIC ANIMALS WHOSE PRIMITIVE LUNGS CANNOT TOLERATE SUCH HIGHLY GASEOUS WATER.
FROM THE SOUND OF A FELLOW CREATURE BEING MERCILESSLY FLOGGED IN THE STREET, HE DERIVES A FEELING OF CALM REASSURANCE.
YES, EVEN THESE OBSTACLES CAN BE OVERCOME.
FFFIT. AY! AY! FFFFIT AY! AY!

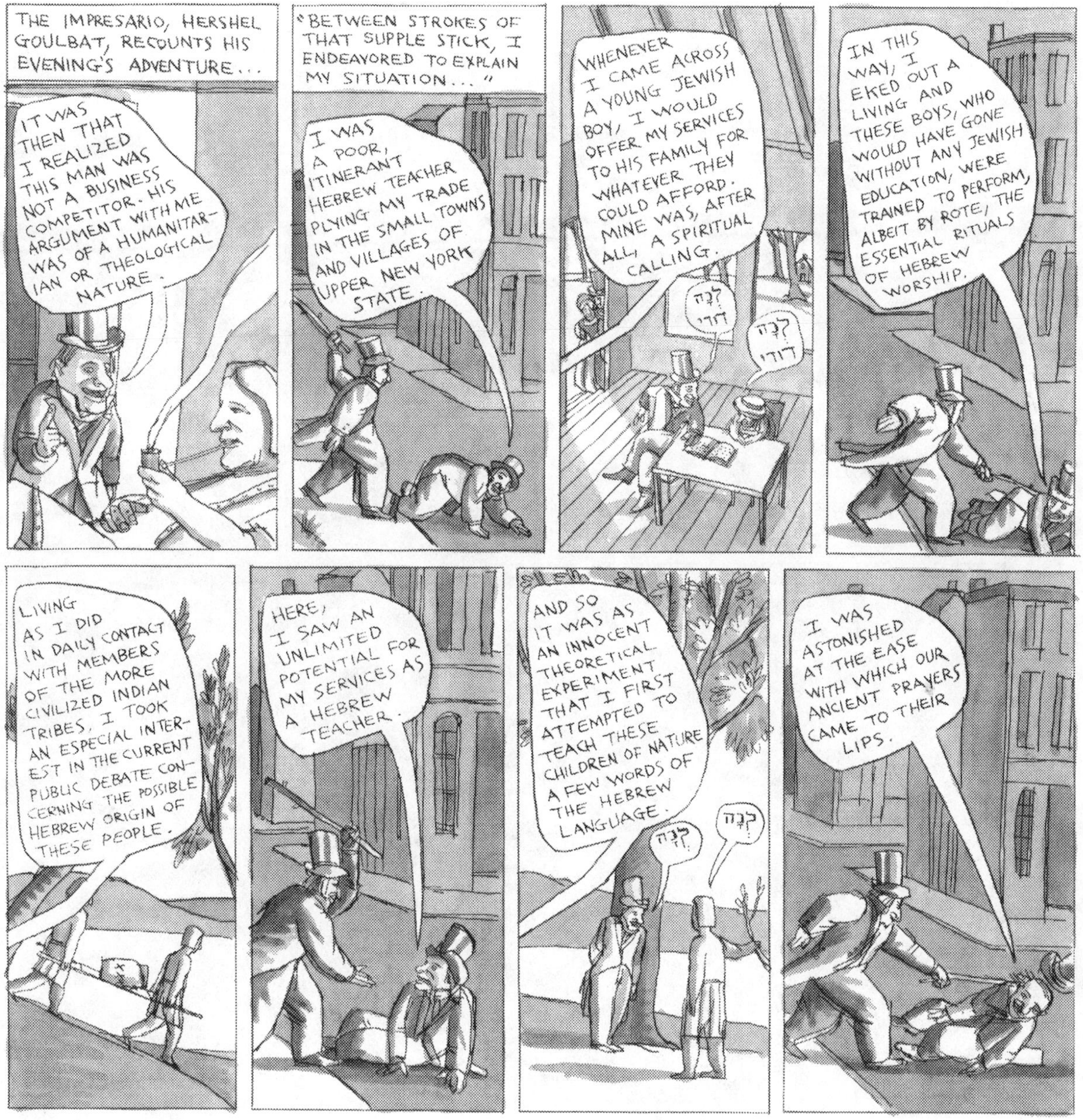
THE IMPRESARIO, HERSHEL GOULBAT, RECOUNTS HIS EVENING'S ADVENTURE...
IT WAS THEN THAT I REALIZED THIS MAN WAS NOT A BUSINESS COMPETITOR. HIS ARGUMENT WITH ME WAS OF A HUMANITARIAN OR THEOLOGICAL NATURE.
"BETWEEN STROKES OF THAT SUPPLE STICK, I ENDEAVORED TO EXPLAIN MY SITUATION..."
I WAS A POOR, ITINERANT HEBREW TEACHER PLYING MY TRADE IN THE SMALL TOWNS AND VILLAGES OF UPPER NEW YORK STATE.
WHENEVER I CAME ACROSS A YOUNG JEWISH BOY, I WOULD OFFER MY SERVICES TO HIS FAMILY FOR WHATEVER THEY COULD AFFORD. MINE WAS, AFTER ALL, A SPIRITUAL CALLING.
לכה דודי
לכה דודי
IN THIS WAY, I EKED OUT A LIVING AND THESE BOYS, WHO WOULD HAVE GONE WITHOUT ANY JEWISH EDUCATION, WERE TRAINED TO PERFORM, ALBEIT BY ROTE, THE ESSENTIAL RITUALS OF HEBREW WORSHIP.
LIVING AS I DID IN DAILY CONTACT WITH MEMBERS OF THE MORE CIVILIZED INDIAN TRIBES, I TOOK AN ESPECIAL INTEREST IN THE CURRENT PUBLIC DEBATE CONCERNING THE POSSIBLE HEBREW ORIGIN OF THESE PEOPLE.
HERE, I SAW AN UNLIMITED POTENTIAL FOR MY SERVICES AS A HEBREW TEACHER.
AND SO IT WAS AS AN INNOCENT THEORETICAL EXPERIMENT THAT I FIRST ATTEMPTED TO TEACH THESE CHILDREN OF NATURE A FEW WORDS OF THE HEBREW LANGUAGE.
לכה
לכה
I WAS ASTONISHED AT THE EASE WITH WHICH OUR ANCIENT PRAYERS CAME TO THEIR LIPS.

YOU MUST MEET MY FRIEND, ISAAC AZARAEL. BROUGHT HERE AS A CHILD FROM AMSTERDAM, HE IS A FINE EXAMPLE OF A JEW RAISED AND NOW HAPPILY THRIVING IN THE FREE AIR OF OUR REPUBLIC.
WHAT HAPPENED TO YOUR FACE?
A THEOLOGICAL DISPUTE LAST NIGHT ACROSS FROM THE GIBRALTAR HOTEL.
YOU'VE NO DOUBT HEARD OF ELIM-MIN-NOPEE, THE WONDER OF BROADWAY... WELL, THERE ARE OTHERS FOLLOWING HIS EXAMPLE!
STANDING ROOM ONLY FOR EIGHT WEEKS AT HIRAM'S MUSEUM.
WILD INDIANS, WITH THE HELP OF CERTAIN UNSCRUPULOUS HEBREW TEACHERS, NOW SEE A CHANCE TO PROFIT FROM THE CURRENT VOGUE FOR SPECULATION UPON THE WHEREABOUTS OF THE LOST TRIBES OF ISRAEL.
THEY SOMEHOW LEARN ENOUGH HEBREW TO PUT ON A GOOD SHOW AND THEN TRAVEL UP AND DOWN THE EAST COAST.
THE IDEA OF A NEW JERUSALEM DISCOVERED IN THE WILDS OF NEW YORK STATE IS IRRESISTIBLE TO THE CASUAL SUNDAY SCHOOL STUDENT OF THE OLD TESTAMENT!
שלום עליכם
BY COMPARISON, WE, THE JEWS OF THE OLD WORLD, APPEAR TO HAVE BEEN THOROUGHLY CORRUPTED BY EUROPEAN CULTURE AND ARE JEWS IN NAME ONLY.
MAY I INTRODUCE YOU TO MY COLLEAGUE, THE EMINENT ACTOR MAYNARD DAIZY.
YOU NEED SOME BUTTONS?

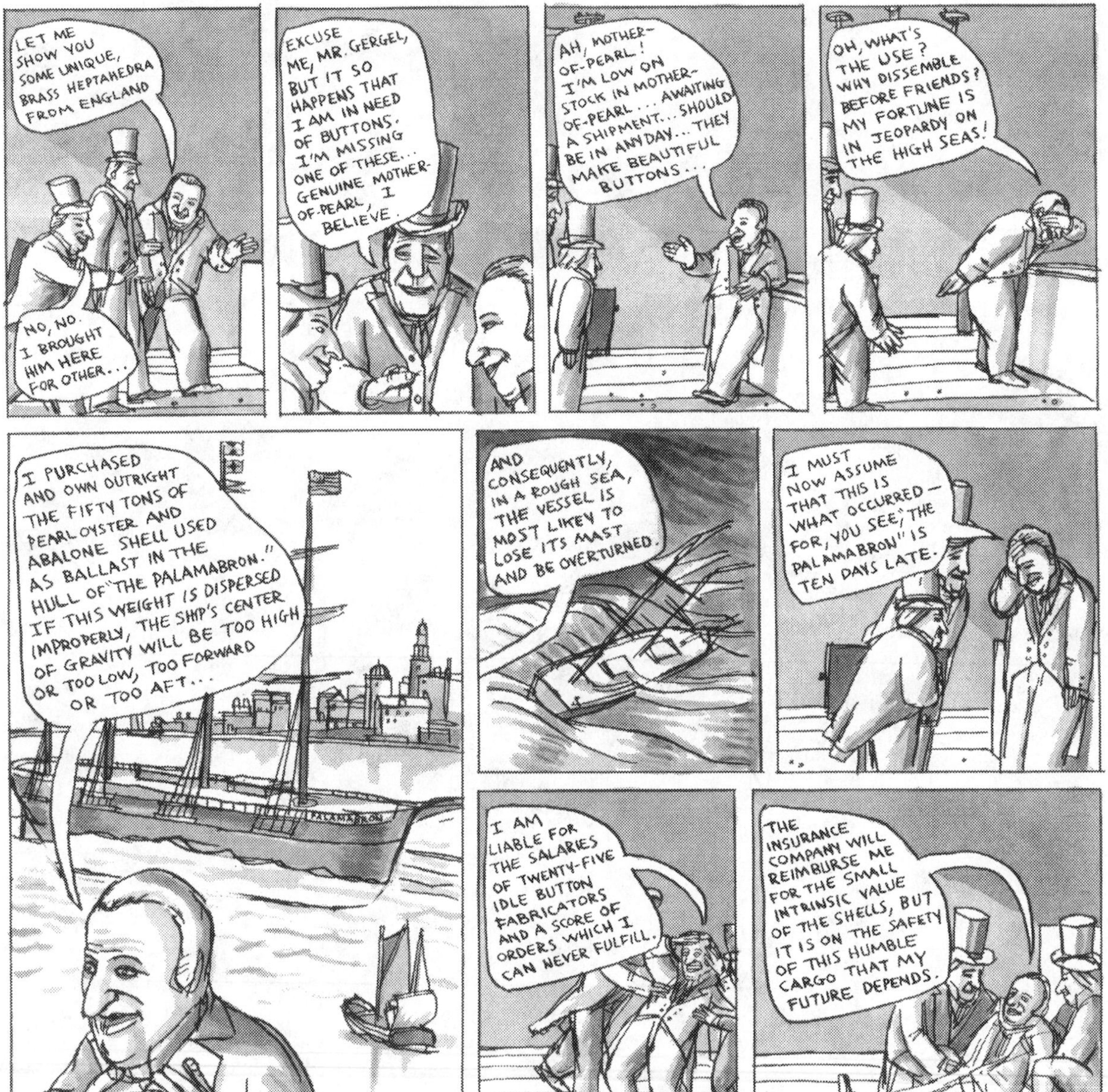

LET ME SHOW YOU SOME UNIQUE, BRASS HEPTAHEDRA FROM ENGLAND
NO, NO. I BROUGHT HIM HERE FOR OTHER...
EXCUSE ME, MR. GERGEL, BUT IT SO HAPPENS THAT I AM IN NEED OF BUTTONS. I'M MISSING ONE OF THESE... GENUINE MOTHER-OF-PEARL, I BELIEVE.
AH, MOTHER-OF-PEARL! I'M LOW ON STOCK IN MOTHER-OF-PEARL... AWAITING A SHIPMENT... SHOULD BE IN ANY DAY... THEY MAKE BEAUTIFUL BUTTONS...
OH, WHAT'S THE USE? WHY DISSEMBLE BEFORE FRIENDS? MY FORTUNE IS IN JEOPARDY ON THE HIGH SEAS!
I PURCHASED AND OWN OUTRIGHT THE FIFTY TONS OF PEARL OYSTER AND ABALONE SHELL USED AS BALLAST IN THE HULL OF "THE PALAMABRON." IF THIS WEIGHT IS DISPERSED IMPROPERLY, THE SHIP'S CENTER OF GRAVITY WILL BE TOO HIGH OR TOO LOW, TOO FORWARD OR TOO AFT...
PALAMABRON
AND CONSEQUENTLY, IN A ROUGH SEA, THE VESSEL IS MOST LIKEY TO LOSE ITS MAST AND BE OVERTURNED.
I MUST NOW ASSUME THAT THIS IS WHAT OCCURRED— FOR, YOU SEE, "THE PALAMABRON" IS TEN DAYS LATE.
I AM LIABLE FOR THE SALARIES OF TWENTY-FIVE IDLE BUTTON FABRICATORS AND A SCORE OF ORDERS WHICH I CAN NEVER FULFILL.
THE INSURANCE COMPANY WILL REIMBURSE ME FOR THE SMALL INTRINSIC VALUE OF THE SHELLS, BUT IT IS ON THE SAFETY OF THIS HUMBLE CARGO THAT MY FUTURE DEPENDS.

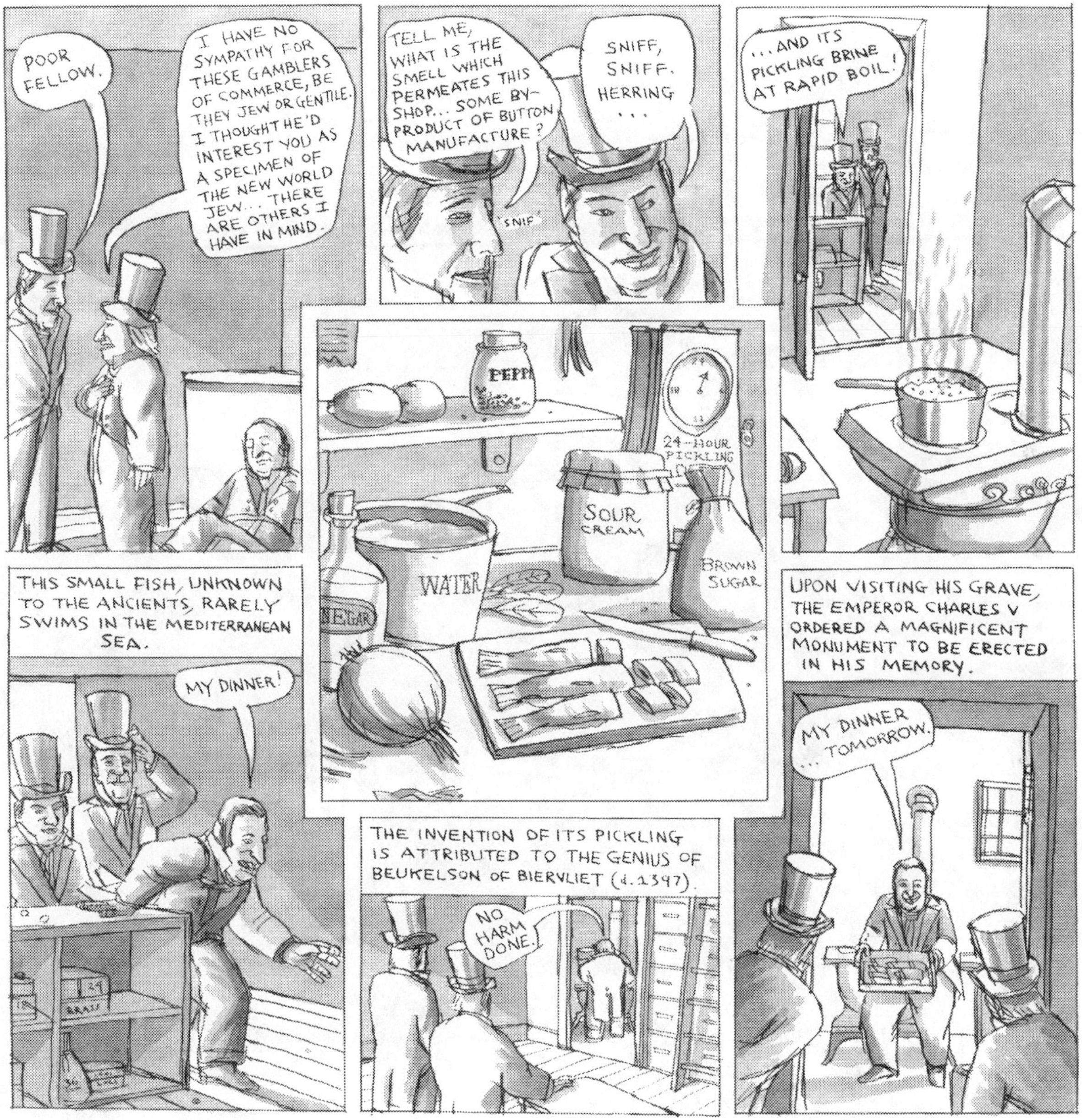
POOR FELLOW.
I HAVE NO SYMPATHY FOR THESE GAMBLERS OF COMMERCE, BE THEY JEW OR GENTILE. I THOUGHT HE'D INTEREST YOU AS A SPECIMEN OF THE NEW WORLD JEW... THERE ARE OTHERS I HAVE IN MIND.
TELL ME, WHAT IS THE SMELL WHICH PERMEATES THIS SHOP... SOME BY-PRODUCT OF BUTTON MANUFACTURE?
SNIF
SNIFF, SNIFF. HERRING ...
...AND ITS PICKLING BRINE AT RAPID BOIL!
24-HOUR PICKLING
SOUR CREAM
WATER
BROWN SUGAR
THIS SMALL FISH, UNKNOWN TO THE ANCIENTS, RARELY SWIMS IN THE MEDITERRANEAN SEA.
MY DINNER!
THE INVENTION OF ITS PICKLING IS ATTRIBUTED TO THE GENIUS OF BEUKELSON OF BIERVLIET (d. 1397).
NO HARM DONE.
UPON VISITING HIS GRAVE, THE EMPEROR CHARLES V ORDERED A MAGNIFICENT MONUMENT TO BE ERECTED IN HIS MEMORY.
MY DINNER ... TOMORROW.

WITH EACH PASSING DAY, FRANCIS ORIOLE'S DREAM OF CARBONATING LAKE ERIE COMES CLOSER TO REALIZATION.
YOU SEE, A PARTNERSHIP OF LIKE-MINDED BUSINESSMEN CAN ACCOMPLISH WONDERS . . .
MR. MARAH, OF THE KISHON FUR TRADING CO., HAS PROMISED ONE HUNDRED THOUSAND DOLLARS . . . MR. YASCO, OF THE N.Y. SAUSAGE CASING CO., TWENTY-FIVE THOUSAND DOLLARS.
WITH THIS SEED MONEY WE WILL ESTABLISH ONE OFFICE HERE, IN NEW YORK CITY, AND ANOTHER ON THE SHORE OF LAKE ERIE . . .
AND WITH WHATEVER MONEY'S LEFT OVER, WE'LL TRY TO RENOVATE YOUR WARDROBE. SOMETHING A LITTLE MORE UP-TO-DATE . . . THE 14th CENTURY, PERHAPS.
SAMSON GERGEL INTRODUCES THE EMINENT ACTOR MAYNARD DAIZY TO A NUMBER OF HIS JEWISH FRIENDS.
MR. ELIEZER YASCO, OF THE N.Y. SAUSAGE CASING CO.
MR. GERSHOM LLAMA, TINSMITH.
MR. SHAUL JUVENAL, PRESIDENT OF THE SHEARITH BATSAL BURIAL SOCIETY.
GETTING SOME IDEA OF THE RANGE OF CHARACTER TYPES?
ALMOST ONE THOUSAND JEWS IN THIS CITY ALONE, YOU SAY?
TONIGHT HEBREW RECITATION ELIM MIN NOPBE 8 P.M. HIRAM'S MUSEUM

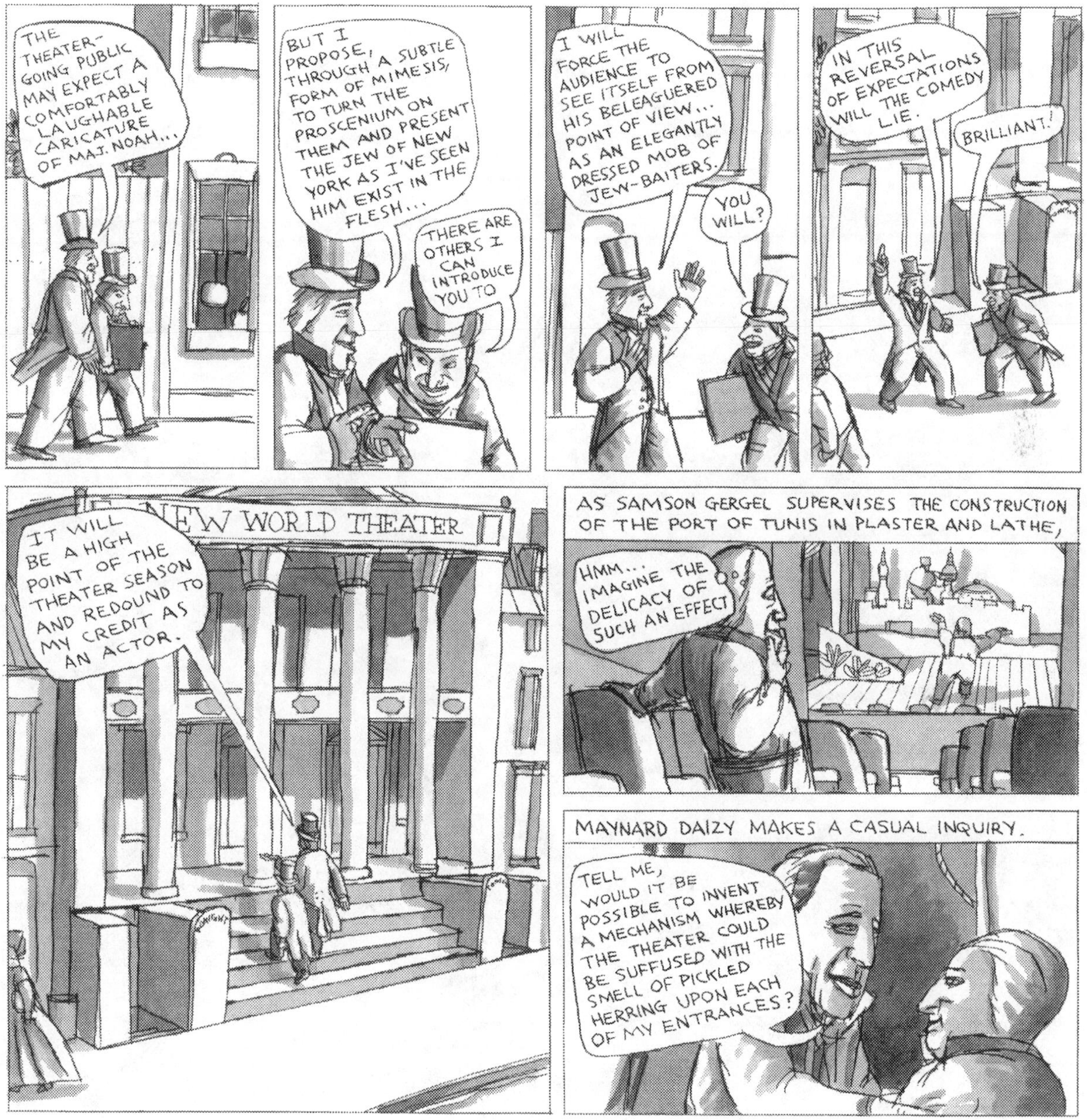
THE THEATER-GOING PUBLIC MAY EXPECT A COMFORTABLY LAUGHABLE CARICATURE OF MAJ. NOAH...
BUT I PROPOSE, THROUGH A SUBTLE FORM OF MIMESIS, TO TURN THE PROSCENIUM ON THEM AND PRESENT THE JEW OF NEW YORK AS I'VE SEEN HIM EXIST IN THE FLESH...
-THERE ARE OTHERS I CAN INTRODUCE YOU TO
I WILL FORCE THE AUDIENCE TO SEE ITSELF FROM HIS BELEAGUERED POINT OF VIEW... AS AN ELEGANTLY DRESSED MOB OF JEW-BAITERS.
YOU WILL?
IN THIS REVERSAL OF EXPECTATIONS WILL THE COMEDY LIE.
BRILLIANT!
NEW WORLD THEATER
IT WILL BE A HIGH POINT OF THE THEATER SEASON AND REDOUND TO MY CREDIT AS AN ACTOR.
AS SAMSON GERGEL SUPERVISES THE CONSTRUCTION OF THE PORT OF TUNIS IN PLASTER AND LATHE,
HMM... IMAGINE THE DELICACY OF SUCH AN EFFECT
MAYNARD DAIZY MAKES A CASUAL INQUIRY.
TELL ME, WOULD IT BE POSSIBLE TO INVENT A MECHANISM WHEREBY THE THEATER COULD BE SUFFUSED WITH THE SMELL OF PICKLED HERRING UPON EACH OF MY ENTRANCES?

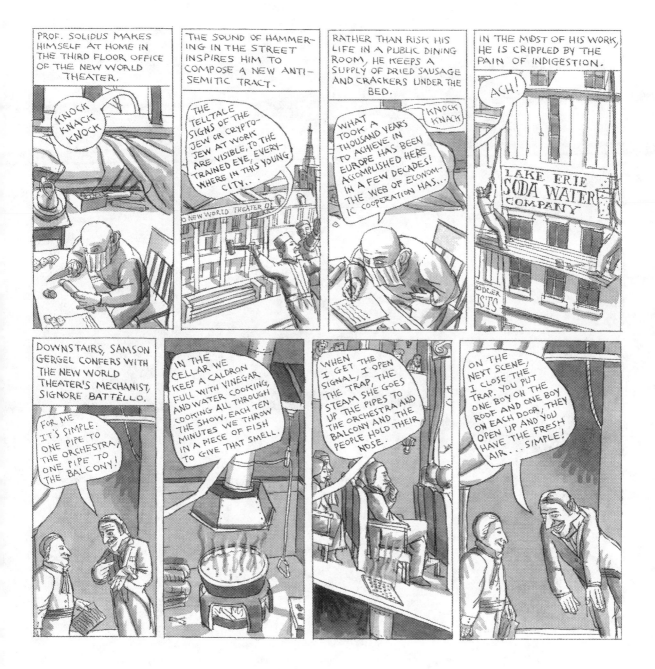

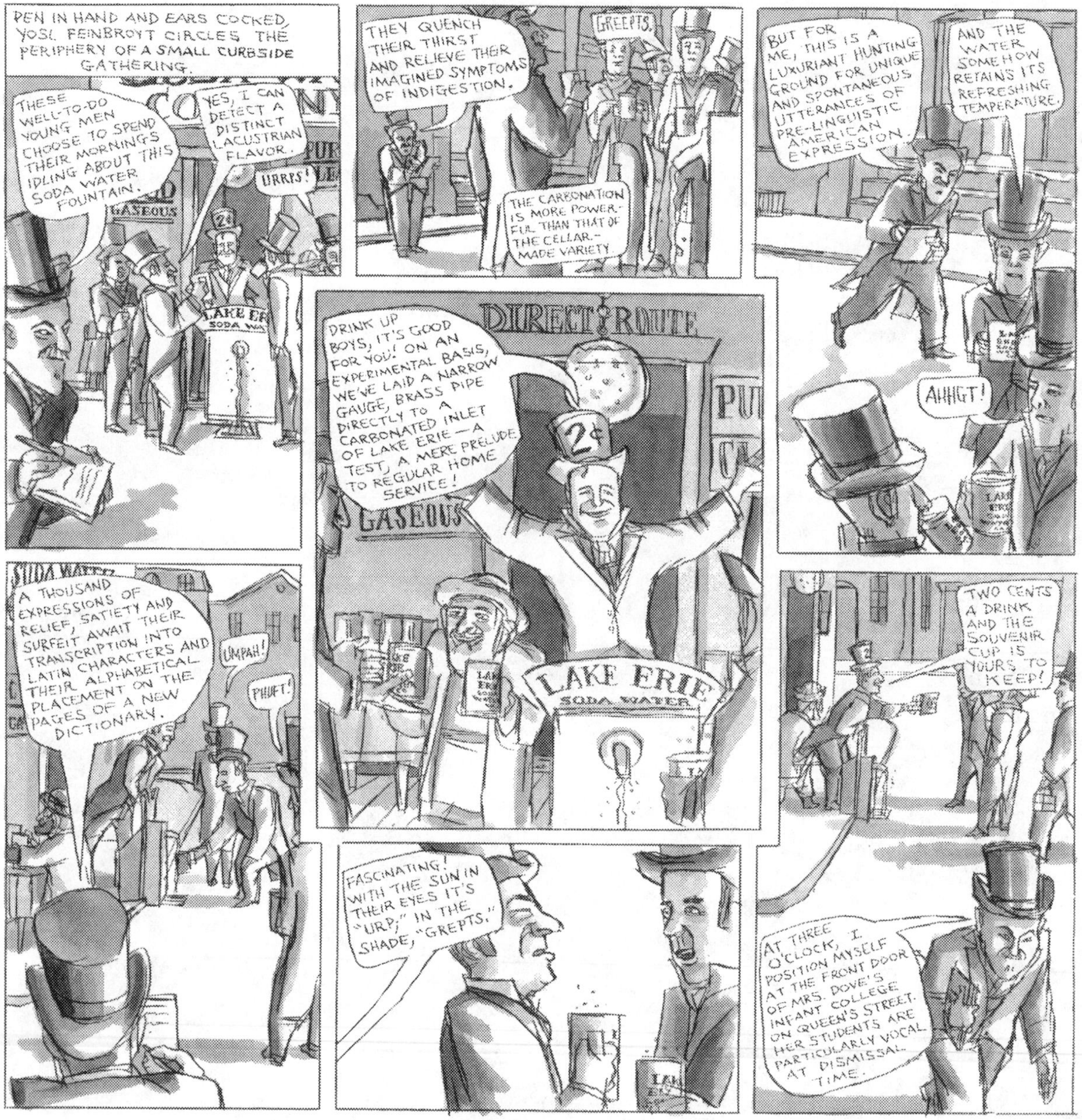
PEN IN HAND AND EARS COCKED, YOSL. FEINBROYT CIRCLES THE PERIPHERY OF A SMALL CURBSIDE GATHERING.
THESE WELL-TO-DO YOUNG MEN CHOOSE TO SPEND THEIR MORNINGS IDLING ABOUT THIS SODA WATER FOUNTAIN.
YES, I CAN DETECT A DISTINCT LACUSTRIAN FLAVOR.
URRPS!
LAKE ERIE SODA WATER
THEY QUENCH THEIR THIRST AND RELIEVE THEIR IMAGINED SYMPTOMS OF INDIGESTION.
GREPTS.
THE CARBONATION IS MORE POWERFUL THAN THAT OF THE CELLAR-MADE VARIETY.
BUT FOR ME, THIS IS A LUXURIANT HUNTING GROUND FOR UNIQUE AND SPONTANEOUS UTTERANCES OF PRE-LINGUISTIC AMERICAN EXPRESSION.
AND THE WATER SOMEHOW RETAINS ITS REFRESHING TEMPERATURE.
AHHGT!
DIRECT ROUTE
DRINK UP BOYS, IT'S GOOD FOR YOU! ON AN EXPERIMENTAL BASIS, WE'VE LAID A NARROW GAUGE, BRASS PIPE DIRECTLY TO A CARBONATED INLET OF LAKE ERIE — A TEST, A MERE PRELUDE TO REGULAR HOME SERVICE!
2¢
GASEOUS
LAKE ERIE SODA WATER
A THOUSAND EXPRESSIONS OF RELIEF, SATIETY AND SURFEIT AWAIT THEIR TRANSCRIPTION INTO LATIN CHARACTERS AND THEIR ALPHABETICAL PLACEMENT ON THE PAGES OF A NEW DICTIONARY.
UMPAH!
PHUFT!
FASCINATING! WITH THE SUN IN THEIR EYES IT'S "URP," IN THE SHADE, "GREPTS."
TWO CENTS A DRINK AND THE SOUVENIR CUP IS YOURS TO KEEP!
AT THREE O'CLOCK, I POSITION MYSELF AT THE FRONT DOOR OF MRS. DOVE'S INFANT COLLEGE ON QUEEN'S STREET. HER STUDENTS ARE PARTICULARLY VOCAL AT DISMISSAL TIME.

THE JEW OF NEW YORK

PAMPHLETS SOLD FOR GOOD

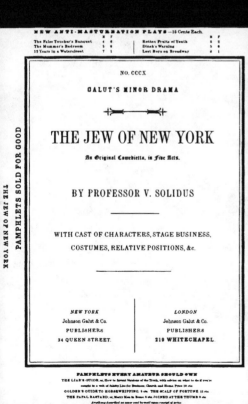

NEW ANTI-MASTURBATION PLAYS—15 Cents Each.

	M	F		M	F
The False Toucher's Banquet	4	6	Rotten Fruits of Youth	8	2
The Mummer's Bedroom	5	0	Dinah's Warning	5	0
12 Years in a Watercloset	7	1	Lost Boys on Broadway	8	1

NO. CCCX

GALUT'S MINOR DRAMA

THE JEW OF NEW YORK

An Original Comedietta, in Five Acts.

BY PROFESSOR V. SOLIDUS

WITH CAST OF CHARACTERS, STAGE BUSINESS, COSTUMES, RELATIVE POSITIONS, &c.

NEW YORK	LONDON
Johnson Galut & Co.	Johnson Galut & Co.
PUBLISHERS	PUBLISHERS
34 QUEEN STREET.	219 WHITECHAPEL.

PAMPHLETS EVERY AMATEUR SHOULD OWN

THE LIAR'S GUIDE; or, How to Invent Versions of the Truth, with advice on what to do if you're caught in a web of falsity. Lies for Business, Church and Home. Price 10 cts.

GOLDER'S GUIDE TO HORSEWHIPPING. 5 cts. THE SCALP OF FORTUNE 11 cts.

THE PAPAL BASTARD; or, Merry Men in Rome 6 cts. JOINED AT THE THUMB 9 cts.

Anything described on cover sent by mail upon receipt of price.

HIRAM'S MUSEUM

No. 472 BROADWAY, BETWEEN GRAND AND BROOME STREETS

EXHIBITIONS OPEN DAY AND NIGHT

A RECITATION

IN PERFECT HEBREW!

BY A RARE AND LIVING MEMBER

OF ONE OF THE LOST TRIBES OF ISRAEL!

ELIM-MIN-NOPEE

RESCUED FROM THE WILDS OF

UPPER NEW YORK STATE!

This prodigy of Nature has been trained to a wonderful degree of intelligence by his Friend and Tutor in the Hebrew Language, Hershel Goulbat.

Welcoming the Sabbath

PSALMS 45 – 99

AND OTHER INSPIRING HYMNS.

UNDER THE DIRECTION OF MR. GOULBAT, AN AUTHENTIC JEWISH SYNAGOGUE HAS BEEN ERECTED FROM WOOD, AT GREAT EXPENSE, FOR THIS PERFORMANCE.

FRIDAY NIGHT

DOORS OPEN AT 7.

ADMISSION 25 CENTS.

NOW ALSO ON EXHIBITION:

THE WILD SOUTH AMERICAN CREATURE RESPONSIBLE FOR THE DEATH OF THE EMINENT ACTOR MAYNARD DAIZY AND SUBSEQUENTLY DESTROYED.

SOUVENIRS AND REFRESHMENTS ARE AVAILABLE IN THE CHINESE ROOMS ON THE FIRST FLOOR.

[71]

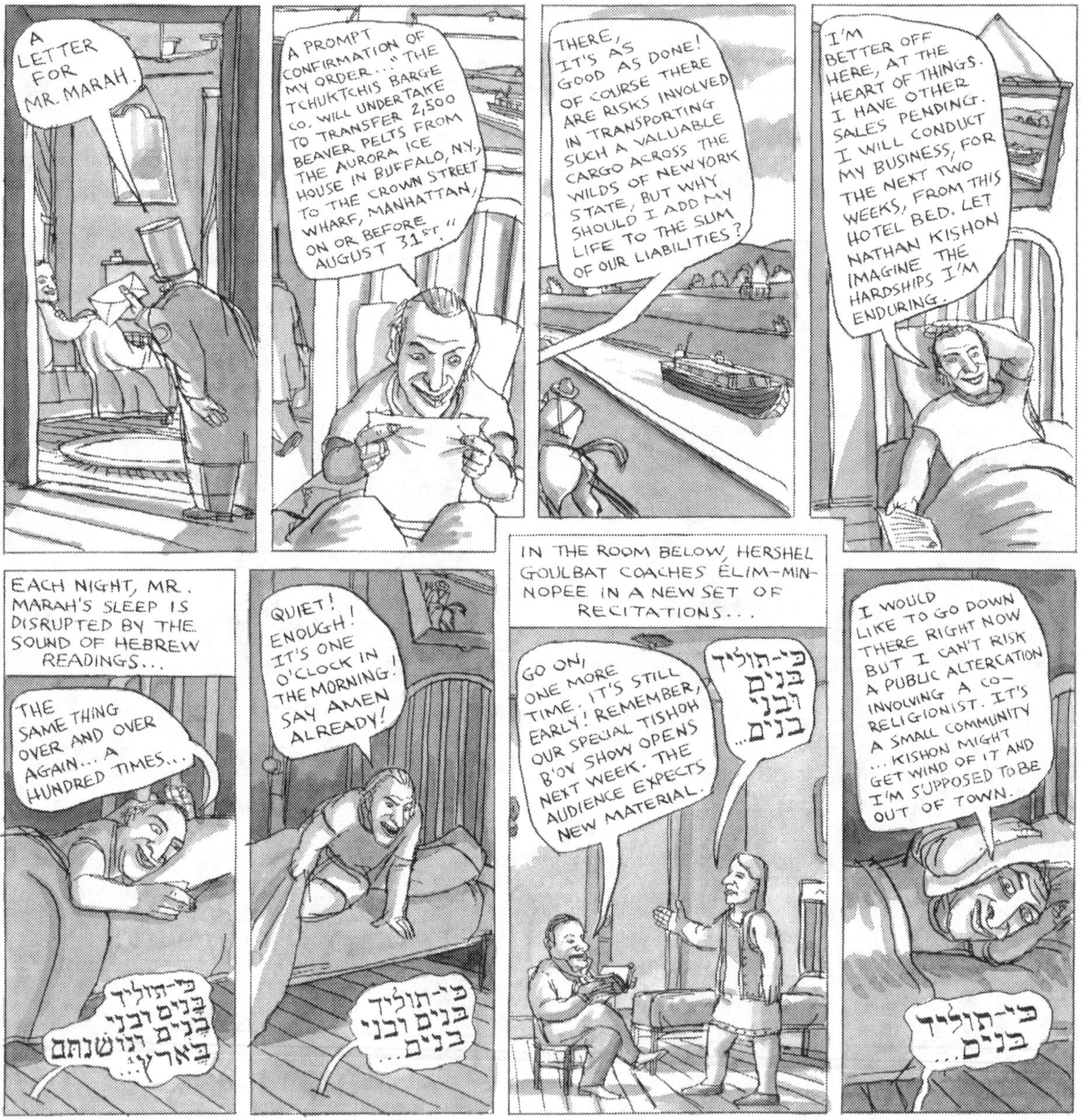
A LETTER FOR MR. MARAH.
A PROMPT CONFIRMATION OF MY ORDER... "THE TCHUKTCHIS BARGE CO. WILL UNDERTAKE TO TRANSFER 2,500 BEAVER PELTS FROM THE AURORA ICE HOUSE IN BUFFALO, N.Y., TO THE CROWN STREET WHARF, MANHATTAN, ON OR BEFORE AUGUST 31ST."
THERE, IT'S AS GOOD AS DONE! OF COURSE THERE ARE RISKS INVOLVED IN TRANSPORTING SUCH A VALUABLE CARGO ACROSS THE WILDS OF NEW YORK STATE, BUT WHY SHOULD I ADD MY LIFE TO THE SUM OF OUR LIABILITIES?
I'M BETTER OFF HERE, AT THE HEART OF THINGS. I HAVE OTHER SALES PENDING. I WILL CONDUCT MY BUSINESS, FOR THE NEXT TWO WEEKS, FROM THIS HOTEL BED. LET NATHAN KISHON IMAGINE THE HARDSHIPS I'M ENDURING.
EACH NIGHT, MR. MARAH'S SLEEP IS DISRUPTED BY THE SOUND OF HEBREW READINGS...
THE SAME THING OVER AND OVER AGAIN... A HUNDRED TIMES...
כי-תוליד בנים ובני בנים ונושנתם בארץ...[1]
QUIET! ENOUGH! IT'S ONE O'CLOCK IN THE MORNING! SAY AMEN ALREADY!
כי-תוליד בנים ובני בנים...
IN THE ROOM BELOW, HERSHEL GOULBAT COACHES ÉLIM-MINNOPEE IN A NEW SET OF RECITATIONS...
GO ON, ONE MORE TIME. IT'S STILL EARLY! REMEMBER, OUR SPECIAL TISHOH B'OV SHOW OPENS NEXT WEEK. THE AUDIENCE EXPECTS NEW MATERIAL.
כי-תוליד בנים ובני בנים...
I WOULD LIKE TO GO DOWN THERE RIGHT NOW BUT I CAN'T RISK A PUBLIC ALTERCATION INVOLVING A CO-RELIGIONIST. IT'S A SMALL COMMUNITY ...KISHON MIGHT GET WIND OF IT AND I'M SUPPOSED TO BE OUT OF TOWN.
כי-תוליד בנים...

[1] Deuteronomy 4:25

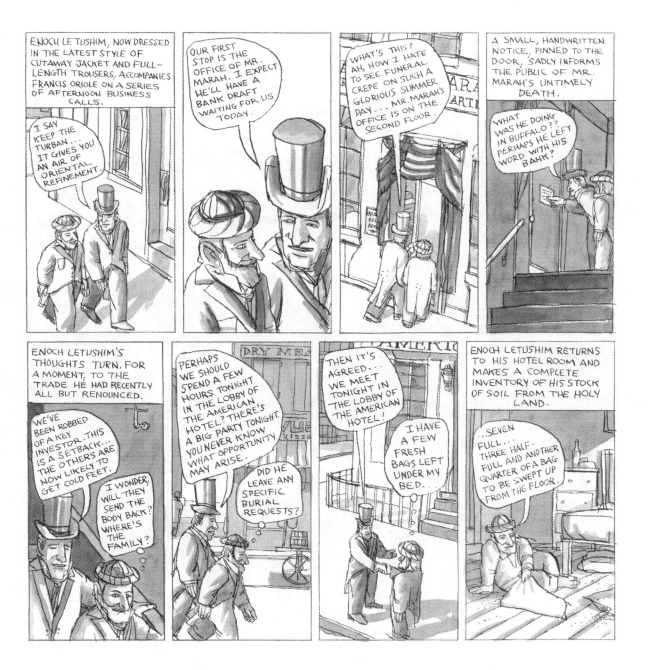

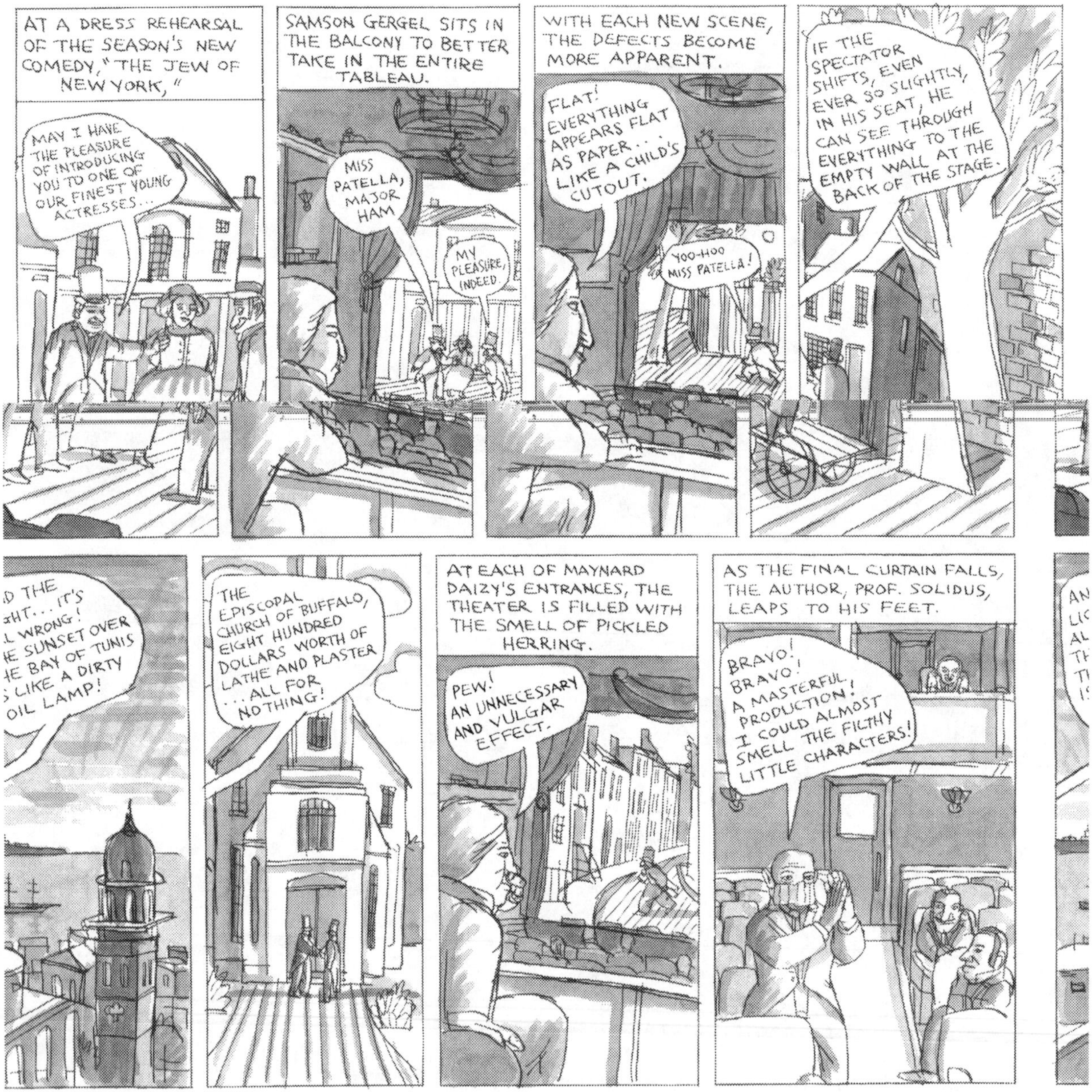
AT A DRESS REHEARSAL OF THE SEASON'S NEW COMEDY, "THE JEW OF NEW YORK,"
MAY I HAVE THE PLEASURE OF INTRODUCING YOU TO ONE OF OUR FINEST YOUNG ACTRESSES...
SAMSON GERGEL SITS IN THE BALCONY TO BETTER TAKE IN THE ENTIRE TABLEAU.
MISS PATELLA, MAJOR HAM
MY PLEASURE, INDEED.
WITH EACH NEW SCENE, THE DEFECTS BECOME MORE APPARENT.
FLAT! EVERYTHING APPEARS FLAT AS PAPER... LIKE A CHILD'S CUTOUT.
YOO-HOO MISS PATELLA!
IF THE SPECTATOR SHIFTS, EVEN EVER SO SLIGHTLY, IN HIS SEAT, HE CAN SEE THROUGH EVERYTHING TO THE EMPTY WALL AT THE BACK OF THE STAGE.
THE ... IT'S WRONG! SUNSET OVER BAY OF TUNIS LIKE A DIRTY OIL LAMP!
THE EPISCOPAL CHURCH OF BUFFALO, EIGHT HUNDRED DOLLARS WORTH OF LATHE AND PLASTER ... ALL FOR NOTHING!
AT EACH OF MAYNARD DAIZY'S ENTRANCES, THE THEATER IS FILLED WITH THE SMELL OF PICKLED HERRING.
PEW! AN UNNECESSARY AND VULGAR EFFECT.
AS THE FINAL CURTAIN FALLS, THE AUTHOR, PROF. SOLIDUS, LEAPS TO HIS FEET.
BRAVO! BRAVO! A MASTERFUL PRODUCTION! I COULD ALMOST SMELL THE FILTHY LITTLE CHARACTERS!

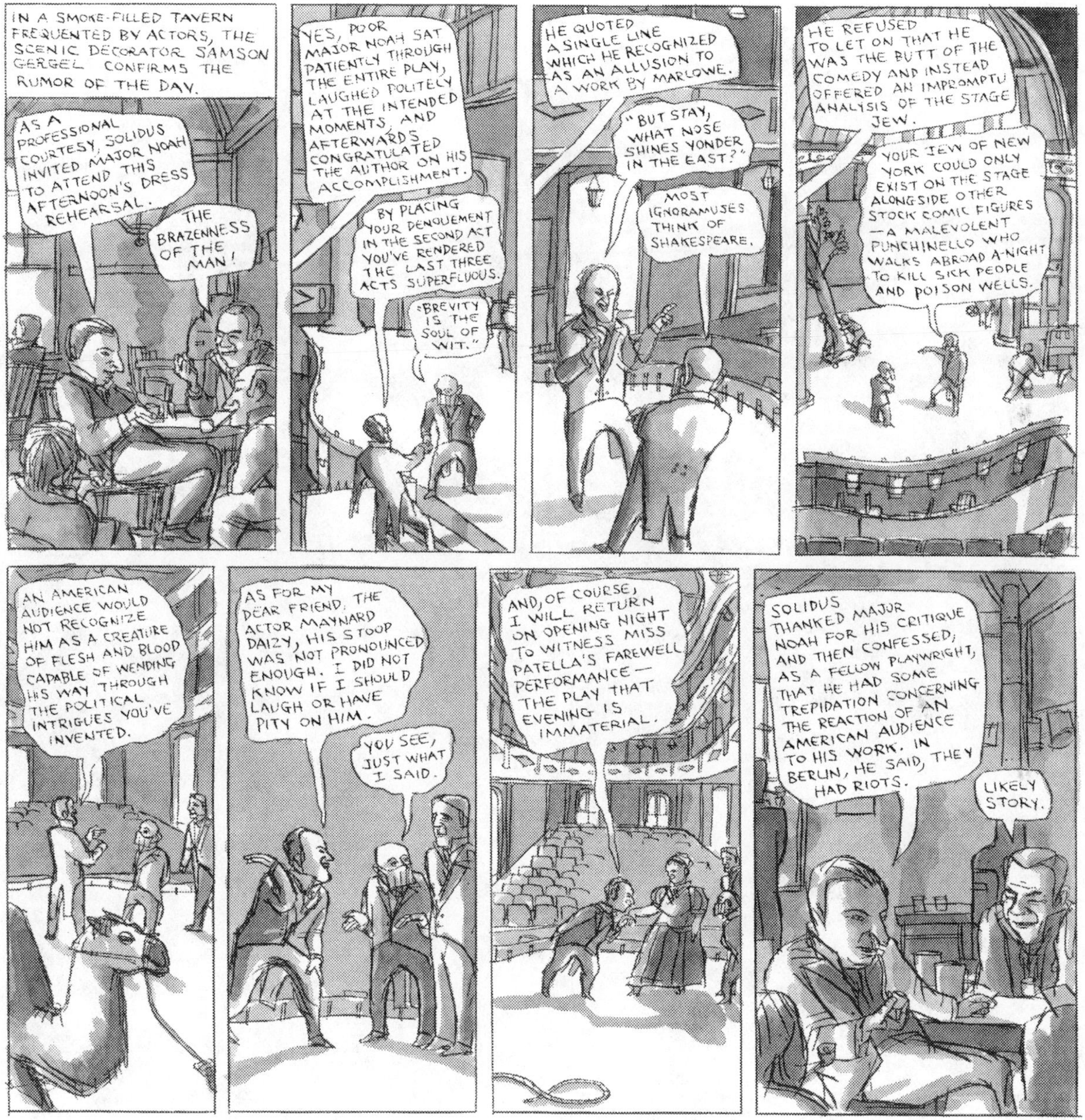
IN A SMOKE-FILLED TAVERN FREQUENTED BY ACTORS, THE SCENIC DECORATOR SAMSON GERGEL CONFIRMS THE RUMOR OF THE DAY.
AS A PROFESSIONAL COURTESY, SOLIDUS INVITED MAJOR NOAH TO ATTEND THIS AFTERNOON'S DRESS REHEARSAL.
THE BRAZENNESS OF THE MAN!
YES, POOR MAJOR NOAH SAT PATIENTLY THROUGH THE ENTIRE PLAY, LAUGHED POLITELY AT THE INTENDED MOMENTS, AND AFTERWARDS CONGRATULATED THE AUTHOR ON HIS ACCOMPLISHMENT.
BY PLACING YOUR DENOUEMENT IN THE SECOND ACT YOU'VE RENDERED THE LAST THREE ACTS SUPERFLUOUS.
"BREVITY IS THE SOUL OF WIT."
HE QUOTED A SINGLE LINE WHICH HE RECOGNIZED AS AN ALLUSION TO A WORK BY MARLOWE.
"BUT STAY, WHAT NOSE SHINES YONDER IN THE EAST?"
MOST IGNORAMUSES THINK OF SHAKESPEARE.
HE REFUSED TO LET ON THAT HE WAS THE BUTT OF THE COMEDY AND INSTEAD OFFERED AN IMPROMPTU ANALYSIS OF THE STAGE JEW.
YOUR JEW OF NEW YORK COULD ONLY EXIST ON THE STAGE ALONGSIDE OTHER STOCK COMIC FIGURES —A MALEVOLENT PUNCHINELLO WHO WALKS ABROAD A-NIGHT TO KILL SICK PEOPLE AND POISON WELLS.
AN AMERICAN AUDIENCE WOULD NOT RECOGNIZE HIM AS A CREATURE OF FLESH AND BLOOD CAPABLE OF WENDING HIS WAY THROUGH THE POLITICAL INTRIGUES YOU'VE INVENTED.
AS FOR MY DEAR FRIEND, THE ACTOR MAYNARD DAIZY, HIS STOOP WAS NOT PRONOUNCED ENOUGH. I DID NOT KNOW IF I SHOULD LAUGH OR HAVE PITY ON HIM.
YOU SEE, JUST WHAT I SAID.
AND, OF COURSE, I WILL RETURN ON OPENING NIGHT TO WITNESS MISS PATELLA'S FAREWELL PERFORMANCE— THE PLAY THAT EVENING IS IMMATERIAL.
SOLIDUS THANKED MAJOR NOAH FOR HIS CRITIQUE AND THEN CONFESSED, AS A FELLOW PLAYWRIGHT, THAT HE HAD SOME TREPIDATION CONCERNING THE REACTION OF AN AMERICAN AUDIENCE TO HIS WORK. IN BERLIN, HE SAID, THEY HAD RIOTS.
LIKELY STORY.

CHAS. LORGNETTE

Cordially Invites the Businessmen, Actors, Private Fanciers and Other Interested Parties to Examine his

FASCINATING STOCK

OF

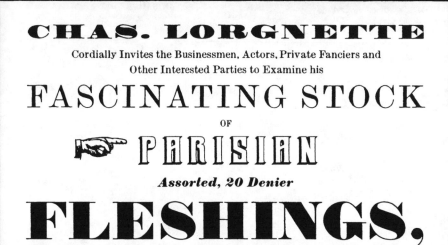

PARISIAN

Assorted, 20 Denier

FLESHINGS,

Manufactured for Professional Theatrical Function

Recently Imported From France, these Garments Represent the Latest Improvements in Design and Translucency of Silken Fabric. From the Stage, they have been Attested to Produce the Unquestionable Illusion of the Unclad Human Form in All Its Glory.

THE INVENTORY OF

- Arabian Harem Slippers.
- Extra-Tight Cambric Shirts.
- British Fox-Hunting Pants.
- Chinese Opium Caps.
- Fancy Half-Pants.
- Disposable Venus Cups.
- Gentlemen's and Ladies' Perspiration Pillows.
- Grecian Houseboy Uniforms.
- Roman Catholic Clerical Vestments in Young Women's sizes.
- And Other Specialty Dry Goods.

CHARLES LORGNETTE,
Proprietor and licensed importer

VINOPER AND SUNCH, PRINTERS AND WASTE-PAPER HANDLERS, BOWERY

Statistical View of the Stocking Trade.

Frames	making		produce	Dozen	consume	Lbs.		valued at	£	wages for making	£	finishing	£	makes in all	£
10,300		fashioned cotton hose		420,000		880,000	cotton yarn		73,000		220,000		32,000		325,000
6,000		cut up, &c.		1,960,000		2,940,000	–		172,000		285,000		98,000		555,000
9,500		fashioned worsted		710,000		2,840,000	worsted		284,000		215,000		41,000		540,000
1,000		cut up, &c.		100,000		400,000	–		40,000		30,000		10,000		80,000
1,300		Angora		95,000		332,500	–		45,000		40,000		19,000		104,000
1,900		lambs' wool		135,000		639,000	–		80,000		50,000		16,000		146,000
3,000		silk		90,000		105,000	silk		120,000		108,000		13,000		241,000
33,000				3,510,000		8,136,500			814,000		948,000		229,000		1,991,000

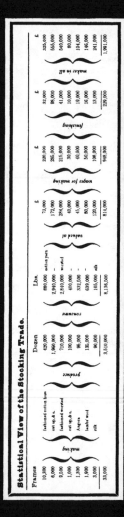

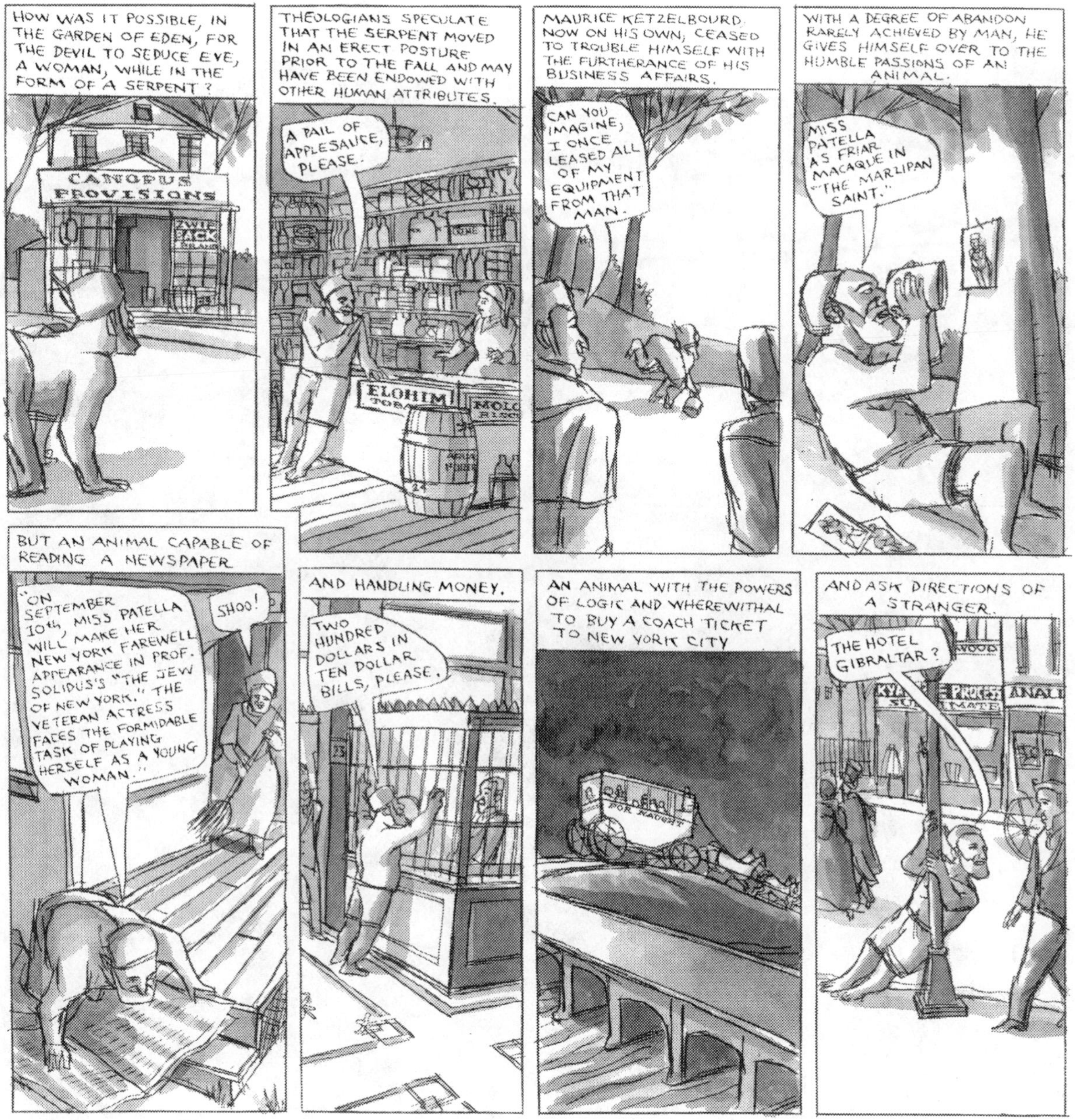
HOW WAS IT POSSIBLE, IN THE GARDEN OF EDEN, FOR THE DEVIL TO SEDUCE EVE, A WOMAN, WHILE IN THE FORM OF A SERPENT?
CANOPUS PROVISIONS
THEOLOGIANS SPECULATE THAT THE SERPENT MOVED IN AN ERECT POSTURE PRIOR TO THE FALL AND MAY HAVE BEEN ENDOWED WITH OTHER HUMAN ATTRIBUTES.
A PAIL OF APPLESAUCE, PLEASE.
ELOHIM
MAURICE KETZELBOURD, NOW ON HIS OWN, CEASED TO TROUBLE HIMSELF WITH THE FURTHERANCE OF HIS BUSINESS AFFAIRS.
CAN YOU IMAGINE, I ONCE LEASED ALL OF MY EQUIPMENT FROM THAT MAN.
WITH A DEGREE OF ABANDON RARELY ACHIEVED BY MAN, HE GIVES HIMSELF OVER TO THE HUMBLE PASSIONS OF AN ANIMAL.
MISS PATELLA AS FRIAR MACAQUE IN "THE MARZIPAN SAINT."
BUT AN ANIMAL CAPABLE OF READING A NEWSPAPER
"ON SEPTEMBER 10TH, MISS PATELLA WILL MAKE HER NEW YORK FAREWELL APPEARANCE IN PROF. SOLIDUS'S "THE JEW OF NEW YORK." THE VETERAN ACTRESS FACES THE FORMIDABLE TASK OF PLAYING HERSELF AS A YOUNG WOMAN."
SHOO!
AND HANDLING MONEY.
TWO HUNDRED DOLLARS IN TEN DOLLAR BILLS, PLEASE.
AN ANIMAL WITH THE POWERS OF LOGIC AND WHEREWITHAL TO BUY A COACH TICKET TO NEW YORK CITY
AND ASK DIRECTIONS OF A STRANGER.
THE HOTEL GIBRALTAR?

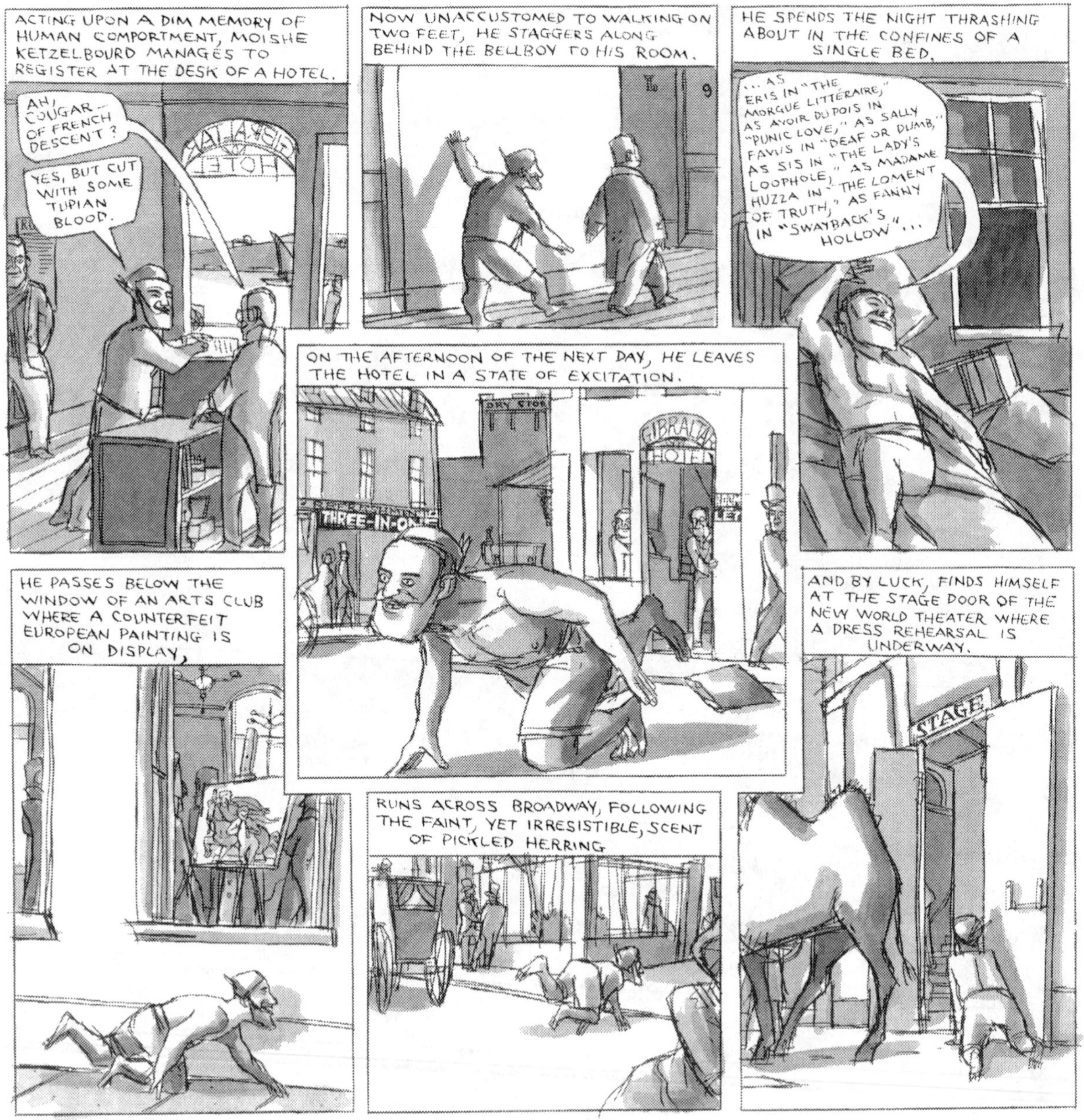
ACTING UPON A DIM MEMORY OF HUMAN COMPORTMENT, MOISHE KETZELBOURD MANAGES TO REGISTER AT THE DESK OF A HOTEL.
AH, COUGAR... OF FRENCH DESCENT?
YES, BUT CUT WITH SOME TUPIAN BLOOD.
GIBRALTAR HOTEL
NOW UNACCUSTOMED TO WALKING ON TWO FEET, HE STAGGERS ALONG BEHIND THE BELLBOY TO HIS ROOM.
9
HE SPENDS THE NIGHT THRASHING ABOUT IN THE CONFINES OF A SINGLE BED.
...AS ERIS IN "THE MORGUE LITTÉRAIRE," AS AVOIR DU POIS IN "PUNIC LOVE," AS SALLY FAVUS IN "DEAF OR DUMB," AS SIS IN "THE LADY'S LOOPHOLE," AS MADAME HUZZA IN "THE LOMENT OF TRUTH," AS FANNY IN "SWAYBACK'S HOLLOW"...
ON THE AFTERNOON OF THE NEXT DAY, HE LEAVES THE HOTEL IN A STATE OF EXCITATION.
THREE-IN-ONE
HE PASSES BELOW THE WINDOW OF AN ARTS CLUB WHERE A COUNTERFEIT EUROPEAN PAINTING IS ON DISPLAY,
RUNS ACROSS BROADWAY, FOLLOWING THE FAINT, YET IRRESISTIBLE, SCENT OF PICKLED HERRING
AND BY LUCK, FINDS HIMSELF AT THE STAGE DOOR OF THE NEW WORLD THEATER WHERE A DRESS REHEARSAL IS UNDERWAY.
STAGE

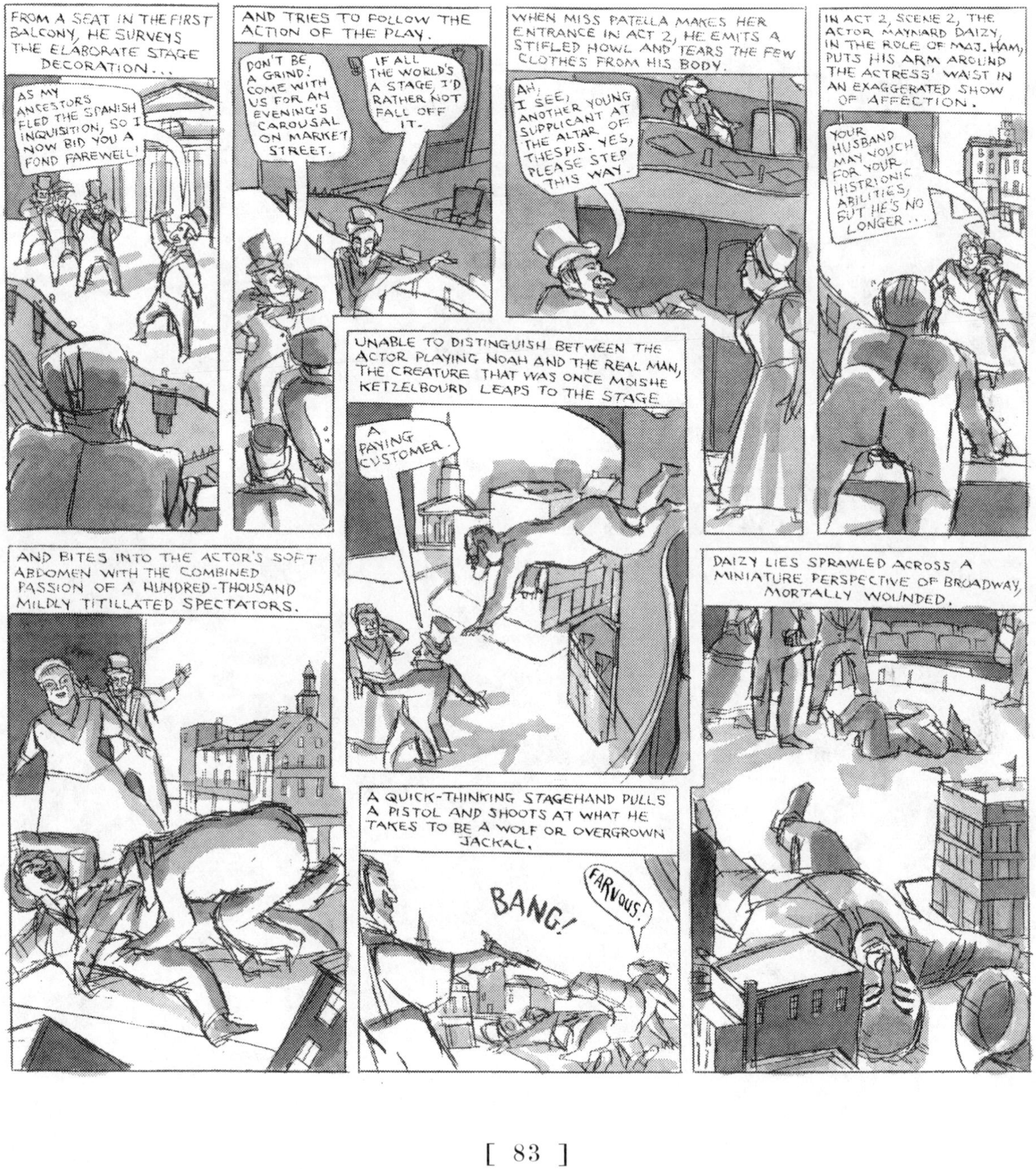
FROM A SEAT IN THE FIRST BALCONY, HE SURVEYS THE ELABORATE STAGE DECORATION...
AS MY ANCESTORS FLED THE SPANISH INQUISITION, SO I NOW BID YOU A FOND FAREWELL!
AND TRIES TO FOLLOW THE ACTION OF THE PLAY.
DON'T BE A GRIND! COME WITH US FOR AN EVENING'S CAROUSAL ON MARKET STREET.
IF ALL THE WORLD'S A STAGE, I'D RATHER NOT FALL OFF IT.
WHEN MISS PATELLA MAKES HER ENTRANCE IN ACT 2, HE EMITS A STIFLED HOWL AND TEARS THE FEW CLOTHES FROM HIS BODY.
AH, I SEE, ANOTHER YOUNG SUPPLICANT AT THE ALTAR OF THESPIS. YES, PLEASE STEP THIS WAY.
IN ACT 2, SCENE 2, THE ACTOR MAYNARD DAIZY, IN THE ROLE OF MAJ. HAM, PUTS HIS ARM AROUND THE ACTRESS' WAIST IN AN EXAGGERATED SHOW OF AFFECTION.
YOUR HUSBAND MAY VOUCH FOR YOUR HISTRIONIC ABILITIES, BUT HE'S NO LONGER...
UNABLE TO DISTINGUISH BETWEEN THE ACTOR PLAYING NOAH AND THE REAL MAN, THE CREATURE THAT WAS ONCE MOISHE KETZELBOURD LEAPS TO THE STAGE.
A PAYING CUSTOMER.
AND BITES INTO THE ACTOR'S SOFT ABDOMEN WITH THE COMBINED PASSION OF A HUNDRED-THOUSAND MILDLY TITILLATED SPECTATORS.
A QUICK-THINKING STAGEHAND PULLS A PISTOL AND SHOOTS AT WHAT HE TAKES TO BE A WOLF OR OVERGROWN JACKAL.
BANG!
FARVOUS!
DAIZY LIES SPRAWLED ACROSS A MINIATURE PERSPECTIVE OF BROADWAY, MORTALLY WOUNDED.

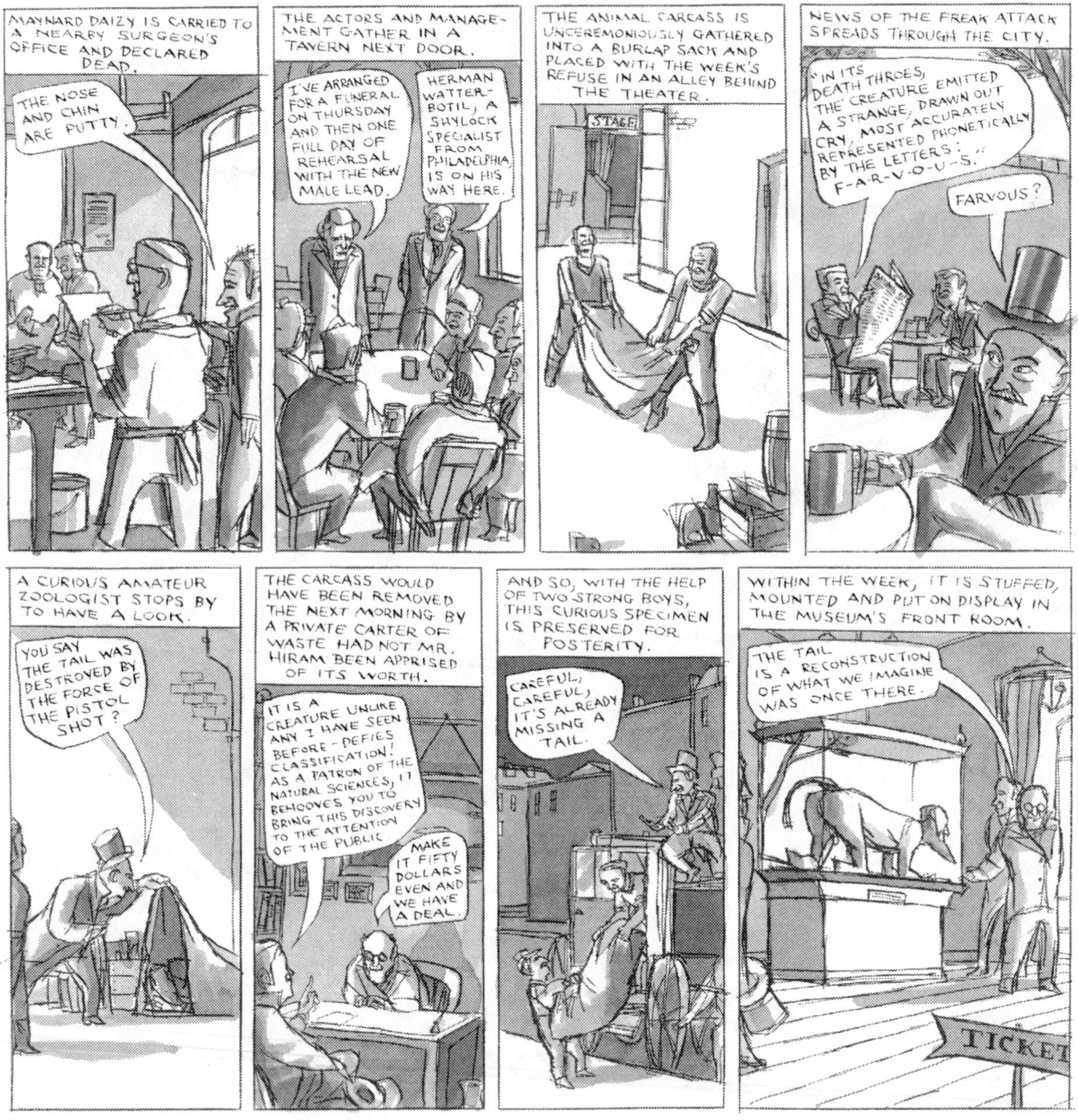
MAYNARD DAIZY IS CARRIED TO A NEARBY SURGEON'S OFFICE AND DECLARED DEAD.
THE NOSE AND CHIN ARE PUTTY.
THE ACTORS AND MANAGEMENT GATHER IN A TAVERN NEXT DOOR.
I'VE ARRANGED FOR A FUNERAL ON THURSDAY AND THEN ONE FULL DAY OF REHEARSAL WITH THE NEW MALE LEAD.
HERMAN WATTERBOTIL, A SHYLOCK SPECIALIST FROM PHILADELPHIA, IS ON HIS WAY HERE.
THE ANIMAL CARCASS IS UNCEREMONIOUSLY GATHERED INTO A BURLAP SACK AND PLACED WITH THE WEEK'S REFUSE IN AN ALLEY BEHIND THE THEATER.
STAGE
NEWS OF THE FREAK ATTACK SPREADS THROUGH THE CITY.
"IN ITS DEATH THROES, THE CREATURE EMITTED A STRANGE, DRAWN OUT CRY, MOST ACCURATELY REPRESENTED PHONETICALLY BY THE LETTERS: F-A-R-V-O-U-S."
FARVOUS?
A CURIOUS AMATEUR ZOOLOGIST STOPS BY TO HAVE A LOOK.
YOU SAY THE TAIL WAS DESTROYED BY THE FORCE OF THE PISTOL SHOT?
THE CARCASS WOULD HAVE BEEN REMOVED THE NEXT MORNING BY A PRIVATE CARTER OF WASTE HAD NOT MR. HIRAM BEEN APPRISED OF ITS WORTH.
IT IS A CREATURE UNLIKE ANY I HAVE SEEN BEFORE - DEFIES CLASSIFICATION! AS A PATRON OF THE NATURAL SCIENCES, IT BEHOOVES YOU TO BRING THIS DISCOVERY TO THE ATTENTION OF THE PUBLIC.
MAKE IT FIFTY DOLLARS EVEN AND WE HAVE A DEAL.
AND SO, WITH THE HELP OF TWO STRONG BOYS, THIS CURIOUS SPECIMEN IS PRESERVED FOR POSTERITY.
CAREFUL, CAREFUL, IT'S ALREADY MISSING A TAIL.
WITHIN THE WEEK, IT IS STUFFED, MOUNTED AND PUT ON DISPLAY IN THE MUSEUM'S FRONT ROOM.
THE TAIL IS A RECONSTRUCTION OF WHAT WE IMAGINE WAS ONCE THERE.
TICKET

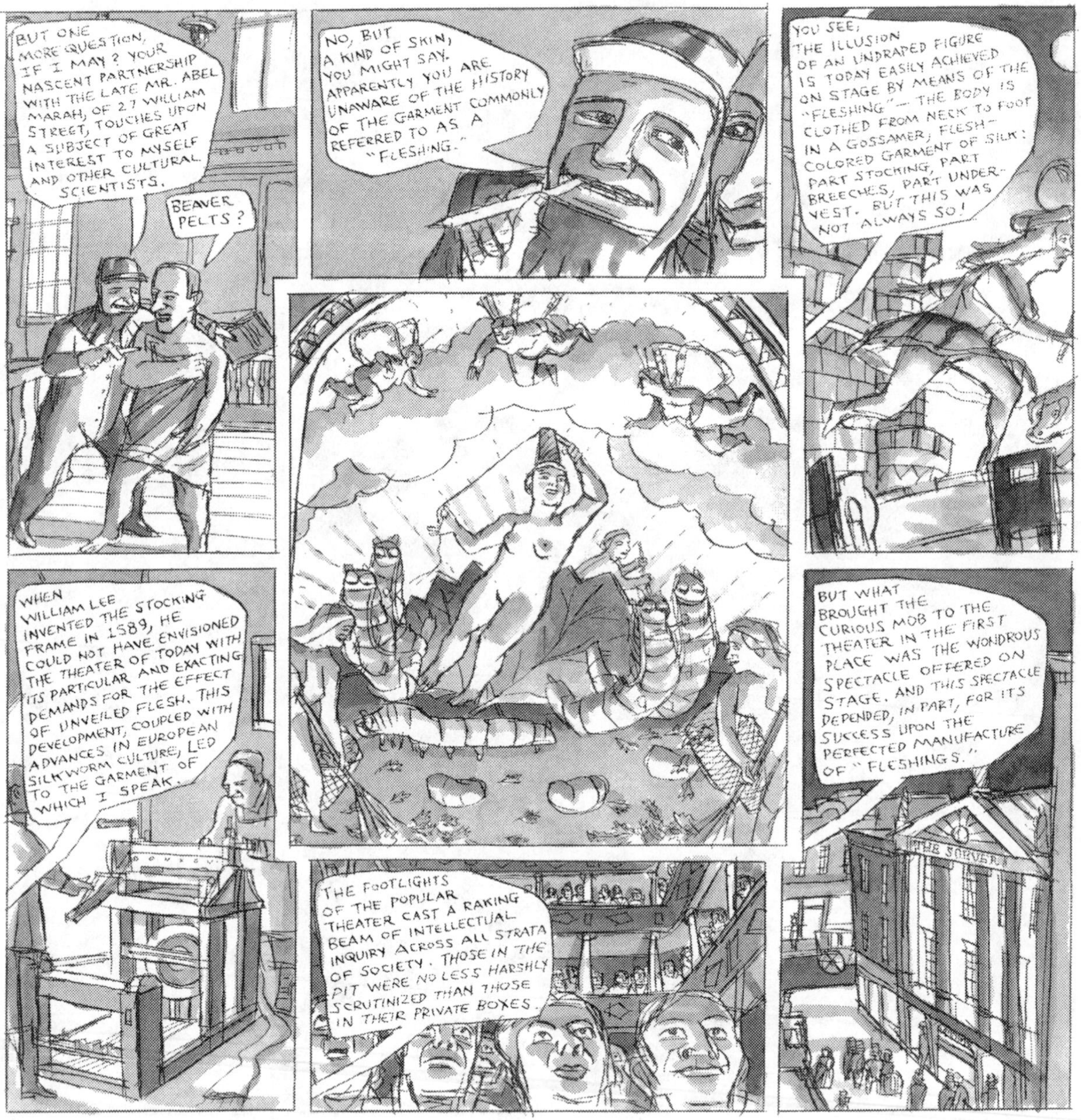
BUT ONE MORE QUESTION, IF I MAY? YOUR NASCENT PARTNERSHIP WITH THE LATE MR. ABEL MARAH, OF 27 WILLIAM STREET, TOUCHES UPON A SUBJECT OF GREAT INTEREST TO MYSELF AND OTHER CULTURAL SCIENTISTS.
BEAVER PELTS?
NO, BUT A KIND OF SKIN, YOU MIGHT SAY. APPARENTLY YOU ARE UNAWARE OF THE HISTORY OF THE GARMENT COMMONLY REFERRED TO AS A "FLESHING."
YOU SEE; THE ILLUSION OF AN UNDRAPED FIGURE IS TODAY EASILY ACHIEVED ON STAGE BY MEANS OF THE "FLESHING"— THE BODY IS CLOTHED FROM NECK TO FOOT IN A GOSSAMER, FLESH-COLORED GARMENT OF SILK: PART STOCKING, PART UNDER-BREECHES, PART UNDER-VEST. BUT THIS WAS NOT ALWAYS SO!
WHEN WILLIAM LEE INVENTED THE STOCKING FRAME IN 1589, HE COULD NOT HAVE ENVISIONED THE THEATER OF TODAY WITH ITS PARTICULAR AND EXACTING DEMANDS FOR THE EFFECT OF UNVEILED FLESH. THIS DEVELOPMENT, COUPLED WITH ADVANCES IN EUROPEAN SILKWORM CULTURE, LED TO THE GARMENT OF WHICH I SPEAK.
BUT WHAT BROUGHT THE CURIOUS MOB TO THE FIRST THEATER IN THE FIRST PLACE WAS THE WONDROUS SPECTACLE OFFERED ON STAGE. AND THIS SPECTACLE DEPENDED, IN PART, FOR ITS SUCCESS UPON THE PERFECTED MANUFACTURE OF "FLESHINGS."
THE FOOTLIGHTS OF THE POPULAR THEATER CAST A RAKING BEAM OF INTELLECTUAL INQUIRY ACROSS ALL STRATA OF SOCIETY. THOSE IN THE PIT WERE NO LESS HARSHLY SCRUTINIZED THAN THOSE IN THEIR PRIVATE BOXES.

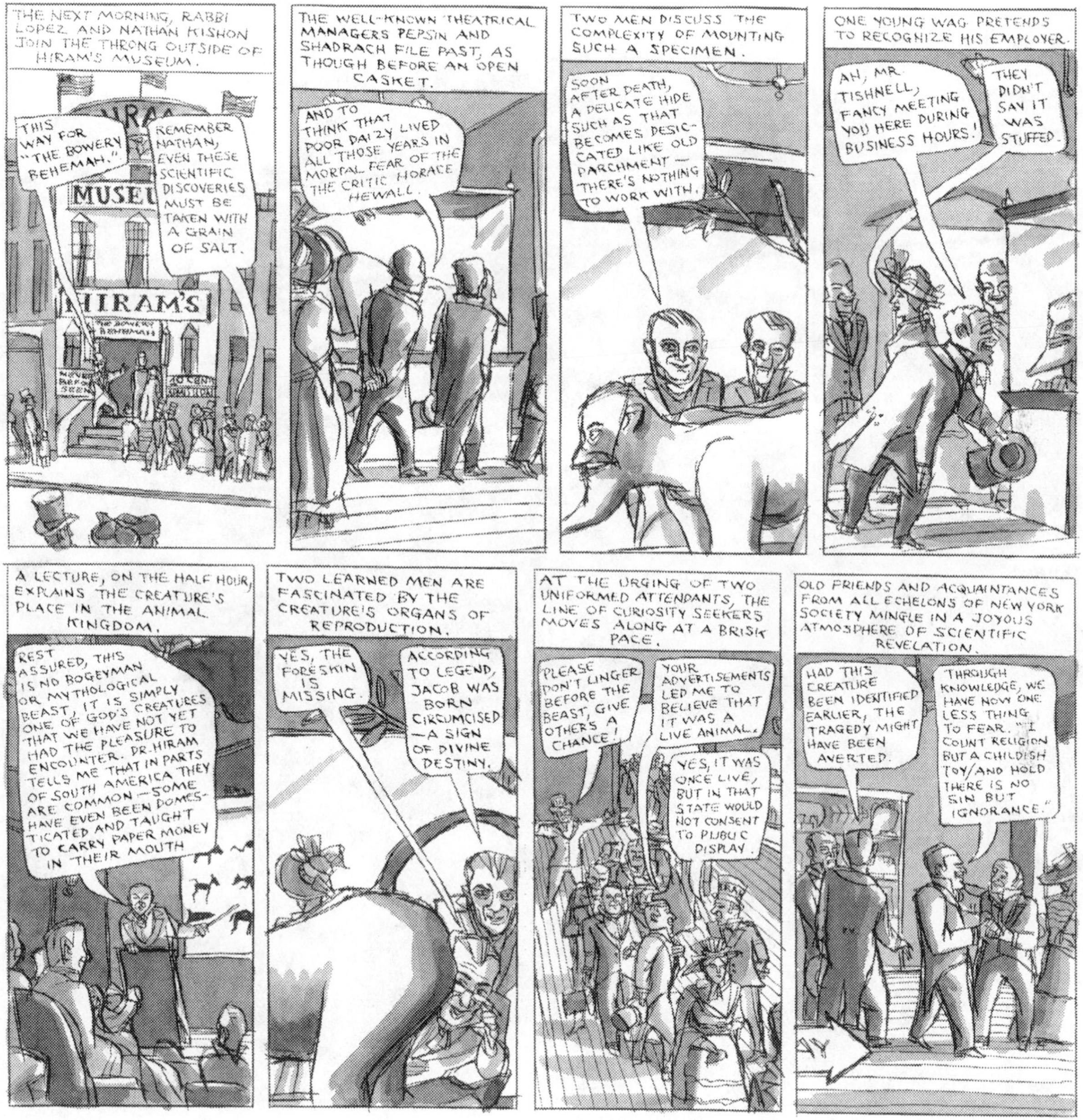

THE NEXT MORNING, RABBI LOPEZ AND NATHAN KISHON JOIN THE THRONG OUTSIDE OF HIRAM'S MUSEUM.
THIS WAY FOR "THE BOWERY BEHEMAH."
REMEMBER NATHAN, EVEN THESE SCIENTIFIC DISCOVERIES MUST BE TAKEN WITH A GRAIN OF SALT.
MUSEU
HIRAM'S
THE WELL-KNOWN THEATRICAL MANAGERS PEPSIN AND SHADRACH FILE PAST, AS THOUGH BEFORE AN OPEN CASKET.
AND TO THINK THAT POOR DAIZY LIVED ALL THOSE YEARS IN MORTAL FEAR OF THE CRITIC HORACE HEWALL.
TWO MEN DISCUSS THE COMPLEXITY OF MOUNTING SUCH A SPECIMEN.
SOON AFTER DEATH, A DELICATE HIDE SUCH AS THAT BECOMES DESICCATED LIKE OLD PARCHMENT — THERE'S NOTHING TO WORK WITH.
ONE YOUNG WAG PRETENDS TO RECOGNIZE HIS EMPLOYER.
AH, MR. TISHNELL, FANCY MEETING YOU HERE DURING BUSINESS HOURS!
THEY DIDN'T SAY IT WAS STUFFED.
A LECTURE, ON THE HALF HOUR, EXPLAINS THE CREATURE'S PLACE IN THE ANIMAL KINGDOM.
REST ASSURED, THIS IS NO BOGEYMAN OR MYTHOLOGICAL BEAST, IT IS SIMPLY ONE OF GOD'S CREATURES THAT WE HAVE NOT YET HAD THE PLEASURE TO ENCOUNTER. DR. HIRAM TELLS ME THAT IN PARTS OF SOUTH AMERICA THEY ARE COMMON — SOME HAVE EVEN BEEN DOMESTICATED AND TAUGHT TO CARRY PAPER MONEY IN THEIR MOUTH
TWO LEARNED MEN ARE FASCINATED BY THE CREATURE'S ORGANS OF REPRODUCTION.
YES, THE FORESKIN IS MISSING.
ACCORDING TO LEGEND, JACOB WAS BORN CIRCUMCISED — A SIGN OF DIVINE DESTINY.
AT THE URGING OF TWO UNIFORMED ATTENDANTS, THE LINE OF CURIOSITY SEEKERS MOVES ALONG AT A BRISK PACE.
PLEASE DON'T LINGER BEFORE THE BEAST, GIVE OTHER'S A CHANCE!
YOUR ADVERTISEMENTS LED ME TO BELIEVE THAT IT WAS A LIVE ANIMAL.
YES, IT WAS ONCE LIVE, BUT IN THAT STATE WOULD NOT CONSENT TO PUBLIC DISPLAY.
OLD FRIENDS AND ACQUAINTANCES FROM ALL ECHELONS OF NEW YORK SOCIETY MINGLE IN A JOYOUS ATMOSPHERE OF SCIENTIFIC REVELATION.
HAD THIS CREATURE BEEN IDENTIFIED EARLIER, THE TRAGEDY MIGHT HAVE BEEN AVERTED.
THROUGH KNOWLEDGE, WE HAVE NOW ONE LESS THING TO FEAR. "I COUNT RELIGION BUT A CHILDISH TOY/AND HOLD THERE IS NO SIN BUT IGNORANCE."

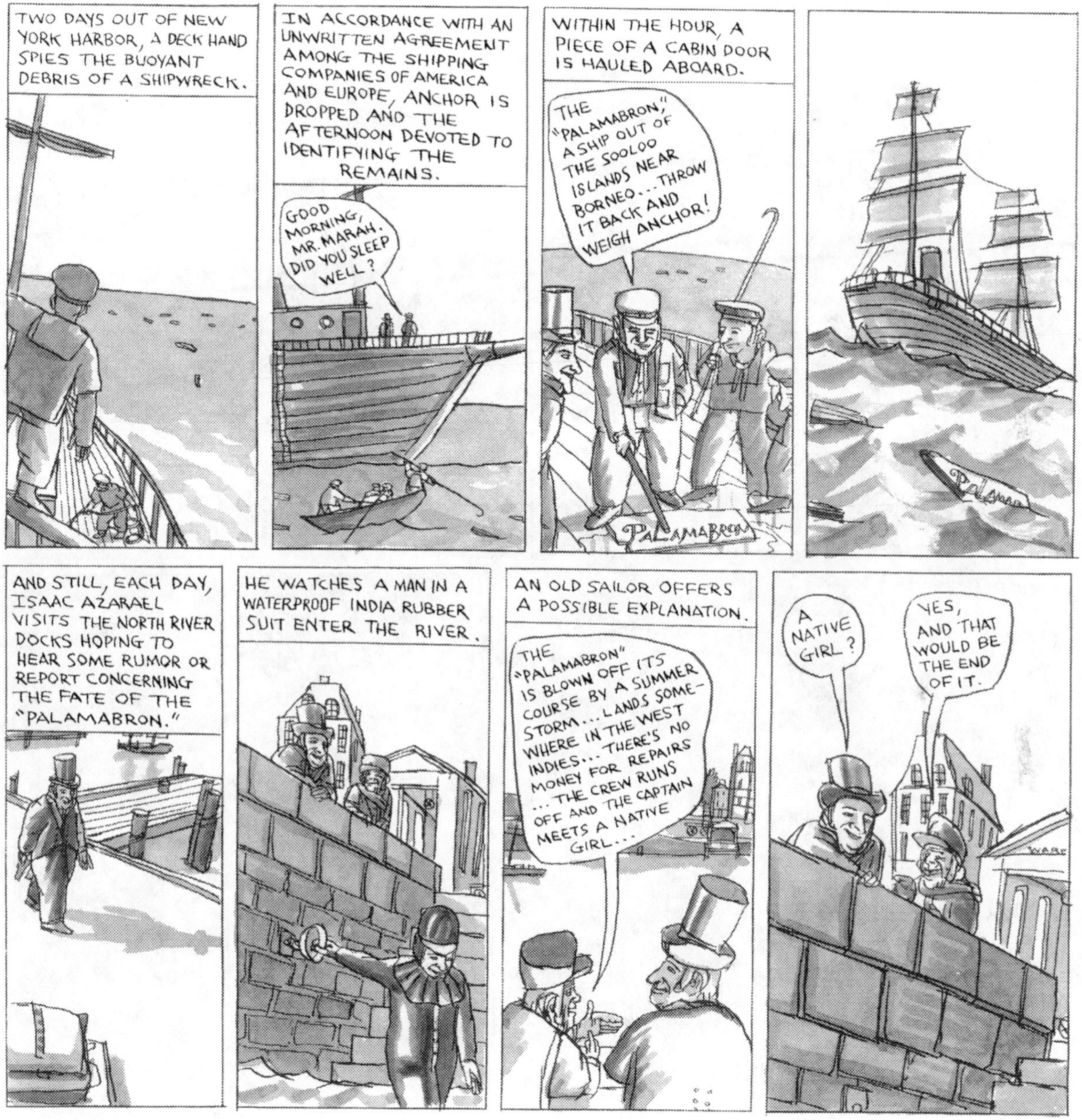
TWO DAYS OUT OF NEW YORK HARBOR, A DECK HAND SPIES THE BUOYANT DEBRIS OF A SHIPWRECK.
IN ACCORDANCE WITH AN UNWRITTEN AGREEMENT AMONG THE SHIPPING COMPANIES OF AMERICA AND EUROPE, ANCHOR IS DROPPED AND THE AFTERNOON DEVOTED TO IDENTIFYING THE REMAINS.
GOOD MORNING, MR. MARAH. DID YOU SLEEP WELL?
WITHIN THE HOUR, A PIECE OF A CABIN DOOR IS HAULED ABOARD.
THE "PALAMABRON," A SHIP OUT OF THE SOOLOO ISLANDS NEAR BORNEO... THROW IT BACK AND WEIGH ANCHOR!
PALAMABRON
AND STILL, EACH DAY, ISAAC AZARAEL VISITS THE NORTH RIVER DOCKS HOPING TO HEAR SOME RUMOR OR REPORT CONCERNING THE FATE OF THE "PALAMABRON."
HE WATCHES A MAN IN A WATERPROOF INDIA RUBBER SUIT ENTER THE RIVER.
AN OLD SAILOR OFFERS A POSSIBLE EXPLANATION.
THE "PALAMABRON" IS BLOWN OFF ITS COURSE BY A SUMMER STORM... LANDS SOMEWHERE IN THE WEST INDIES... THERE'S NO MONEY FOR REPAIRS... THE CREW RUNS OFF AND THE CAPTAIN MEETS A NATIVE GIRL...
A NATIVE GIRL?
YES, AND THAT WOULD BE THE END OF IT.

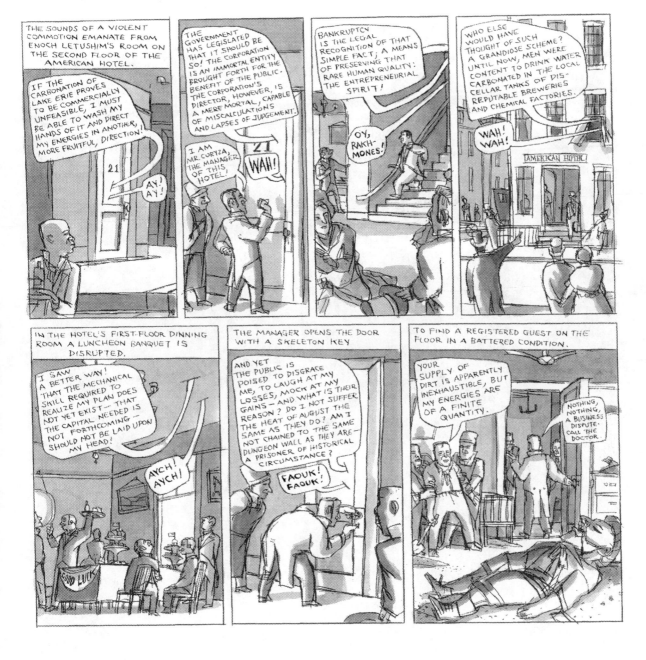

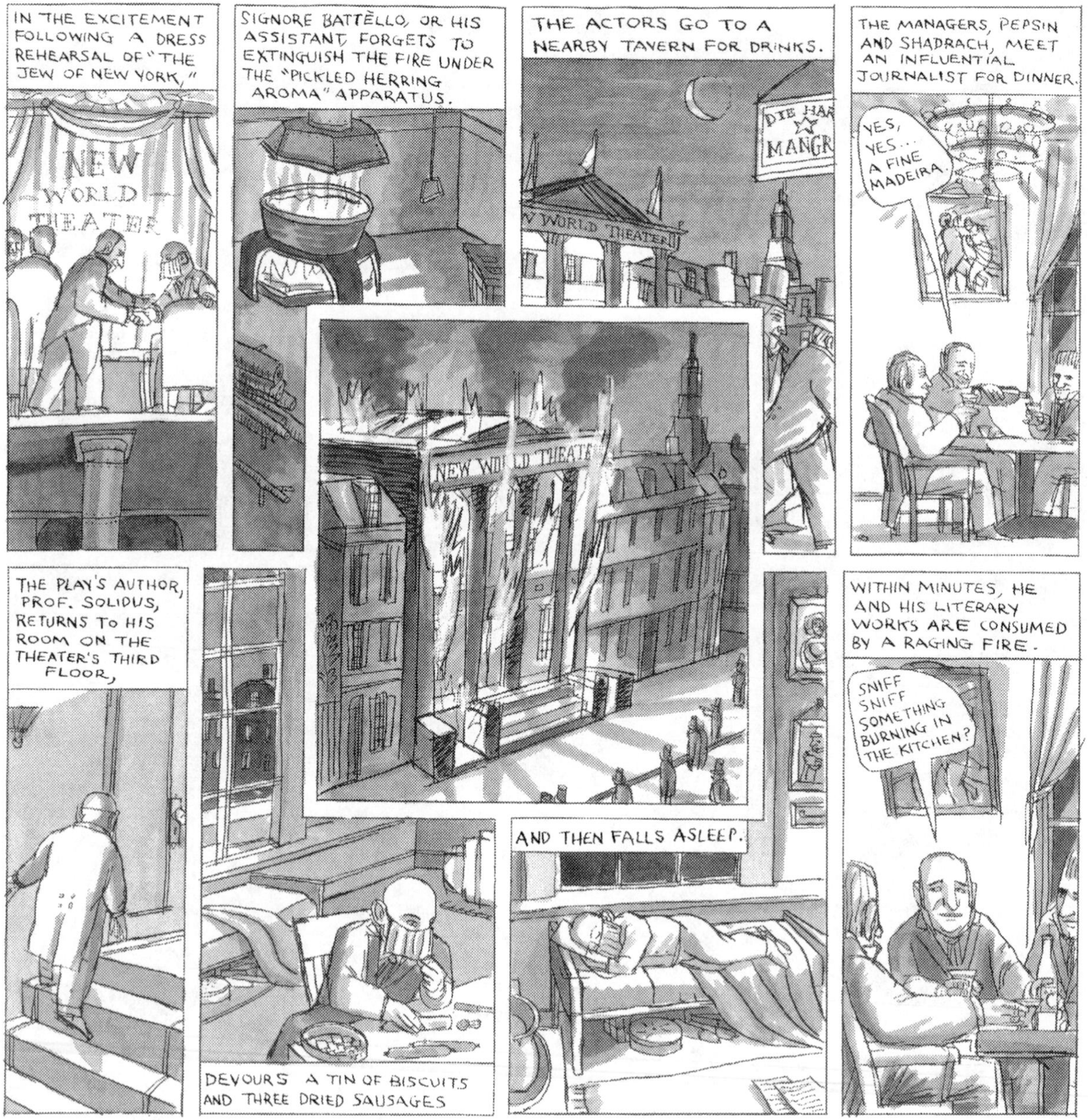
IN THE EXCITEMENT FOLLOWING A DRESS REHEARSAL OF "THE JEW OF NEW YORK,"
NEW WORLD THEATER
SIGNORE BATTÈLLO, OR HIS ASSISTANT, FORGETS TO EXTINGUISH THE FIRE UNDER THE "PICKLED HERRING AROMA" APPARATUS.
THE ACTORS GO TO A NEARBY TAVERN FOR DRINKS.
THE MANAGERS, PEPSIN AND SHADRACH, MEET AN INFLUENTIAL JOURNALIST FOR DINNER.
YES, YES... A FINE MADEIRA.
NEW WORLD THEATER
THE PLAY'S AUTHOR, PROF. SOLIDUS, RETURNS TO HIS ROOM ON THE THEATER'S THIRD FLOOR,
DEVOURS A TIN OF BISCUITS AND THREE DRIED SAUSAGES
AND THEN FALLS ASLEEP.
WITHIN MINUTES, HE AND HIS LITERARY WORKS ARE CONSUMED BY A RAGING FIRE.
SNIFF SNIFF SOMETHING BURNING IN THE KITCHEN?

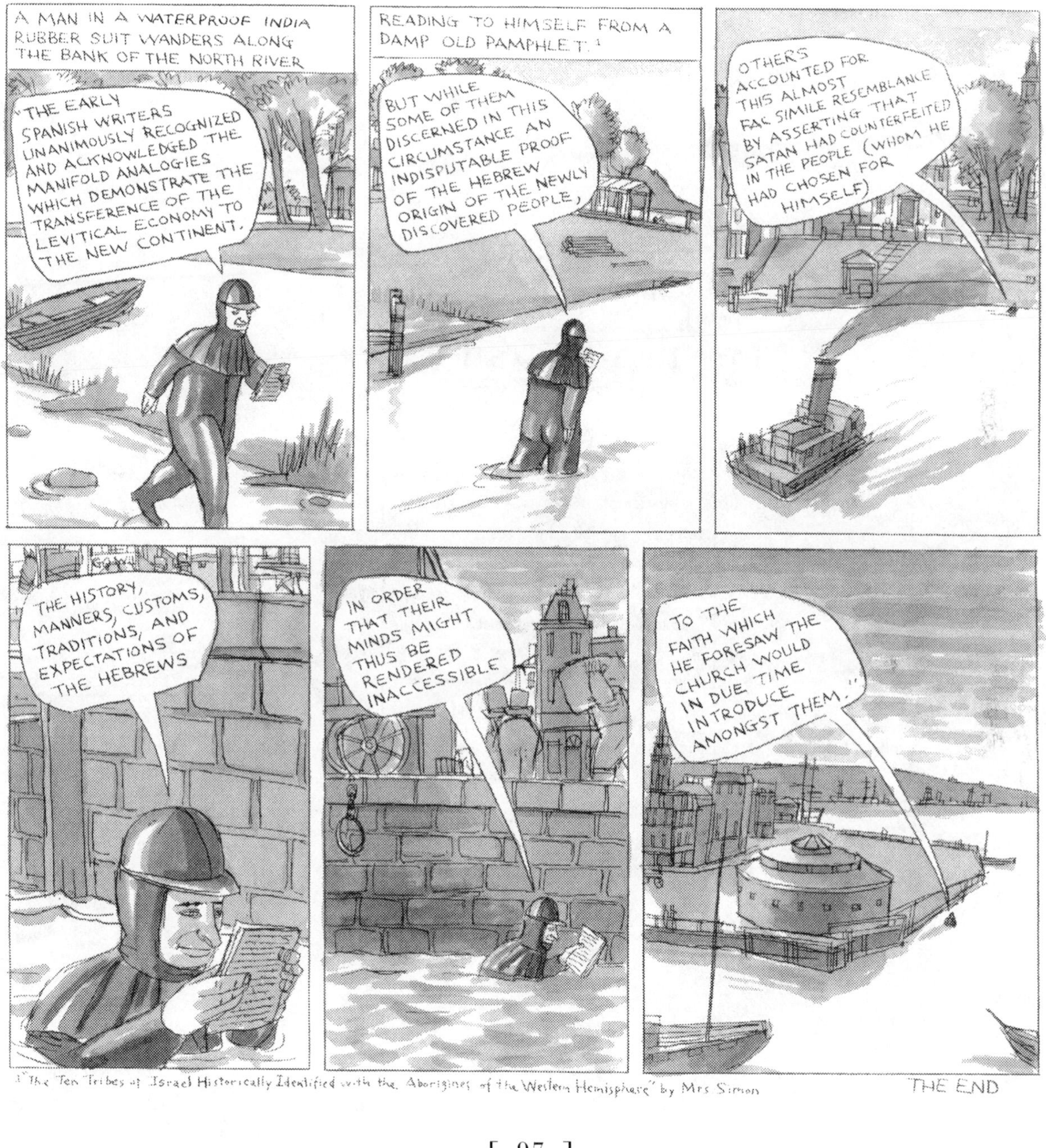
A MAN IN A WATERPROOF INDIA RUBBER SUIT WANDERS ALONG THE BANK OF THE NORTH RIVER
"THE EARLY SPANISH WRITERS UNANIMOUSLY RECOGNIZED AND ACKNOWLEDGED THE MANIFOLD ANALOGIES WHICH DEMONSTRATE THE TRANSFERENCE OF THE LEVITICAL ECONOMY TO THE NEW CONTINENT,
READING TO HIMSELF FROM A DAMP OLD PAMPHLET.[1]
BUT WHILE SOME OF THEM DISCERNED IN THIS CIRCUMSTANCE AN INDISPUTABLE PROOF OF THE HEBREW ORIGIN OF THE NEWLY DISCOVERED PEOPLE,
OTHERS ACCOUNTED FOR THIS ALMOST FAC SIMILE RESEMBLANCE BY ASSERTING THAT SATAN HAD COUNTERFEITED IN THE PEOPLE (WHOM HE HAD CHOSEN FOR HIMSELF)
THE HISTORY, MANNERS, CUSTOMS, TRADITIONS, AND EXPECTATIONS OF THE HEBREWS
IN ORDER THAT THEIR MINDS MIGHT THUS BE RENDERED INACCESSIBLE
TO THE FAITH WHICH HE FORESAW THE CHURCH WOULD IN DUE TIME INTRODUCE AMONGST THEM."

[1] "The Ten Tribes of Israel Historically Identified with the Aborigines of the Western Hemisphere" by Mrs Simon

THE END

.at can ...

for sure.

or
of
ine
ose
ion
the
ood,
atter
bate
and
lis-
w,
are
ead.
ng to
public
ever

Portraits of Eminent Men

BEN KATCHOR,

THE author of this book lives in New York City. He is well known for his weekly comic-strip work published under the titles "Julius Knipl, Real Estate Photographer," and "The Cardboard Valise." These strips appear in the *Forward* and a dozen other newspapers around the country. He also produces a monthly comic-strip for the magazine *Metropolis*.

LEFT-OVER FROM DINNER

After a heavy meal, one is not dispos...
taking on heavy mental labor

t
is
art
but
the
upo
sch
tor
the
rela
On

THE LAKE ERIE SODA-WATER COMPANY.

A Cross-sectional View Showing the Wastage of Soda-Water on a Representative City Street.

AN INQUIRY INTO PROFLIGATE BEHAVIOR.

At this time in history, the population of The City of New York is close to 1,000,000 souls—each consuming an average of six glasses of soda-water each day, or 375,000 gal. of liquid. The amount of carbonated waters drawn each day from the Canadian shore of Lake Erie is approximately 100,000,000 gal. Careful investigation has revealed that 96,250,000 gal. of this precious commodity are wasted each day.

How can the rational mind explain this prodigious loss of liquid wealth? By what mechanism of abuse does the average soda-water drinker discard a quantity of beverage equal to that which he consumes?

Subscribers who are not on the meter system have been known to let their tap "run" until the soda-water reaches the temperature of a chilled drink. They have no regard for the fact that thousands of dollars in capital improvements to the entire system are worn-down by heedless "running" of their tap.

If the present wastage of soda-water is not curtailed, through educational or compulsory means, the Great Lake Erie will be drained dry in the next hundred years.

Furthermore, the supply of this exquisite beverage is maintained at the expense of a privately held corporation. For how long can The Lake Erie Soda-Water Company absorb these crippling losses? What is the future of carbonated water in our great metropolis? Can the Federal government be called upon to underwrite the pleasures of a few well-to-do New Yorkers?

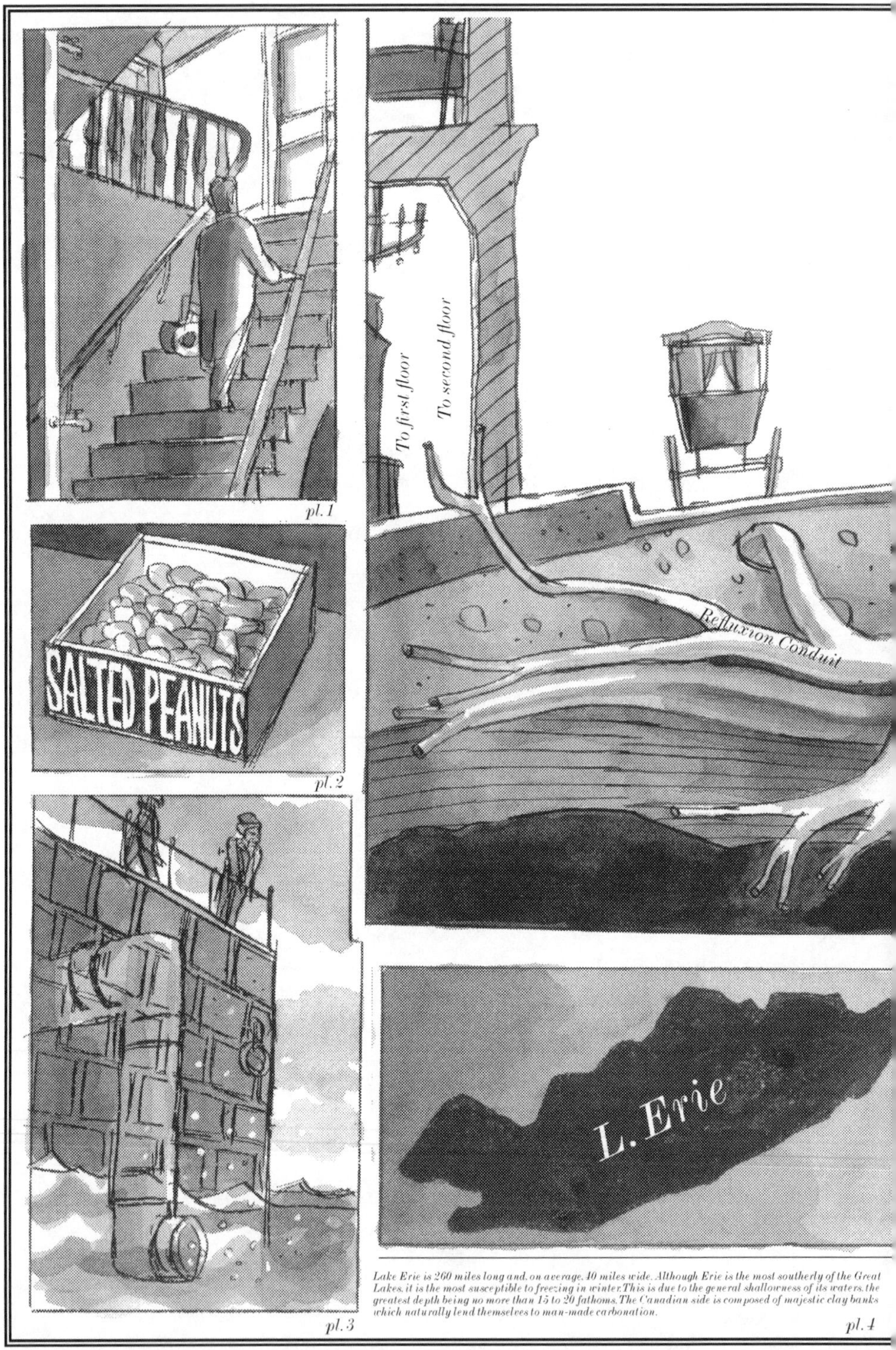
pl. 1
SALTED PEANUTS
pl. 2
pl. 3
To first floor
To second floor
Refluxion Conduit
L. Erie

Lake Erie is 260 miles long and, on average, 40 miles wide. Although Erie is the most southerly of the Great Lakes, it is the most susceptible to freezing in winter. This is due to the general shallowness of its waters, the greatest depth being no more than 15 to 20 fathoms. The Canadian side is composed of majestic clay banks which naturally lend themselves to man-made carbonation.

pl. 4

Printed in the United States
by Baker & Taylor Publisher Services